UNRAVEL

A DARK DRABBLES ANTHOLOGY

Compiled & Edited by D Kershaw

Also available from Black Hare Press

DARK DRABBLES ANTHOLOGIES

WORLDS
ANGELS
MONSTERS
BEYOND

Twitter: @BlackHarePress
Facebook: BlackHarePress
Website: www.BlackHarePress.com

ISBN978-1-925809-26-8

Cover Design by Dawn Burdett
Book Formatting by Ben Thomas

"It seemed to me that a careful examination of the room and the lawn might possibly reveal some traces of this mysterious individual. You know my methods, Watson. There was not one of them which I did not apply to the inquiry. And it ended by my discovering traces, but very different ones from those which I had expected."

The Adventure of the Crooked Man, Arthur Conan Doyle, 1893

Table of Contents

Foreword

While undoubtedly there are smatterings through history, the unchallenged fathers of crime fiction must be Edgar Allan Poe and Arthur Conan Doyle.

From Poe's, at the time, visionary role of the detective in *The Cask of Amontillado*, to Sherlock Holmes—arguably the most famous detective of all time—in Doyle's prolific tales about the crime-solving mastermind, we find ourselves immersed in the trail of unravelling clues, often only finding out the true perpetrator at the very moment the detective unveils it.

And so began our love of dark and vicarious adventures into the depravities of those living in the shadows.

Love and kisses
D. Kershaw & Ben Thomas
Black Hare Press

Whoosh
by Virginia Carraway Stark

Homeless people are the worst. Don't you think? That's why I do what I do. They're scum. I've got rid of a lot of them like this; a can of gasoline and a lighter, *whoosh*, one last drain on society!

I carried the can down an alley, looking for a target, and crumpled when something heavy hit me on the head. I woke up, a cop was standing over me. I tried to get up but I was handcuffed to an old iron pipe.

"You aren't the first I've gotten rid of like this," he said with a smile.

Whoosh!

Virginia Carraway Stark has a diverse portfolio and has many publications. Over the years she has developed this into a wide range of products from screenplays to novels to articles to blogging to travel journalism. She has been published by many presses from grassroots to Simon and Schuster. She has been an honourable mention at Cannes Film Festival for her screenplay, "Blind Eye" and was nominated for an Aurora Award. She also placed in the final top three screenplay shorts as well as numerous other awards for her anthologies, novels, blogs and other projects.

Missing Persons
by Wondra Vanian

"Honey?" Alfred's wife called from the kitchen. "Can you give me a hand, please?"

He went to see what culinary disaster Sue had gotten herself into this time. Expecting her to be covered in flour and pastry, he was surprised to find her with a cop.

A dead cop.

There was blood everywhere.

"Dear Lord! What happened?"

"Well," she said, "Officer Hussein had a few questions about the Lampton kid's disappearance."

Alfred frowned. "Why would— Oh. Is that why we had to buy a chest freezer last week?"

Sue looked sheepish. "Good thing we went for the larger one, huh?"

Wondra Vanian is an American living in the United Kingdom with her Welsh husband and their army of fur babies. A writer first, Wondra is also an avid gamer, photographer, cinephile, and blogger. She has music in her blood, sleeps with the lights on, and has been known to dance naked in the moonlight. Wondra was a multiple Top-Ten finisher in the 2017 and 2018 Preditors and Editors Reader's Poll, including ithe Best Author category. Her story, "Halloween Night," was named a Notable Contender for the Bristol Short Story Prize in 2015.
Website : www.wondravanian.com

Law and Disorder
by Tracy Davidson

I've seen worse crime scenes. Decapitations, exsanguinations, body parts chopped up and hung from branches of a tree. As gore goes, this one's tame.

Sure, there's some blood. But bruising on her neck gives cause of death away. A domestic that escalated. Seen it a hundred times.

Yet, I sit, shaking in a corner, unable to move as colleagues do their duty. I've worked with many for years. They've never seen their chief like this before.

My sergeant shuffles forwards, holding out handcuffs. I offer no resistance.

He escorts me from my house, forensics still bustling over my wife's body...

Tracy Davidson lives in Warwickshire, England, and writes poetry and flash fiction. Her work has appeared in various publications and anthologies, including: Poet's Market, Mslexia, Atlas Poetica, Writing Magazine, Modern Haiku, The Binnacle, A Hundred Gourds, Shooter, Journey to Crone, The Great Gatsby Anthology, WAR and In Protest: 150 Poems for Human Rights.

Sisters of Perpetual Mercy
by Raven Corinn Carluk

"Mister Dalton. I wasn't expecting your call for another week."

"There isn't much I can do about that, Sister Agnes."

"Is that to say his condition is deteriorating?"

"Faster than the others. The supplements aren't keeping the symptoms at bay."

"Perhaps he ate too many too fast."

"Perhaps it's the inferior quality of the product."

"What are you saying?"

"You heard me. They're far too skinny. Feed them better before you send them to us."

"If the senator does not like our Venezuelan orphans, he is welcome to find his own pituitary glands there in America."

"...we'll double our order."

Raven Corinn Carluk *writes dark fantasy, paranormal romance, and anything else that catches her interest. She's authored five novels, where she explores themes of love and acceptance. Her shorter pieces, usually from her darker side, can be found in Black Hare Press anthologies, at Detritus Online, and through Alban Lake Publishers.*
Twitter: @ravencorinn
Website: RavenCorinnCarluk.Blogspot.Com

Worse, Much Worse
by David Bowmore

It was like the shower scene from Pyscho—but worse, much worse.

As a copper, I'd seen many brutal things—death, amputations, disfigurement.

But this, I'd seen nothing like this.

She must have had more than a hundred knife wounds. One of her breasts was three feet from the body. He'd burned her eyes out with cigarettes. The sick bastard had even sexually assaulted her…post mortis.

With all the evil in the world, what could I do?

I looked at everyone as a potential target.

I'd turned from the path. My new life goal was to be like him.

David Bowmore has lived here, there and everywhere, but now lives in Yorkshire with his wonderful wife and a small white poodle. He has worn many hats in his time; head chef, teacher and landscape gardener. His first collection of short stories 'The Magic of Deben Market' is available from Clarendon House.
Website: davidbowmore.co.uk
Facebook: davidbowmoreauthor

Calling Card
by Susanne Thomas

FBI Agent and former Army Captain Trisha Brooks screamed. Her face was red, and her breaths came shallow and fast.

She had been sure that the dead animals, left as decoration at each murder, had been the killer's cry to be found.

But every single lead had dried up, and each time a photo of the next victim had been held down by another dead beast's body. This last time her sister's face had stared out at her from beneath a hare that had been ripped to shreds. Now Rachel was nowhere to be found and time was almost up.

Susanne Thomas reads, writes, parents, and teaches from the windy west in Wyoming, and she loves fantasy, science fiction, speculative fiction, poetry, children's books, science, coffee, and puns.
Website: www.themightierpenn.com
Facebook: SusanneThomasAuthor

False Lead
by Terry Miller

The sight was unbelievable. Grayson had been a local Taxidermist yet there he stood displayed motionless and stiff in the corner, him and several others. *There goes my only lead*, Detective Dietrich thought to himself.

The next room was the expected trophies, all posed on their respective bases. Dietrich explored the house further, finding much the same. He sighed in disappointment.

Back in the main room, a cellphone rang. Dietrich followed the noise to stuffed Mr. Grayson's jeans pocket.

"Hello?"

"Hope you enjoy my work, Detective. Say hello to Mr. Grayson for me, won't you?"

CLICK!

Dietrich screamed in frustration.

Terry Miller is an author and 2017 Rhysling Award-nominated poet residing in Portsmouth, OH, USA. He has self-published a dark poetry collection on Amazon and one short story to date. His work has also appeared in Sanitarium, Devolution Z, Jitter Press, Poetry Quarterly, O Unholy Night in Deathlehem, and the 2017 Rhysling Anthology from the Science Fiction and Fantasy Poetry Association.
Facebook: tmiller2015

Things That Go Bump in the Light
by Chris Bannor

Horrific acts shouldn't be committed in the light—that was an unspoken rule. It made it easier for him; a smile at the neighbour, a friendly wave to a coach as he passed by. No one suspected such dark behaviour in the light of day, as if the sun itself was protection.

No one remembered who he was or how he managed to get the young girl's attention. No one remembered anything out of the ordinary.

All they remembered was a sobbing parent, the discarded, disfigured dead body, and a trail of clues that spiralled back around to her grave.

Chris Bannor is a science fiction and fantasy writer who lives in Southern California. Chris learned her love of genre stories from her mother at an early age and has never veered far from that path. She also enjoys musical theater and road trips with her family, but is a general homebody otherwise. Twitter: @BannorChris

Dust to Dust
by Jason Holden

Adam had been bullied his whole life.

The two working in the mill now were the worst of them. They made his life hell.

They made him let them work without a permit or safety checks. They hadn't even isolated the system; if it started now, they would be buried in a fine lime powder that would burn their skin and sear their lungs as they inhaled it. The massive rollers inside would grind them to dust.

No one would know, there was no proof they were ever there.

His finger hovered over the button. "Dust to dust," he whispered.

*After giving up a full-time job as a quarry operator so that his wife could follow her dream career as an academic in the field of chemistry, **Jason Holden** and his family left England and temporarily moved to Spain where they currently reside. While there, he took on the role of full-time parent and began to create stories for his daughter. Now that she is in school, he creates stories for himself and hopes to share those stories with others.*

Night Shift
by Carole de Monclin

Anticipation was everything. The act itself required too much concentration to truly savour the moment. Imagining the aftermath gave him chills. Everybody loved a hero.

His cue came as a shout, "Code blue!"

He rushed in with the already waiting crash cart and took charge. A well-practiced dance: CPR, intubation, defibrillation...

But tonight, no grateful family would congratulate their saviour.

He hated losing a patient. How many had it been over the years?

He must have overestimated the dose he injected. As expected, the heart had stopped, but resuscitation should have remained possible.

Better luck next time, the nurse thought.

Carole de Monclin travels both the real world and imaginary ones. She's lived in France, Australia, and the USA; visited 25+ countries; and explored Mars, Ceres, and many distant planets. She writes to invite people on a journey. Stories have found her for as long as she can remember, be it in a cave in Victoria, the smile of a baby in Paris, or a museum in Florida.
Website: CaroledeMonclin.com
Twitter: @CaroledeMonclin

Not Worthy
By Eddie D. Moore

Wesley glanced at the badge on his chest before stepping into the nearly empty saloon. The barkeep nodded toward a man sitting in the corner. A Bible sat between a whiskey bottle and a pistol on the stranger's table. Wesley cleared his throat as he approached the stranger.

"I've heard that you've been taking things that aren't yours and harassing people."

The stranger shrugged. "The preacher didn't know his Bible, and the wannabe gunslinger was rather slow."

"And the whiskey?"

The stranger leaned back exposing the gun he was pointing at the sheriff. "They weren't thirsty either. Leave the badge."

Eddie D. Moore travels hundreds of hours a year, and he fills that time by listening to audiobooks. When he isn't playing with his grandchildren, he writes his own stories. You can find a list of his publications on his blog or by visiting his Amazon Author Page. While you're there, be sure to pick up a copy of his mini-anthology Misfits & Oddities. Website: eddiedmoore.wordpress.com Amazon: amazon.com/author/eddiedmoore

The Love of a Good Wife
by Nicola Currie

I never thought I'd be the type of person who peered into someone else's window, who would follow them home, stalk them online. No one would think it to look at me, a mother in her forties who dresses in florals and pastels, who makes cupcakes for the school fete.

She strips her clothes off and I see she is as beautiful as my tortured mind imagined. I can see why she captured my husband's attention, why he grins as he approaches her, touches her.

I watch them together and cry. How could he cheat me like this? She's mine.

Nicola Currie is 34, from Cambridge, UK where she works in educational publishing. She has published poetry in literary magazines, including Mslexia and Sarasvati, and has also completed her first novel, which was longlisted for the Bath Children's Novel Award.
Website: writeitandweep.home.blog

Fingers in the Cookie Jar
by Gregg Cunningham

"I don't know where the money is, sir. I swear, I honestly don't know." He wept as his eyes glanced towards the door, praying for another customer to walk in wanting to fill up their gas tank.

But the robber wasn't fooled for a second.

"I suggest you quit fucking stalling and tell me where you stashed the goddam money!"

Jack squirmed, wincing at the pain he was about to receive again.

"It's been a slow night, takings are down."

"Wrong answer!"

Jack's howling screams drowned out the shrill of the cash register as the coinage tray slammed shut again.

Gregg Cunningham 48, short story writer who has had to pick up his game since stumbling into facebook writer's groups. He has stories published by 559 Publishing in in 13 Bites volume 3,4,5, Plan 9 from Outer space, Other Realms, Heard It on The Radio, 559 Ways to Die, short stories publishing by Zombie Pirate Publishing in Relationship add Vice, Full Metal Horror, Phuket Tattoo, World War four and Flash Fiction Addiction (flash) with Zombie Pirate Publishing, and also in Daastan Magazine Chapter 11 and Brian,Rich and the Wardrobe.
Amazon: www.amazon.com/-/e/B016OTHX0K
Website: cortlandsdogs.wordpress.com

Scratches on Paper and Skin
by Shelly Jarvis

"The fingernails. That's how they all get caught," Rick says.

He lifts the hand towards me, fingers purpled, nails tattered. He uses scissors and tweezers to remove what is left and carefully drops the remains in a plastic baggie.

I watch in rapt attention, taking notes with my leaky blue pen.

Rick says, "Stop writing down all this shit I'm telling you. The last thing you want is someone to come across that notebook and tie you to one of the bodies."

"I've picked strangers each time," I say, smirking.

He shrugs. "Doesn't matter. The fingernails always tell the truth."

Shelly Jarvis is a speculative fiction author from West Virginia, US. She found a life-long love of sci-fi and fantasy in the 3rd grade when she found Madeleine L'Engle's "A Wrinkle in Time." Shelly is an avid reader, a Whovian, the ideal viewer of dog rescue videos, and undoubtedly Ravenclaw. She currently has three YA sci-fi books available for purchase on Amazon.
Website: www.ShellyJarvis.com

Skull
by Andrew Anderson

"Captain, they've found another skeleton. We're unable to confirm if it's Lieutenant Poulsen yet; its skull is missing, so we can't check it against his dental records. A DNA test will take weeks."

Williams nodded. "Thanks, Jones. I fear Poulsen is dead, probably hidden where no-one can find him."

Sighing, she placed her head in her hands. Jones tactfully left Williams to grieve the loss of her partner of twelve years.

When the door closed, Williams locked it. Opening her bottom desk drawer, she grinned at Poulsen's skull, caressing the bullet hole.

"Yes, where no one will *ever* find him."

Andrew Anderson is a full-time civil servant, dabbling in writing music, poetry, screenplays and short stories in his limited spare time, when not working on building himself a fort made out of second-hand books. He lives in Bathgate, Scotland with his wife, two children and his dog.
Twitter: @soorploom

One Last Case
by Alexander Pyles

There was always that one. Your white whale. The one that got away. It has been almost 20 years. The case you couldn't solve. The case that went cold. After that it was nothing but politics, paper pushing, and human pettiness.

Standing at the grave of one of the kids, Benjamin, the frustration comes back. The liver spots on your hands stretch as you clench your fists. "I just wanted an answer. A relief from the wondering."

"What if you could have it all?"

You turn to find a suit standing there, with a gun barrel levelled at your heart.

Alexander Pyles resides in IL with his wife and children. He holds an MA in Philosophy and an MFA in Writing Popular Fiction. His short story chapbook titled, "Milo (01001101 01101001 01101100 01101111)," from Radix Media, is due out fall 2019. His other short fiction has appeared on 101fiction.org, River and South Review, and other venues.
Website: www.pylesofbooks.com
Twitter: @Pylesofbooks

What Remains
by Liam Hogan

"You be respectful of his remains," the Acting Superintendent snarls. "He was one of us!"

I blink. "I always am."

More so than the forensic pathologist, scraping away. Or photographers, flashing-flash-flashing. Or the investigators, clomping around looking for the murder weapon. Crime scene cleaners care. Truly we do.

He slams the door and I'm alone. The corpse is gone, of course. Just a lake of his blood and fragments of skull and hair.

I lift the handle of my heavy mop, tut at the stain at its blunt end.

Subcontracting out to some domestic cleaning agency?

Not on my watch.

Liam Hogan is a London based short story writer, the host of Liars' League, and a Ministry of Stories mentor. His story "Ana", appears in Best of British Science Fiction 2016 (NewCon Press) and his twisted fantasy collection, "Happy Ending Not Guaranteed", is published by Arachne Press. Website: happyendingnotguaranteed.blogspot.co.uk Twitter: @LiamJHogan

The Intruder
by Gregg Cunningham

Barry's hand reached for the wall, blindly sliding along the wallpaper until he found the doorway and inched through.

His heart was beating so fast as he tried to keep his thoughts of who lurked inside the house at bay. He knew he had to be so careful, one wrong footfall on the squeaky wooden flooring under the carpet would give away his position. But as Barry entered the bedroom, he realised he was right, the Millers were still on holiday and the house was vacant.

He smiled, unzipped his backpack and began packing it with whatever he could find.

Gregg Cunningham 48, short story writer who has had to pick up his game since stumbling into facebook writer's groups. He has stories published by 559 Publishing in in 13 Bites volume 3,4,5, Plan 9 from Outer space, Other Realms, Heard It on The Radio, 559 Ways to Die, short stories publishing by Zombie Pirate Publishing in Relationship add Vice, Full Metal Horror, Phuket Tattoo, World War four and Flash Fiction Addiction (flash) with Zombie Pirate Publishing, and also in Daastan Magazine Chapter 11 and Brian,Rich and the Wardrobe.
Amazon: www.amazon.com/-/e/B016OTHX0K
Website: cortlandsdogs.wordpress.com

Maggie
by Rhiannon Bird

"Ma'am, I have to ask you to move away," I said, stepping towards her. Silent tears ran down her face and her hands fisted into her gown.

"This is my house. I need to know what's going on."

"I know. Calm down and please move away from the crime scene."

"Crime scene?" I winced at her tone; it was bordering on hysterics. She gasped, "My daughter. What are you doing with Maggie?"

I sighed. Of course, I had to be the one to tell her that her husband was in the hospital and it was Maggie that put him there.

Rhiannon Bird is a young aspiring author. She has a passion for words and storytelling. Rhiannon has her own quotes blog; Thoughts of a Writer. She has had 4 works published. This includes 3 short stories and 2 poems. These are published on Eskimo pie, Literary yard, Down in the Dirt Magazine and Short break fiction. She can be found on Facebook, Instagram, and Pinterest.

Project Infertility
by Aditya Deshmukh

"Look at me." D784 dragged P030 up.

P030 glanced away.

"Is it possible?" D784 forced his head towards hers. "Did you corrupt the System?" Her eyes twinkled.

P030 nodded. "I had to. Remember the days before the System?"

"Days of chaos."

"No, Freedom. Now we just follow orders from a stupid computer. Free will is extinct."

D784 unlocked his hand cuffs.

"You're releasing me?"

"The System estimated my child wouldn't contribute much to the society. They took my fertility." D784 smiled. "Go, merge the rebellions into one single invincible force. I'll assist you. It's time to make the System infertile."

Aditya Deshmukh is a mechanical engineering student who likes exploring the mechanics of writing as much as he likes tinkering with machines. He writes dark fiction and poetry. He is published in over three dozen anthologies and has a poetry book "Opium Hearts" and a collection of drabbles coming out soon. He likes chatting with people who share similar interests, so feel free to check him out.
Facebook: adityadeshmukhwrites
Website: www.adityadeshmukh.com

Cliché
by Rennie St. James

The world is a stage and all men are actors. Everyone wears a mask. They are trite and overused, but true. I set my stage and wore my mask. No one was the wiser…until you.

There was a spurt of something like joy because I was no longer alone. You saw the real me.

Here's another cliché—two people can only keep a secret if one of them is dead.

My mask remains in place, and my stage is still set. The lack of your tell-tale smile on stage with me is a price I'm willing and able to pay.

Rennie St. James shares several similarities with her fictional characters (heroes and villains alike) including a love of chocolate, horror movies, martial arts, history, yoga, and travel. She doesn't have a pet mountain lion but is proudly owned by three rescue kitties. They live in relative harmony in beautiful southwestern Virginia (United States). The first three books of Rennie's urban fantasy series, The Rahki Chronicles, are available now. A new series and several standalone stories are already in the works as future releases.
Website: writerRSJ.com

The Knife
by Alanna Robertson-Webb

The tool I used to liberate my son is sitting on my dresser, like a trophy. I'm happy that I was finally able to free him, and I couldn't be more proud of his cheerful attitude.

Right now he's sitting next to me, his cute little face upturned in a grin. Some of his baby teeth have left gaps in his roguish grin, but I can fix that. I'll also need to sew the slit I made in his throat, but getting his blood out of our clothes will be harder.

At least he's free from years of cancer now.

Alanna Robertson-Webb is a sales support member by day, and a writer and editor by night. She loves VT, and live in PA. She has been writing since she was five years old, and writing well since she was seventeen years old. She lives with a fiance and a cat, both of whom take up most of her bed space. She loves to L.A.R.P., and one day she aspired to write a horrifyingly fantastic novel. Her short horror stories have been published before, but she still enjoys remaining mysterious.
Reddit: MythologyLovesHorror

The Price
by Chris Bannor

Some crimes never got solved. Some deaths didn't make sense. He looked around the hallowed ground, eyes roaming over green grass and sparsely populated trees. A pond rested on the outer edges of the quiet where a woman sat near a newly made grave.

It was one of many such scenes that would decorate his career. This was his first big case but even when the murderer was caught, it didn't bring the dead back. He memorised the moment so that he would never grow callused against it. No matter how many they caught, the price was always too high.

Chris Bannor is a science fiction and fantasy writer who lives in Southern California. Chris learned her love of genre stories from her mother at an early age and has never veered far from that path. She also enjoys musical theater and road trips with her family, but is a general homebody otherwise. Twitter: @BannorChris

An Eye for an Eye
by Beth W. Patterson

I don't like the term "cyber-creeping." I just want to have a little fun. It's been almost ten years since John and I called off our wedding, but I have to put his new girlfriend in her place.

At first, I was careless, and she blocked me on social media. But I know her favourite place to sit in City Park: a bench under a huge oak tree full of wind chimes. The Google Maps satellite passes right over it. I'll zoom in…

What is she doing with my children on her lap? Oh God, why are their eyes missing?

Beth W. Patterson was a full-time musician for over two decades before diving into the world of writing, a process she describes as "fleeing the circus to join the zoo". She is the author of the books Mongrels and Misfits, and The Wild Harmonic, and a contributing writer to thirty anthologies. Patterson has performed in eighteen countries, expanding her perspective as she goes. Her playing appears on over a hundred and seventy albums, soundtracks, videos, commercials, and voice-overs (including seven solo albums of her own). She lives in New Orleans, Louisiana with her husband Josh Paxton, jazz pianist extraordinaire.
Website: www.bethpattersonmusic.com
Facebook: bethodist

An Eerie Homage
By Olivia Arieti

Lady Lucinda's murder had to be re-examined; nobody could believe that such a reserved and devoted soul had been so brutally assassinated.

Since friends and family appeared quite forgetful of whatever detail, the investigator had the coffin re-opened.

Surprisingly, the gardener's corpse, a blood crusted knife in his hand, was lying above the woman as though he had just stabbed her while their decomposed jaws touched like in a final kiss.

Sir Reginald, after killing his wife, and shortly afterwards, her lover, had him secretly placed in the same grave; his homage to the adulterers for masking his deadly deeds.

Olivia Arieti has a degree from the University of Pisa and lives in Torre del Lago Puccini, Italy, with her family. Besides being a published playwright, she loves writing retellings of fairy tales, and at the same time is intrigued by supernatural and horror themes. Her stories appeared in several magazines and anthologies like Enchanted Conversations, Enchanted Tales Literary Magazine, Fantasia Divinity Magazine, Cliterature, Medieval Nightmares, Static Movement, 100 Doors To Madness Forgotten Tomb Press, Black Cats Horrified Press, Bloody Ghost Stories Full Moon Books, Death And Decorations Thirteen O'Clock Press, Infective Ink, Pandemonium Press, Pussy Magic Magazine.

Find Me
by Susanne Thomas

The police had failed Tim once again.

He'd left three fingerprints this time, and they hadn't found even one of them.

He'd left a hair two fires ago, and they'd missed it in all the soot.

At this next fire, he was going to leave a piece from a shirt identical to the one he always wore.

If that didn't work, he had no idea what else he could do. He needed to light the matches. These buildings would burn bright, and it was going be beautiful.

But if they didn't stop him soon, someone was going to get hurt.

Susanne Thomas reads, writes, parents, and teaches from the windy west in Wyoming, and she loves fantasy, science fiction, speculative fiction, poetry, children's books, science, coffee, and puns.
Website: www.themightierpenn.com
Facebook: SusanneThomasAuthor

Shared Goals
By Eddie D. Moore

Sheriff Johnson lifted the crime scene tape as Detective Morgan slipped under it. The detective stepped carefully around blood splatter as he studied the apartment. He inspected the corpse on the floor and eyed the bloody knife beside it.

"Is this the work of our vigilante?" asked the Sheriff.

The detective nodded and opened an evidence bag. "Yes, the victim is a human trafficking suspect, but we didn't have enough evidence to charge him."

The detective wiped the fingerprints from the knife before bagging it.

The Sheriff's jaw dropped open. "What are you doing?"

"I'm keeping the crime rate down."

Eddie D. Moore travels hundreds of hours a year, and he fills that time by listening to audiobooks. When he isn't playing with his grandchildren, he writes his own stories. You can find a list of his publications on his blog or by visiting his Amazon Author Page. While you're there, be sure to pick up a copy of his mini-anthology Misfits & Oddities. Website: eddiedmoore.wordpress.com Amazon: amazon.com/author/eddiedmoore

Crop Circle
by Pamela Jeffs

The sunflower crop is ruined. Claw-toed footprints pepper my front yard. A crop circle is branded into the far hill.

And there are noises coming from the barn.

I approach holding a shovel close. My only weapon. There's another high, yowling shriek. Carefully, I unlock the rear door. It swings open silently. I peer around the corner, the shovel held high.

It's the Donoghue twins—surrounded by broken flowers, rakes and petrol cans.

"Some aliens come visit ya last night, Mrs Pettigrew?" they snigger.

Little bastards.

I grit my teeth and raise the shovel high.

I'll give them bloody aliens!

Pamela Jeffs is a speculative fiction author living in Queensland, Australia with her husband and two daughters. She is a member of the Queensland Writers' Centre and has had numerous short fiction pieces published in recent national and international anthologies. In 2017 and again in 2018, Pamela was nominated for an Australian Aurealis Award in the category of 'Best Science Fiction Short Story'. Her debut collection titled 'Red Hour and Other Strange Tales' was released in March 2018.
Website: www.pamelajeffs.com
Facebook: pamelajeffsauthor

The Poison Poisoner
by Shawn M. Klimek

Detective Givens signalled the waiters to refill every champagne glass and then chimed his own to signal a toast. "Forgive this break from tradition," he pleaded, bowing towards the head table, "but I cannot wait to toast two of the boldest, most cold-blooded poisoners to ever crash a wedding." He raised an arresting palm to silence the gasps and mutterings. "Have no fear! The waiters are even now distributing an antidote to the first poison. At twice the dosage, however, this antidote itself becomes deadly, which makes me the second poisoner. Now, shall we all drink to discover the first?"

Shawn M. Klimek is the middle child of seven creative siblings, a globetrotting, U.S. military spouse, an internationally best-selling short-story writer, award-winning poet, and butler to a Maltese. More than one hundred of his stories and poems have been published in digital magazines or anthologies, including BHP's Deep Space, Eerie Christmas and every book so far in the Dark Drabbles series.
Website: jotinthedark.blogspot.com
Facebook: shawnmklimekauthor

A Note
by Joel R. Hunt

When he got home from work, he found the driveway vacant, the house abandoned. His wardrobe had been emptied of his wife's clothing. His children's rooms had been ransacked.

There was a note in the kitchen, ink still drying.

I'M LEAVING YOU. I TOOK THE KIDS. DON'T TRY TO FIND US.

He went straight to the police, who said he was in denial. To them, it was clear that his wife had been dissatisfied and left when she had the chance.

He begged. He shouted. He waved the note in their faces.

Why wouldn't they listen?

It wasn't her handwriting.

Joel R. Hunt is a writer from the UK who dabbles in the darker aspects of life, particularly through horror, science fiction and the supernatural. He has been published here and there (though likely nowhere you've heard of) and hopes to have released his first anthology of short stories later this year.
Twitter: @JoelRHunt1
Reddit: JRHEvilInc

The King
by Alanna Robertson-Webb

Being a Scotland Yard detective is a rough job. Day in and day out I solve cases for His Royal Majesty, always without so much as a "Thank you, good job!"

His dogs show more love towards his subjects than he does.

I've been at this job for twenty-six years, and last night my bonus came through.

I awoke this morning to shouts of "The King is dead!" Mourners lined the streets, and babies wailed at the commotion.

The best part?

They put me on the case, and I know a little secret they don't: I'll never turn myself in.

Alanna Robertson-Webb is a sales support member by day, and a writer and editor by night. She loves VT, and live in PA. She has been writing since she was five years old, and writing well since she was seventeen years old. She lives with a fiance and a cat, both of whom take up most of her bed space. She loves to L.A.R.P., and one day she aspired to write a horrifyingly fantastic novel. Her short horror stories have been published before, but she still enjoys remaining mysterious.
Reddit: MythologyLovesHorror

Trapped by the Payroll
by Abi Linhardt

They hired me to find missing girls. Followed a few leads, waited outside a bar. Tracked one drunk sorority girl to another and I found out the girls were in love with suave out-of-towners with fancy accents and mysterious eyes.

"They ran away together," one of the sisters told me. No note? No last-ditch *fuck you* to their parents?

Late at night, I scoped out the last known location of the guys. A truck pulled up, screaming inside. I called a cop I knew. He knew the names of the guys. Underground payrolls can't be cracked.

Abi Linhardt has been a gamer all her life but is a teacher at heart. When she is not writing, you can find her slaying enemies online or teaching in a college classroom. She has published works of fiction, poetry, college essays, and even won two literary awards for her short stories in science fiction and horror. Abi lives and writes in the grey world of northern Ohio.

Bad Luck
by Jonathan Inbody

Tom smashed at the front of the small safe with a claw hammer, knocking off the combination dial and denting the door enough that he could pry it open. Behind him, Jackson reloaded his gun. His hands were shaking, but he had done what needed to be done. With the kind of money they were about to get, they could do anything.

"It's empty," Tom said quietly.

In the corner of the room, the house's owner sat dead in a puddle of his own blood and brain matter. He really shouldn't have lied to his friends about winning the lottery.

Jonathan Inbody is a filmmaker, author, and podcaster from Buffalo, New York. He enjoys B-movies, pen and paper RPGs, and New Wave Science Fiction novels. His short story "Dying Feels Like Slowly Sinking" is due to be published in the anthology Deteriorate from Whimsically Dark Publishing. Jon can be heard every other week on his improvisational movie pitch podcast X Meets Y.
Website: xmeetsy.libsyn.com

The Walk
by A.L. King

Their fortune afforded them retirement on vast acreage. It was through their woodland they took walks, even after Eleanor's diagnosis. Herman led her.

"Seeing the grandkids was great," she said, unaware of just how far they'd walked since bidding their kin goodbye.

"Great until you mentioned the robbery," he countered. "I played it like you were confusing TV with memory, but you kept talking about the teller we shot dead in sixty-eight."

Suddenly, her eyes sparkled sharply—and sadly.

"Was it an accident?"

"It was," he answered. "But this isn't."

Herman sprinted toward home. Eleanor never found her way back.

A.L. King is an author of horror, fantasy, science fiction, and poetry. As an avid fan of dark subjects from an early age, his first influences included R.L. Stine, Edgar Allan Poe, and Stephen King. Later stylistic inspirations came from foreign horror films and media, particularly Japanese. He is a graduate of West Liberty University, has dabbled in journalism, and is actively involved in his community. Although his creativity leans toward darker genres, he has even written a children's book titled "Leif's First Fall." He was raised in the town of Sistersville, West Virginia, which he still proudly calls home.

Auto-da-Fe
by Donald Jacob Uitvlugt

He lies in Bloom Memorial's ICU, swaddled in bandages. Umbilicals of IVs and wires web around him. Only the monitor beeps show him to be alive.

He has no nerve endings, but after-memories of the pain play in an endless loop. The smell of burning flesh. Skin melting like wax. Heat pressing in all around. The cloying, bitter taste of smoke.

Through the pain comes certainty. He had known it would come. Knew it when he bought the gasoline. Knew when he heard the hiss of the match.

Baptism by fire.

And on his bed of pain, he smiles.

Donald Jacob Uitvlugt lives on neither coast of the United States, but mostly in a haunted memory palace of his own design. His short fiction has appeared in numerous print and online venues, including Cirsova Magazine and the Flame Tree Press anthology Murder Mayhem. He works primarily in speculative fiction, though he loves blending and stretching genres. He strives to write what he calls "haiku fiction," stories that are small in scale but big in impact.
Website: haikufiction.blogspot.com
Twitter: @haikufictiondju

The Masked Surrender
by Shawn M. Klimek

"This question is for Detective Givens," said the final reporter.

"Go ahead," said Givens.

"You've said that the Masked Butcher leaves behind a rubber mask as his calling card not only to taunt police, but because he wants to be caught."

"Correct. He primarily wants fame."

"If that's true, why does he use disguises? And follow-up question, if he's helping, why haven't you caught him?"

"Let me reverse the question," said Givens. "If the Masked Butcher did not want to be caught, why else would he sneak into a phony press conference and identify himself by asking an off-script question?"

Shawn M. Klimek is the middle child of seven creative siblings, a globetrotting, U.S. military spouse, an internationally best-selling short-story writer, award-winning poet, and butler to a Maltese. More than one hundred of his stories and poems have been published in digital magazines or anthologies, including BHP's Deep Space, Eerie Christmas and every book so far in the Dark Drabbles series.
Website: jotinthedark.blogspot.com
Facebook: shawnmklimekauthor

Deep in the House of Watobra
by Stuart Conover

Pyer'Eal had been practicing holding her breath.

The air was poison in the House of Watobra.

Yet, she slipped inside one moonless night.

Two minutes and the pressure built.

She swallowed it down.

Just shy of three minutes, she snuck into The Warlord's private chambers.

A beast of a creature lay naked upon the bed.

Four minutes and trapped air burned to be free.

She unsheathed the knife.

Exhaling, she drove the blade into the Orc's heart.

Inhaling death, she smiled as the creature took its final breath.

Her life a small price to pay for revenge against The Warlord.

Stuart Conover is a father, husband, rescue dog owner, published author, blogger, journalist, horror enthusiast, comic book geek, science fiction junkie, and IT professional. With all of that to cram in daily, we have no idea if or when he sleeps or how he gets writing done! (We suspect it has to do with having evil clones.) Stuart is a Chicago native and runs the author resource Horror Tree.

Innocently Guilty
by Terri A. Arnold

I am innocent. Why doesn't anyone believe me? I'll tell you. I'm not a good person. I've done unspeakable things, but I swear I didn't do this. As I sit here and stare at the cold metal bars that make up two walls of my cell, I wonder how this happened. I sit in silence as I contemplate the crime I will serve time for; arson. I laugh quietly, being convicted of this crime gives me the alibi I need for the crime I did commit. For I am innocent, but also guilty of the worse crime there is, murder.

Terri A Arnold has recently begun to share stories that she has been writing for years. She is from a small town in Nova Scotia and loves to put words to paper. By day she works as a registered nurse, but any other time she can be found reading or writing, and is loving it more and more every day.

Rush Job
by G. Allen Wilbanks

"When we arrived at this secluded little getaway two days ago, there were ten of us. Over the past forty-eight hours, someone has been picking us off, one by one," explained Detective Frank Antic. "I brought us all together tonight to put an end to this sick little game."

"Perhaps there is more than one killer in this house, Detective," suggested a mousy, blonde woman.

"No," he said. "The killer acted alone. I'm positive of that." The detective reached under his coat and removed a nickel-plated, Colt semi-automatic pistol. "I'm just tired of killing you assholes one at a time."

G. Allen Wilbanks is a member of the Horror Writers Association (HWA) and has published over 50 short stories in various magazines and on-line venues. He is the author of two short story collections, and the novel, When Darkness Comes.
Website: www.gallenwilbanks.com
Blog: DeepDarkThoughts.com

Homemade
by Abi Linhardt

Working the deep south was the detective's least favourite. All the TV shows made it look fun and hip, but really it was just swamps, mosquitos, cafes, and macabre toothless smiles.

He stood under the Spanish Moss, eyeing the lady in question. A husband killer. The man's car had been found burned out on a highway heading north. Standing behind her white fence, hanging laundry, she looked innocent.

"Ma'am," he said, stiffly as he could, his necktie suffocating. "I have some questions about your husband's whereabouts."

The lady smiled like sun tea. "Can I offer you my homemade meat pie?"

Abi Linhardt has been a gamer all her life but is a teacher at heart. When she is not writing, you can find her slaying enemies online or teaching in a college classroom. She has published works of fiction, poetry, college essays, and even won two literary awards for her short stories in science fiction and horror. Abi lives and writes in the grey world of northern Ohio.

The Curator
by Cameron Marcoux

Pictures. Photographs everywhere. Splayed across the room, all face up. Flesh jaggedly sewn together. Hair in matted clumps. Teeth in a dish. Blood.

The detective closed his eyes. The images were still there. This was too much. But what choice did he have? Weakness wouldn't catch this lunatic. He took a breath and opened them again.

Limbs hacked from bodies. Fingers in small piles. Intestines hanging from a ladder. People had been dissected and put on display in the likeness of a museum. He called himself the Curator. On the bottom of each polaroid was a single word: Sight. Passion. Discord. Revelation.

Cameron Marcoux is a writer of stories, which, considering where you are reading this, makes a lot of sense. He also teaches English to the lovely and terrifying creatures we call teenagers. He lives in the quiet, northern reaches of New England in the U.S. with his girlfriend and scaredy dog.

Bad Math
by Glenn R. Wilson

I thought I had killed them all.

I guess I calculated wrong.

Therefore, there's a chance I might be caught. Unless I pull the trigger.

Across the pathway, reaching for the keys to her apartment, is the daughter in hiding. The one I didn't know of until yesterday. He had so many liaisons, but this offspring I almost missed. I'd rather do it subtly. Not my style to be so crude. And ruthless. Out in the open. Seems so wrong.

But, what the hell.

A couple quick pops and it's over. So much blood…

At least I'll sleep well tonight.

Glenn R. Wilson has come full circle. Making a point to mature, like fine wine, before diving head-first into his long list of writing projects, he's approaching them with a plan. That strategy is to build with one brick at a time. He's accumulated a few bricks already and is adding more. Over time, with persistence and determination, he'll have a home. But for now, a solid foundation is the goal. Please, enjoy the process with him.

Dressed for Carnage
by Rowanne S. Carberry

Gun hidden in the dip of her back, she stalks her prey, light as a cat.

"Go ahead, I need a piss," the man says.

A sly smile spreads across her face.

Sliding out the gun she moves closer, waiting for the girlfriend to walk off.

Hearing the zipper sliding down, she places her finger on the trigger, pulling without a second thought, slipping away the moment she sees blood splatter up the wall.

She blends in with crowds leaving the clubs. Hidden from cameras she melts away. Ticking off hit number 100, she smiles knowing she won't be caught.

Rowanne S. Carberry was born in England in 1990, where she stills lives now with her cat Wolverine. Rowanne has always loved writing, and her first poem was published at the age of 15, but her ambition has always been to help people. Rowanne studied at the University of Sunderland where she completed combined honours of Psychology with Drama. Rowanne writes to offer others an escape. Although Rowanne writes in varied genres each story or poem she writes will often have a darkness to it, which helped coin her brand, Poisoned Quill Writing – Wicked words from a poisoned quill.
Facebook: PoisonedQuillWriting
Instagram: @poisoned_quill_writing

The Sting of Justice
by Shawn M. Klimek

Twin "goth chicks" sat across from Detective Givens in the interrogation room.

"To whichever of you is Ivy, the true goth," he said, addressing both, "security footage proves you shot the bartender. End this charade now, and I'll recommend lenience."

"Iris, your plan to frustrate identification by impersonating Ivy is doomed and you risk an obstruction charge."

Both women remained defiant.

"I give up," said Givens. "Constable, return their nose rings."

As the women accessorised, Givens pointed at the twin who didn't wince. "Arrest that one for murder," he said.

Grinning, he revealed, "I ordered them sterilised in lemon juice."

Shawn M. Klimek is the middle child of seven creative siblings, a globetrotting, U.S. military spouse, an internationally best-selling short-story writer, award-winning poet, and butler to a Maltese. More than one hundred of his stories and poems have been published in digital magazines or anthologies, including BHP's Deep Space, Eerie Christmas and every book so far in the Dark Drabbles series.
Website: jotinthedark.blogspot.com
Facebook: shawnmklimekauthor

Dirty Tricks
by John H. Dromey

To begin cross-examination, the criminal defence lawyer picked up Exhibit A.

"Is it just my imagination or does this package weigh less than it did the last time I handled it?"

"A few of the seeds were removed for testing," the witness said.

"For what purpose?"

"To verify they're from a cannabis plant and to see if they'd germinate."

"Using hydroponics? Or did you place the seeds in potting soil?"

"The latter."

The lawyer turned to the judge. "Your Honour, I ask that all charges against my client be dropped. This witness has just admitted under oath he *planted* evidence."

John H. Dromey was born in northeast Missouri, USA. He enjoys reading—mysteries in particular—and writing in a variety of genres. He's had short fiction published in Alfred Hitchcock's Mystery Magazine, Martian Magazine, Stupefying Stories Showcase, Thriller Magazine, Unfit Magazine, and elsewhere, as well as in a number of anthologies, including Chilling Horror Short Stories (Flame Tree Publishing, 2015).

Grave Oversight
by Diana Grove

It's a good spot—lonely bush, far from roads. Only dirt bike riders come out here. I open the Land Rover's boot and fling aside rope and plastic. Idiot! You left the bloody shovel behind. Can't go back. Too risky.

The girl seems smaller wrapped in plastic. I think about her while I dig with an empty first aid kit, and the sky darkens. That last terrified look she gave me will stay with me forever. Smiling, I shove her in the grave with my foot. Only one misstep…

It was easier than I expected to get away with murder.

Diana Grove writes weird short stories for children and adults that seldom have happy endings. Her chilling children's story 'Mr Grimwood's Curse' is in the Spring issue of The Caterpillar. Other stories have been published in the zine Trembling With Fear and the print anthologies Freak Pure Slush Vol. 13, Trembling With Fear: Year One and Witches vs Wizards.
Twitter: @ImaginaryGrove

The Unmaker
by Nicola Currie

They whisper in corners as I scrub the tiles beneath the throne. They do not notice me, these clever men who think they see. Already they conspire and politick, wondering which one of them did it.

The new king had sat alone on his throne; a just prize for one who had survived the schemes and plots of the road to coronation.

He hadn't noticed me either, until I cried out, the fire I stoked spitting sparks at my eye. The king laughed at my distress. When he turned, I put the poker to good use and laughed at his.

Nicola Currie is 34, from Cambridge, UK where she works in educational publishing. She has published poetry in literary magazines, including Mslexia and Sarasvati, and has also completed her first novel, which was longlisted for the Bath Children's Novel Award.
Website: writeitandweep.home.blog

Heist
by C.L. Williams

I enter the police station to drop off a package. A signature is required from the sergeant.

This isn't any regular package purchased from the internet. It's evidence from one holding cell to another. I tell the woman I see I require a specific signature. She looks for the man in charge while I'm asked to wait. I see the keys and make my way to evidence. I open the door and take what I need. I then go back to the van and let out the guy meant to do this job. I get in the van and leave.

*C.L. Williams is an independent author from central Virginia. He has written eight poetry books, four novellas, one novel, and a contributor to multiple anthologies, with the most recent appearance being an all-ages anthology titled Temoli from Thazbook. His most recent poetry book, The Paradox Complex, features the poem "Sad Crying Clown" that is now a video on YouTube directed by Matthew Mark Hunter of MMH Productions. C.L. Williams is currently working on his first sci-fi book, an all-ages book titled Novo: Away from Earth. When not writing, C.L. Williams is reading and sharing the work of other independent authors.
Facebook: writer434
Twitter: @writer_434*

The Unfortunate Record
by Galina Trefil

The teacher expected a mundane report on the local history. So naturally the gothic teenager, rather than do a run-of-the-mill internet search, instead checked the library's 19th century obituary records.

She flipped through the pages, hungry for the weirdest, juiciest thing she could find. And then…a suicide. A suicide allegedly committed via shotgun blast to the back of the head.

"For my assignment," she told the class, "I discovered an actual murder."

She relayed the details to her audience, all of whom were deliciously titillated—all but the teacher, whose violent and impulsive greatgrandfather had once been the town coroner.

Galina Trefil is a novelist specializing in women's, minority, and disabled rights. Her short stories and articles have appeared in Neurology Now, UnBound Emagazine, The Guardian, Tikkun, Romea.CZ, Jewcy, Jewrotica, Telegram Magazine, Ink Drift Magazine, The Dissident Voice, Open Road Review, and the anthologies "Flock: The Journey," "First Love," "Sea of Secrets," "Organic Ink," and "Suspense Unimagined."

The Best Resource
by Cindar Harrell

"What are you saying? That the thief is a ghost or something? No one can just walk through walls," I heard the detective say from my hiding spot in the ceiling.

"We can't explain it. The sensors would have been triggered no matter where they may have come in. No fingerprints, no fibres. No evidence that the crown was here at all."

"Just give up, no one is going to catch this one. Whoever it is, they must have amazing resources," said a second detective.

I smiled and blew him a secret kiss. He was by far my best resource.

Cindar Harrell loves fairy tales, especially ones with a dark twist. Her stories are often fairy tale inspired, but she is also working on a mystery series. Her stories can be found on Amazon and in various anthologies. You can follow her on Facebook and visit her blog, which she promises to try and update more often,
Website: cindarharrell.wordpress.com
Facebook: CindarHarrell

Down by the Water
by Laura Hughes

As the water's surface glitters like sparkling diamonds in the glow of the full moon, a fierce cry breaks the silence of the night. It's eerie sound echoing through the darkness of the trees. Then a loud splash, as a large mass pierces the tranquillity of the water, causing ripples and waves to perpetrate outward from the disturbance. All grows quiet again, except for the chirp of the crickets and the occasional hoot from an owl, as the water calms back to its original state of glistening diamonds. As if nothing happened to disturb the peaceful splendour of the night.

Laura Hughes was born and raised in Memphis, Tennessee. She is a high school graduate now residing in a small town in West Tennessee. She began writing poetry at the age of eighteen, after being diagnosed with Schizo-Affective Disorder. She used her writing as a form of therapy to help deal with the issues her illness caused. She shares her work, in the hopes that she can help others that are also afflicted and having difficulties in their lives.

The Smuggler
by Cecelia Hopkins-Drewer

"It looks like a drug deal gone wrong," Detective Booker said, checking the residue on the gunshot victim's fingers.

"If you look closer, you will see the drugs are still here," Coroner Smith pointed to the bloated abdomen.

"How would anyone get them?" Booker exclaimed.

"Simple," Smith said. He drew a sharp scalpel out of his investigative kit; slit the body open from pubic bone to ribcage and pulled out a plastic bag full of powder. "Unique method of delivery, eh?"

Booker retched. He had a sudden urge to escape from the locked morgue. Smith had turned crooked months ago.

Cecelia Hopkins-Drewer lives in Adelaide, South Australia. She has written a Masters paper on H.P. Lovecraft, and her weird poetry has been published in THE MENTOR (edited by Ron Clarke), and SPECTRAL REALMS (edited by S.T. Joshi). Her novels include a teenage vampire series comprised of three volumes, MYSTIC EVERMORE, SAINTS AND SINNERS & AUTUMN SECRETS. Short stories have been published in WORLDS, ANGELS & MONSTERS (Dark Drabbles anthologies edited by Dean Kershaw).
Amazon: amazon.com/Cecelia-Hopkins-Drewer/e/B071G968NM
Website: chopkin39.wixsite.com/website

Mass Madness
by D.J. Elton

Brien was only four when a man in the street went crazy. Brien and Mum had just come out of Coles with three full bags, and they heard *rat-a-tat tat* like those machine guns you hear in the movies. Mum screamed, dropped the shopping, and pulled Brien behind a postbox.

"Help!" "Move!" "Jesus!" People ran into each other, yelling and swearing to God. Some were dropping on the ground, groping at a body part that was oozing red. Hell had come alive.

Later, the man with two guns said that he couldn't remember anything. "Some evil just took me over."

D.J. Elton writes fiction and poetry, and is currently studying writing and literature which is improving her work in unexpected ways. She spends a lot of time in northern India and should probably live there, however there is much to be done in Melbourne, so this is the home base. She has meditated daily for the past 35 years and has worked in healthcare for equally as long, so she's very happy to be writing, zoning in and out of all things literary.
Twitter: @DJEltonwrites

An Eye for Detail
by Mason Harold Hilden

Entering the crime scene, Leta Diaz was met by Detective Smith.

"Ok, Diaz, do your magic".

Diaz began her analysis.

"The victim was slashed across the throat at the urinal. Arterial spraying shows the perp's a pro, severing both artery and vein. The victim died covered in blood and piss. There was no attempt to approach the victim. Spray patterns here show partial outlines of the perp's shoes, size ten".

Like always, Smith was amazed.

Her investigation done, Diaz unlocked the maintenance door and retrieved her cleaning cart. Thirty years of her dealing with this shit had taken its toll.

Mason Harold Hilden has dabbled in animation and comic-book scripting.

In a Warehouse
By Stephen Herczeg

The fireman had finished their job. The flames were out. The warehouse now just a smouldering ruin.

And there he was.

A lone body lying in the middle of the floor. Clothes singed but not burnt. No signs of trauma. My mind screamed, something didn't seem right.

I opened his mouth and pushed a cotton swab into his throat with my forceps. I moved it across every surface. It came back clean and white. No ash or soot. He hadn't breathed in any smoke.

I looked up at the detective.

"This man was dead before the fire. This was murder."

Stephen Herczeg is an IT Geek based in Canberra Australia. He has been writing for over twenty years and has completed a couple of dodgy novels, sixteen feature length screenplays and numerous short stories and scripts. His horror work has featured in Sproutlings, Hells Bells, Below the Stairs, Trickster's Treats #1 and #2, Shades of Santa, Behind the Mask, Beyond the Infinite; The Body Horror Book, Anemone Enemy, Petrified Punks and Beginnings. He has also had numerous Sherlock Holmes stories published through the Belanger Books - Sherlock Holmes anthologies.

Fire Starter
by Paula R.C. Readman

Beyond the rooftops, the sun explodes in a brilliant show of reds and oranges in the fading light. Such a simple joy to share before the noose digs in deep tomorrow. Some say it is no more than I deserve. How sweet the sun is to share its fiery light with me.

Between the heat and the screaming, I cannot tell you which I most prefer. Such a silly mistake brought me here. I lingered too long. The dancing colours held me captured as I grasped the petrol can. Caught in a blue flashing light, I had nowhere to run.

Paula R C Readman left school at 16 with no qualifications and worked in low paying jobs. In 1998, with no understanding of English grammar, she decided to beat her dyslexia by setting herself a challenge to become a published author. She taught herself 'How to Write' from books which her husband purchased from eBay. After 250 purchases, he finally told her 'just to get on with the writing'. Since 2010, she had 24 stories published and is now waiting to see if her first novel is accepted.
Website: paulareadman1.wordpress.com

The Velvet Purse
by Peter J. Foote

Silk slippers find traction on stones, leather gloves locate gaps in the mortar, and the assassin makes silent progress up the castle wall.

Perched in the windowsill's shadow, the assassin confirms that the climb didn't crush the velvet purse, before taking out a slim dagger.

With a nimble stroke, the assassin slides the dagger between the shutters, eases them wide, and slips into the noble's bedroom.

Eyes adjust and the snoring noble on the bed materialises.

Soundless, the assassin reaches the bed, opens the velvet purse, releasing the venomous spider within to discover its victim.

"No one cheats the Brotherhood."

Peter J. Foote is a bestselling speculative fiction writer from Nova Scotia. Outside of writing, he runs a used bookstore specialising in fantasy & sci-fi, cosplays, and alternates between red wine and coffee as the mood demands. His short stories can be found in both print and in ebook form, with his story "Sea Monkeys" winning the inaugural "Engen Books/Kit Sora, Flash Fiction/Flash Photography" contest in March of 2018. As the founder of the group "Genre Writers of Atlantic Canada", Peter believes that the writing community is stronger when it works together.
Twitter: @PeterJFoote1
Website: peterjfooteauthor.wordpress.com

Driving for a Living
by Jason Holden

The van rumbled along, bumping up and down as its tyres dipped in and out of holes littering the track.

Driving was Joe's pleasure—he had bought a panel van, had turned listening to his tunes and looking at the amazing Derbyshire scenery into a job.

Unfortunately, it was a job that didn't pay well. He was forced to look for other means of income.

His instructions were, "Don't mess with the cargo! Don't ask questions!"

Joe turned up the music, hoping to drown out the muffled cries for help that came from the duct taped mouths in the back.

*After giving up a full-time job as a quarry operator so that his wife could follow her dream career as an academic in the field of chemistry, **Jason Holden** and his family left England and temporarily moved to Spain where they currently reside. While there, he took on the role of full-time parent and began to create stories for his daughter. Now that she is in school, he creates stories for himself and hopes to share those stories with others.*

Orange Crumbs
by Ximena Escobar

The sun rose on the desert of his body, a television casting blue lights on his bare skin.

Ross felt unexpectedly relaxed. It was the man's expression; once he'd put the plastic bag around his head, he'd stopped wrestling—he wanted to die, deep down, free himself from the curse of his body's twisted appetites. As the bag of Cheetos rustled around his fingers, he felt emancipated too, from his own prison of mediocrity.

How many boys had he saved with just one bag?

He didn't untie him.

When people began to scurry out of their doors, so did Ross.

Ximena Escobar is an emerging author of literary fiction and poetry. Originally from Chile, she is the author of a translation into Spanish of the Broadway Musical "The Wizard of Oz", and of an original adaptation of the same, "Navidad en Oz". Clarendon House Publications published her first short story in the UK, "The Persistence of Memory", and Literally Stories her first online publication with "The Green Light". She has since had several acceptances from other publishers and is working very hard exploring new exciting avenues in her writing.
She lives in Nottingham with her family.
Facebook: Ximenautora

HomiCider
by Gregg Cunningham

My shift was done, and the drive had been long. I was dying for a beer, but the usual fuckwits lined the roads, cutting in front of my rig and really pissing me off, and it was me who had to ease off the gas.

At the bar, all the little shit had to do was serve me and I would have been out of his face and well on my way to being out of mine.

But no. I get the smug attitude.

"Sorry mate, no high vis vests allowed!"

I snapped and picked up the empty Bulmer's bottle.

Gregg Cunningham 48, short story writer who has had to pick up his game since stumbling into facebook writer's groups. He has stories published by 559 Publishing in in 13 Bites volume 3,4,5, Plan 9 from Outer space, Other Realms, Heard It on The Radio, 559 Ways to Die, short stories publishing by Zombie Pirate Publishing in Relationship add Vice, Full Metal Horror, Phuket Tattoo, World War four and Flash Fiction Addiction (flash) with Zombie Pirate Publishing, and also in Daastan Magazine Chapter 11 and Brian,Rich and the Wardrobe.
Amazon: www.amazon.com/-/e/B016OTHX0K
Website: cortlandsdogs.wordpress.com

Bittersweet Justice
by John H. Dromey

The drawing room was crowded with miscreants of every stripe.

"This isn't my cup of tea," one of the men said.

"What's that? Are you trying to tell me you don't like this situation where a pompous amateur detective has once again persuaded the police to assemble all the murder suspects in one room so he can dramatically reveal the guilty party that no one else suspects?"

"No. I'm saying I ordered sweet tea and this is bitter."

Just then the amateur sleuth—a remorseful killer—entered the room, glanced at the empty teacup and asked, "Who drank my hemlock?"

First published in *The Literary Hatchet*, 2013

John H. Dromey was born in northeast Missouri, USA. He enjoys reading—mysteries in particular—and writing in a variety of genres. He's had short fiction published in Alfred Hitchcock's Mystery Magazine, Martian Magazine, Stupefying Stories Showcase, Thriller Magazine, Unfit Magazine, and elsewhere, as well as in a number of anthologies, including Chilling Horror Short Stories (Flame Tree Publishing, 2015).

Jetsam and Flotsam
by Pamela Jeffs

The river hides my secrets. In the jetsam and flotsam of her flow. She conceals what I have done—the sinking of Pirate Lionheart's ship.

Lengths of rope slither through the water. Barrels roll by. A boot, laces streaming in the water. The newspapers claimed it was a pleasure craft scuttled higher up the river, but it wasn't. How did they miss the smaller clues? The bodies floating past me look nothing like pleasure seekers. Each one has a pirate brand scored into the shoulder. But it concerns me not. I'm just waiting for the treasure map to float by.

Pamela Jeffs is a speculative fiction author living in Queensland, Australia with her husband and two daughters. She is a member of the Queensland Writers' Centre and has had numerous short fiction pieces published in recent national and international anthologies. In 2017 and again in 2018, Pamela was nominated for an Australian Aurealis Award in the category of 'Best Science Fiction Short Story'. Her debut collection titled 'Red Hour and Other Strange Tales' was released in March 2018.
Website: www.pamelajeffs.com
Facebook: pamelajeffsauthor

Good Friends
by J.A. Hammer

There were ways not to be caught. Of course, the best way was to never have a dead body in your possession, but Amelia knew how hard that rule was to follow. The other rules though, if they were obeyed, then she was unstoppable.

- No souvenirs.
- No family members (not even annoying Ethan).
- No life insurance policies.

And always keep a friend to help out. She grinned. Florida had great friends too, the brackish creek behind her house home to both alligators and bull sharks. A little blood in the water, a little push...and good friends came to her rescue.

J.A. Hammer lives off of coffee (mostly Dead Eyes) and stress in the wild concrete city of Tokyo, where zombies are living and using the train lines every day. Known as CoffeeQuills online, they're mostly safe to talk to (bites only happen in the name of science) but be wary if approaching before dawn. The cake is not a lie, but you'll have to get it yourself. If you're interested in steampunk/paranormal Japan, check out their Patreon, or if you'd like daily drabbles and pictures from Japan, follow CoffeeQuills on either Instagram or Twitter.
Website : www.patreon.com/coffeequills

Too Late
by E.L. Giles

The cold morning waves bathed the sandy shore, bringing a eerie chill as the tide rose and enveloped the dead, naked body of a woman.

At the crack of dawn, a scream pierced the tranquil morning. The shore buzzed with activity. Thumbs rested on the screens of phones as the mutilated body was dragged out of the water, giving momentum to the rising speculation.

A message lay engraved on her dead body, her skin swelling and turning blue where the blade had slashed the epidermis, filling every witness with the most dreadful kinds of nightmares.

"You're too late," it read.

E.L. Giles is a dreamer, passionate about art, a restless worker and a bit of a weird human. He started his artistic journey as a music composer until the need to put his thoughts and stories down on paper grew too strong for him to resist it any longer. He lives in the French Province of Quebec, Canada, with his girlfriend and two boys.
Facebook: elgilesauthor
Website: www.elgilesauthor.com

Mabel
by Sinister Sweetheart

Grandpa Cyril was on his last days. My brother and I sat at his bedside until the bitter end. With quavering breaths, he unburdened his soul through confession.

"Kids, there's something to need to know. Your Aunt Mabel, she's not right. She disappeared in the woods for two days as a child. She showed back up to the house dirtier than normal, but basically unaffected.

"Two weeks later, police officers found the dead body of a young girl in the same woods. Fingerprints and dental records reported it to be the body of seven-year-old Mabel, having died sixteen days earlier."

*Since **Sinister Sweetheart** made her first post to a popular Internet forum, she's taken the horror community by storm. Her ability to create, terrify, and drive home her stories is insurmountable. Sinister Sweetheart's published works can be found in multiple anthologies for all to read, but be forewarned, if you do... you may want to call your therapist after, her stories are terrifying, disturbing and devilishly unsettling. She is not only a fright visually, but also has a creepy tentacle in horror podcasting as well. Sinister Sweetheart writes, voice acts and is the media director of the Scarecrow Tales podcast.*
Website: Sinistersweetheart.wixsite.com/sinistersweetheart
Facebook: NMBrownStories

Cleared
by Gabriella Balcom

Falling down, Ellen dropped her popcorn. "Oh, no!" she wailed. Some people helped her. Others stared.

During the movie, she changed seats, pulled a wig and dark jacket from her bag, then slipped outside. She jogged to her destination, but quickly returned to the theatre.

Two days later, a maid let herself into a hotel room. She screamed, seeing the man riddled with bullet holes.

"The suspect list is never-ending," Officer Lane told his superior. "He swindled bosses, co-workers, used women, owed ex-wives, and almost everyone hated him. The only person we know is innocent is his current wife, Ellen."

Gabriella Balcom lives in Texas with her family, loves reading and writing, and thinks she was born with a book in her hands. She works in a mental health field, and writes fantasy, horror/thriller, romance, children's stories, and sci-fi. She likes travelling, music, good shows, photography, history, interesting tales, and animals. Gabriella says she's a sucker for a great story and loves forests, mountains, and back roads which might lead who knows where. She has a weakness for lasagne, garlic bread, tacos, cheese, and chocolate, but not necessarily in that order.
Facebook: GabriellaBalcom.lonestarauthor

New York Night
by Ann Christine Tabaka

The New York skyline was silhouetted against a starry night. The streets were abuzz with theatre goers leaving for restaurants or for home. All of a sudden, a scream rang out and everyone froze, quiet. The crowd parted, and there he stood with a wild look in his eyes and a bloody knife in his hand. He fell to his knees, then collapsed face down. There were two dead bodies on the street. The police arrived within minutes and started asking questions.

Meanwhile, no one noticed as a shadowy figure slowly walked away and disappeared into the New York night.

Ann Christine Tabaka was nominated for the 2017 Pushcart Prize in Poetry, has been internationally published, and won poetry awards from numerous publications. She is the author of 9 poetry books. Christine lives in Delaware, USA. She loves gardening and cooking. Chris lives with her husband and two cats. Her most recent credits are: Burningword Literary Journal; Ethos Literary Journal, North of Oxford, Pomona Valley Review, Page & Spine, West Texas Literary Review, The Hungry Chimera, Sheila-Na-Gig, Pangolin Review, Foliate Oak Review, Better Than Starbucks!, The Write Launch, The Stray Branch, The McKinley Review, Fourth & Sycamore.

Until It Happens to Your Child
by Carole de Monclin

On that fine spring day at 1.46 pm, everything changed.

With prom days away, Sarah had bought an elegant red gown.

That dress will never be worn.

Witnesses' accounts only give me a glimpse into her nightmare.

Room 234. A resounding bang interrupts the teacher. Paralysis sinks its claws into every soul. Another deafening crack echoes. Closer. Menacing. Incomprehensible. Kids scramble under their desks.

The door bursts open. The gunshot roars so loudly, Sarah doesn't immediately understand she's hit. Life flows out too fast for goodbyes or regrets.

Farewell, daughter. My only comfort is knowing your friend held your hand.

Carole de Monclin travels both the real world and imaginary ones. She's lived in France, Australia, and the USA; visited 25+ countries; and explored Mars, Ceres, and many distant planets. She writes to invite people on a journey. Stories have found her for as long as she can remember, be it in a cave in Victoria, the smile of a baby in Paris, or a museum in Florida.
Website: CaroledeMonclin.com
Twitter: @CaroledeMonclin

No Evidence to Find
by Radar DeBoard

Joseph chuckled lightly to himself.

When he had killed the first one, there was a definite fear he would be caught. A fear the police would find his DNA, or some other traces of him on the bodies.

Then he came up with the idea to use his good works to help him.

So far it had worked for seven victims—soon to be eight.

He poured a ladle of stew into the bowl of another unsuspecting homeless person.

The police can't start a murder investigation without a body. No one ever said that community service couldn't benefit the volunteer.

Radar DeBoard is a horror movie and novel enthusiast who resides in the small town of Goddard, Kansas. He occasionally dabbles in writing and enjoys making dark tales for people to enjoy.

The Dead Wife
by J.M. Meyer

Seamus Quin was convicted of murdering his wife in 1409. The shovel he slammed into her arm caused a deep gash which became infected. Sepsis set in and painful death followed. With his brother and best friend as witnesses, he appealed, on the grounds of his wife's incompetence and cruelty. She kept an untidy house, berated him in public, and had not had a child during three years of marriage.

"I meant to teach, not kill. 'Twas her fault for not tending her wound."

The court agreed and Seamus was permitted to wed his dead wife's sister, as was custom.

J.M. Meyer is writer, artist and small business owner living in New York., where she received her master's degree from Teacher's College, Columbia University. Jacqueline loves the science fiction and horror genres. Reading Ray Bradbury was a mind-blowing experience for her in 8th grade. Alfred Hitchcock and Rod Serling were the horror heroes of her youth. Mercedes M. Yardley is her current horror writing hero. Jacqueline also enjoys the company of her husband Bruce and their three children, Julia, Emma and Lauren. Jacqueline's mantra: The only time it's too late to try something new is when you are dead.
Website: jmoranmeyer.net
Twitter: @moran_meyer

Monster Hunter
by Donald Jacob Uitvlugt

I see you.

You know that tingle you feel on the back of your neck while you're driving? Or shopping for groceries? Or in the shower?

That's me.

I know all of your secrets. Those crimes you hide, even from your lover.

You disgust me.

Walking around like you're not a monster. Like the sun won't burn you or the ground won't swallow you up. You just think you're safe. Keep on thinking that way. You'll see.

You're a thing masquerading in human skin. Soon my knife will reveal the truth to the world. It always does.

I see you...

Donald Jacob Uitvlugt lives on neither coast of the United States, but mostly in a haunted memory palace of his own design. His short fiction has appeared in numerous print and online venues, including Cirsova Magazine and the Flame Tree Press anthology Murder Mayhem. He works primarily in speculative fiction, though he loves blending and stretching genres. He strives to write what he calls "haiku fiction," stories that are small in scale but big in impact.
Website: haikufiction.blogspot.com
Twitter: @haikufictiondju

Hitchhiker's Delight
by Kelly A. Harmon

Nick fingered the knucklebones on his key chain as he pulled over.

The bearded man slid into the back, smelling of...something...and body odour.

"Where to?" Nick asked.

"West."

"Odessa?"

The hitchhiker nodded, then gestured toward the rearview mirror. "Nice dream catcher. Rabbit skin?"

"Something like that." Nick smiled.

Suddenly, the hitchhiker slid forward, wrapping an arm around Nick's neck. "Most folks aren't brave enough to stop—weren't you afraid you'd pick up a serial killer?"

Nicolas laughed, finally recognising the tangy odour of blood. He pulled a switchblade from his pocket. "What are the odds? One killer picking up another?"

Kelly A. Harmon *is an award-winning journalist and author, and a member of the Science Fiction & Fantasy Writers of America and Horror Writers of America. A Baltimore native, she writes the Charm City Darkness series. The fourth book in the series, In the Eye of the Beholder, is now available. Find her short fiction in many magazines and anthologies, including Occult Detective Quarterly; Terra! Tara! Terror! and Deep Cuts: Mayhem, Menace and Misery.*
Website: kellyaharmon.com
Twitter: @kellyaharmon

Who's Is It?
by Wendy Roberts

Detective Whit steps through the abandoned warehouse and stops at the wall splattered with blood before he looks at the report in his hand.

"No leads."

The officer next to him shakes his head. "Nothing yet, but we're running the bit of hair samples..."

"It's from wigs." Detective Whit shuts the folder. "Their heads are shaved weeks before they're killed."

"And the fingers?" The officer glances at the ground where a pool of blood is left behind.

"Previous victims."

"We've got a fingerprint." The officer holds up the evidence.

"Yeah, who's is it?"

The man fumbles a bit. "Um."

"Exactly."

Writing short stories and novels started as a past time for **Wendy Roberts** *and has now become a fully fledged passion. She posts short stories on her website and can be found most days on Twitter.*
Website: flippinscribbler.wordpress.com
Twitter: @_WARoberts

Love Letter
by Raven Corinn Carluk

Detective,

I've enjoyed watching you dance to my tune. You've been more entertaining than that slob you replaced. You seemed to care about the young women I disassembled.

Have you seen yourself in them? I have.

Regardless of the joy you've brought me, I must leave. I would have left long ago, but for the entertainment value your investigation provided.

Since the futility of finding me surely keeps you up, marinating in frustration, I've left you one clue. A single hair, somewhere in this house. I look forward to seeing you again, my sweet Nicole.

Always one step ahead,

Whistler

Raven Corinn Carluk writes dark fantasy, paranormal romance, and anything else that catches her interest. She's authored five novels, where she explores themes of love and acceptance. Her shorter pieces, usually from her darker side, can be found in Black Hare Press anthologies, at Detritus Online, and through Alban Lake Publishers.
Twitter: @ravencorinn
Website: RavenCorinnCarluk.Blogspot.Com

Duty Calls
by Amber M. Simpson

An hour after her lights go out, I break a window and crawl inside.

I watch her awhile; the rise and fall of her chest, little sounds she makes in her sleep.

So beautiful.

Squeezing my hands around her throat, she jerks and her eyes pop open. She tries to scream but I tighten my grip, slowly crushing her wind pipe.

I tuck her in, kiss her goodnight, and leave through the front door, whistling.

In the car, the radio crackles, "Dorchester Street, hit and run."

Duty calls.

Buckling up, I hit my sirens and take off into the night.

Amber M. Simpson is a chronic nighttime writer with a penchant for dark fiction and fantasy. When she's not editing for Fantasia Divinity Magazine, she divides her creative time (when she's not procrastinating) between writing a mystery/horror novel, working on a medieval fantasy series, and coming up with new ideas for short stories. Above all, she enjoys being a mom to her two greatest creations, Max and Liam, who keep her feet on the ground even while her head is in the clouds.
Website: ambermsimpson.com

Under the Microscope
by A.R. Johnston

Bits of bone, blood, tissue were just all parts of a whole. "Or what used to be a whole," Colleen mused as she placed her next sample on a slide to put under a microscope.

"You think you can sort out all of this mess and make matches?" Jones stood in the doorway staring at all the slides.

Colleen slowly looked up from the microscope, scribbling a note before looking at Jones.

"Have I ever not been able to figure it out?" She smirked.

Jones laughed. "You're amazing, Colleen."

She was the one that brought concrete evidence. Evidence in blood.

A.R. Johnston is a small-town girl from Nova Scotia, Canada. Her style of writing is considered Urban Fantasy. Her first major publication is part of an anthology called First Love and she has several more titles lined up. She is a lover of coffee, good tv shows, horror flicks, and reader of books. She pretends to be a writer when real life doesn't get in the way. Pesky full-time job and adulting!

Going Back to Mexico
by Isabella Fox

"They'll know we're keeping back some of the money," Hugo said. "We're already paid well, don't be greedy."

"Nah, he won't miss a couple of grand," Eduardo replied. "I want to end my days back in Mexico, enjoying the scenery before I'm old."

***

"Carlos, you know those young punks are robbing us blind. Teach them you don't cross Santos," the drug lord ordered.

Eduardo opened his eyes. He and Hugo were buried in the hot sand, only their heads visible. He had his wish, he was going to end his days in Mexico looking at the scenery, while still young.

Isabella Fox teaches primary aged students to love writing by making it challenging. In her spare time she reads, goes for long walks with her husband and works hard on her farm.

Blind Pursuit
by Ann Christine Tabaka

As she worked her way through the forest at night, she touched each tree. The rough bark reminded her of braille, since she could not see. She kept moving, trying to get away from them. She didn't know who they were, or why, but they were after her.

As she tripped and fell, she held her breath, trying not to cry out in alarm. She tried to remain quiet and unnoticed, but it was too late. As she looked up, she saw them standing over her. Her name is now listed among the missing, on the back of milk cartons.

Ann Christine Tabaka was nominated for the 2017 Pushcart Prize in Poetry, has been internationally published, and won poetry awards from numerous publications. She is the author of 9 poetry books. Christine lives in Delaware, USA. She loves gardening and cooking. Chris lives with her husband and two cats. Her most recent credits are: Burningword Literary Journal; Ethos Literary Journal, North of Oxford, Pomona Valley Review, Page & Spine, West Texas Literary Review, The Hungry Chimera, Sheila-Na-Gig, Pangolin Review, Foliate Oak Review, Better Than Starbucks!, The Write Launch, The Stray Branch, The McKinley Review, Fourth & Sycamore.

The Cross and Dollar Gang
by Pamela Jeffs

Smoke rises from the end of Inspector Carnegie's cigar. A man in a suit, murdered, lies at his feet uncaring of the fumes.

There's only one clue in the room. Bloody footprints on the carpet. Carnegie's partner, Phillips, rolls the body over.

Another clue.

The corpse has two symbols painted on its forehead. A cross and a dollar sign.

Phillips recoils. "Is that what I think it is?"

Carnegie sucks in another breath of smoke. The burning end of his cigar brightens then fades back to dull ember. "Yup. Looks like the Cross and Dollar gang are back in town."

Pamela Jeffs is a speculative fiction author living in Queensland, Australia with her husband and two daughters. She is a member of the Queensland Writers' Centre and has had numerous short fiction pieces published in recent national and international anthologies. In 2017 and again in 2018, Pamela was nominated for an Australian Aurealis Award in the category of 'Best Science Fiction Short Story'. Her debut collection titled 'Red Hour and Other Strange Tales' was released in March 2018.
Website: www.pamelajeffs.com
Facebook: pamelajeffsauthor

New Message
by Brian Rosenberger

To: Melody

CC:

BC:

Subject: Update

Sorry for the chaos. My upstairs neighbour (that one) had her apt broken into. Her TV, a bag of frozen tater tots and jewellery were stolen.

The cops questioned me. I said I wasn't home.

Later, I surveyed the crime scene and saw no visible damage.

Anyway, dinner is still on. About 7 yrs old. Poor little thing. I know you prefer the taste of tender flesh. She's still draining. About to don the butcher's apron (and nothing else). How's that for a tease?

See you soon. Bring an appetite. No snackin!!!

The Chef

Brian Rosenberger lives in a cellar in Marietta, GA (USA) and writes by the light of captured fireflies. He is the author of As the Worms Turns and three poetry collections. He is also a featured contributor to the Pro-Wrestling literary collection, Three-Way Dance, available from Gimmick Press.
Facebook: HeWhoSuffers

Obsession
by Carole de Monclin

I'd spotted him or found proof he'd lurked undetected enough times to know anywhere, anytime existed the possibility he was watching me. Despite having repeatedly cheated and lied, the bastard claimed he loved me.

He'd created a nightmare where he was always on my mind.

Just when I considered involving the police, he vanished. No more calls, messages, or sightings. Friends told me he was seeing someone.

How sweet freedom tasted.

Months passed before I accepted another man's invitation.

I was leaving my apartment to meet my date when a hard hand closed over my mouth.

"You belong to me."

Carole de Monclin travels both the real world and imaginary ones. She's lived in France, Australia, and the USA; visited 25+ countries; and explored Mars, Ceres, and many distant planets. She writes to invite people on a journey. Stories have found her for as long as she can remember, be it in a cave in Victoria, the smile of a baby in Paris, or a museum in Florida.
Website: CaroledeMonclin.com
Twitter: @CaroledeMonclin

The World's Greatest Artist
by Charlotte O'Farrell

Verity made the trip to see the world's most famous painting every year with her elderly father. They waited for the quieter times so they could be alone with it.

They admired the artistry, the pure talent. They gushed over each masterful brushstroke.

She took his hand.

"You did a great job, Dad," she whispered. It was the same thing she told him every year. And he had: in the fifty years since he'd replaced the painting with his forgery, no-one had guessed.

They left the museum and looked forward to seeing the real thing hanging up in their cellar.

Charlotte O'Farrell is a lifelong horror fan who writes about all manner of the weird and wonderful. Her work can be found at the Drabble, the Rock N Roll Horror Zine and Horror Tree, among other places.
Twitter: @ChaOFarrell

Caught Red-Handed
by Rowanne S. Carberry

Sammie looks up as she hears the bell above the door. Her heart skips a beat as two officers walk into the shop.

"Good morning, officers."

"We're here about Chris."

Straight to the point. It takes all her strength not to look down.

"I haven't seen Chris in weeks," Sammie replies.

After asking a few questions the officers go to leave until they look down.

Both pulling out a Taser, they're pointed at Sammie.

"Hands in the air!"

Everything freezes. She tries to work out how she's been caught, then she sees the stream of blood from under the counter.

Rowanne S. Carberry was born in England in 1990, where she stills lives now with her cat Wolverine. Rowanne has always loved writing, and her first poem was published at the age of 15, but her ambition has always been to help people. Rowanne studied at the University of Sunderland where she completed combined honours of Psychology with Drama. Rowanne writes to offer others an escape. Although Rowanne writes in varied genres each story or poem she writes will often have a darkness to it, which helped coin her brand, Poisoned Quill Writing – Wicked words from a poisoned quill.

Facebook: *PoisonedQuillWriting*
Instagram: *@poisoned_quill_writing*

Living Forever
by Charlotte O'Farrell

WHAT SHOULD I DO? I'M SCARED. Fiona texted, tears in her eyes.

After a pause, the reply appeared: FOLLOW YOUR HEART.

Grandpa was the wisest person when he was alive. It was comforting to have his sayings frozen in time and repeated back to her via the Live Forever app. As soon as his funeral was done, she'd uploaded all their old conversations into it.

But it didn't help her decide where to hide the bodies, and the smell in her basement was starting to get unbearable. Grandpa always dumped his victims in the quarry, but that seemed too predictable.

Charlotte O'Farrell is a lifelong horror fan who writes about all manner of the weird and wonderful. Her work can be found at the Drabble, the Rock N Roll Horror Zine and Horror Tree, among other places.
Twitter: @ChaOFarrell

Thieves and Cigarettes
by Rhiannon Bird

He puffed his last cigarette as he crept towards the store. There was no one else in the street.

"You sure that it's disabled?" he said into the phone.

"No alarms, just like every other time, Boss," the youngster replied lazily. He took a last glance around and threw a rock through the glass. Instantly an alarm rang out. "Shit, there must be a secondary system we didn't know about," the youngster said, but he was already running, he would not be caught.

It was only once he was a safe distance away he realised the half-smoked cigarette was gone.

Rhiannon Bird is a young aspiring author. She has a passion for words and storytelling. Rhiannon has her own quotes blog; Thoughts of a Writer. She has had 4 works published. This includes 3 short stories and 2 poems. These are published on Eskimo pie, Literary yard, Down in the Dirt Magazine and Short break fiction. She can be found on Facebook, Instagram, and Pinterest.

Mrs. McAdilly's Garden
by Shelly Jarvis

Alice McAdilly was eighty-seven years old when they found the bodies.

She lived in a nursing home in the Garden District, with views of devil's trumpet and yellow queen, the air thickly scented with coral honeysuckle.

She watched officers pass under thick-limbed trees that offered swathes of shade from the oppressive New Orleans heat.

"We found thirteen bodies under your house."

She shook her head. "Should be fifteen."

"Why'd you do it?"

Her milky eyes took on a faraway look. "Why does anyone do anything? Because I wanted to. Because I could. I just gave the bastards what they deserved."

Shelly Jarvis is a speculative fiction author from West Virginia, US. She found a life-long love of sci-fi and fantasy in the 3rd grade when she found Madeleine L'Engle's "A Wrinkle in Time." Shelly is an avid reader, a Whovian, the ideal viewer of dog rescue videos, and undoubtedly Ravenclaw. She currently has three YA sci-fi books available for purchase on Amazon.
Website: www.ShellyJarvis.com

The Rat
by Roxanne Dent

Bennie the Rat knocked back his seventh Blue Ruin as the blonde bombshell with gams that wouldn't quit walked in. Her eyes passed over me and settled on Bennie as she sauntered up to the bar.

The doll leaned over, and I heard her whisper, "Eddy the Carp sends his regards." She straightened up and winked at me before she sashayed out.

Bennie was so sloshed it took three minutes for him to drop, another five for the rest of us to realise the dame had buried a shiv in his ribs and Bennie the rat was stone cold dead.

Roxanne Dent has sold nine novels and dozens of short stories in a variety of genres including Paranormal Fantasy, Regency, Mystery, Horror and YA. She has also co-authored short stories and plays with her sister, Karen Dent. Member of New England Horror Writers, The Fiction Writers Guild, Berlin Writers Group, Essex Writers and Artists Group.

Third Round
by Sam M. Phillips

My opponent might look tough—a mean faced boxer ready to knock my block off—but what he has to dish out is nothing compared to the punishment waiting for me if I don't deliver.

I suppose, in the end, it's just my stupid pride getting hurt. Yeah, I'm thirteen for zero, all of them knockouts, but everyone loses eventually. It's just the business we're in.

Off to the side of the ring, I can see his goons watching. I'll be dead before I leave the building if I don't take a dive, third round.

And they've got my daughter.

Sam M. Phillips is the co-founder of Zombie Pirate Publishing, producing short story anthologies and helping emerging writers. His own work has appeared in dozens of anthologies and magazines such as Full Moon Slaughter 2, 13 Bites Volumes IV and V, Rejected for Content 6, and Dastaan World Magazine. He lives in the green valleys of northern New South Wales, Australia, and enjoys reading, walking, and playing drums in the death metal band Decryptus.
Website: zombiepiratepublishing.com
Blog: bigconfusingwords.wordpress.com

The Colour Red
by Lyndsey Ellis-Holloway

"It's a beautiful view, isn't it?" she asked with a smile, glancing over her shoulder at the detective.

"Put the weapon down, Ma'am," the detective replied gently, hand lingering over his own gun.

"What a perfect sunset! What stunning colours! That red! I'll miss this."

She smiled before she took a long sip of wine. "I do so love the colour red...he always looked good in it, too."

Placing her wine glass and the gun on the table beside her she turned to face the detective, her blue eyes lingering on her husband's corpse. "Goodbye, darling. Rest in peace."

Lyndsey Ellis-Holloway is a writer from Knaresborough, UK. She writes fantasy, sci-fi, horror and dystopian stories, focussing on compelling characters and layering in myth and legend at every opportunity. When she's not writing she spends time with her husband, her dogs and her friends enjoying activities such as walking, movies, conventions and of course writing for fun as well!

Jack and Jill
by Gabriella Balcom

"Let me show you the best way to cut," Jack said, demonstrating with a knife. "You want to hit the jugular the first time and not have to try again." He smiled because killing was enjoyable, regardless of how it was done. Afterward, he guided Jill in washing the body in the shower, wiping down everything, checking the drain for hair and debris, and vacuuming.

"Here's my favourite way," he said days later, pointing to the vat of acid he'd prepared.

"Nice." Jill nodded approvingly. "I love these names you've chosen for us, too."

Jack grinned. "They'll never catch us."

Gabriella Balcom lives in Texas with her family, loves reading and writing, and thinks she was born with a book in her hands. She works in a mental health field, and writes fantasy, horror/thriller, romance, children's stories, and sci-fi. She likes travelling, music, good shows, photography, history, interesting tales, and animals. Gabriella says she's a sucker for a great story and loves forests, mountains, and back roads which might lead who knows where. She has a weakness for lasagne, garlic bread, tacos, cheese, and chocolate, but not necessarily in that order.
Facebook: GabriellaBalcom.lonestarauthor

Eye on the Prize
by Crystal L. Kirkham

The necklace sparkled under the dim illumination from the security lights. A one of a kind that she couldn't wait to hold. Lifting the protective glass, she held her breath. Silence.

She exhaled with relief and lifted her sparkly prize from the display. It was heavier than she'd expected. Knowing she shouldn't, she placed it around her neck. It suited her.

Too bad this was for a client. Slipping it in her pocket, she crept out, locking doors behind her. No one would know she'd been here. One last job and she'd spend the rest of her life in luxury.

Crystal L. Kirkham *resides in a small hamlet west of Red Deer, Alberta. She's an avid outdoors person, unrepentant coffee addict, part-time foodie, servant to a wonderful feline, and companion to two delightfully hilarious canines. She will neither confirm nor deny the rumours regarding the heart in a jar on her desk and the bottle of reader's tears right next to it. Her paranormal urban fantasy series, Saints and Sinners, is available on Amazon and her YA Fantasy, Feathers and Fae will be released October 11, 2019, from Kyanite Publishing.*
Website: www.crystallkirkham.com

To See Myself Bleed
by Cindar Harrell

I've always wondered what my insides look like. I suppose it is an obsession of mine. What colour is my blood? How pink are my lungs as they take in air? How fast does my bleeding heart beat?

I look at myself all day, but it's not really me. They always say that it's what's inside that counts.

Today, I prove them right. I take the scalpel and turn to view my face, contorted in terror as my sister struggles.

"That's the thing I love about twins…our minds are different, but inside and out, we are just the same."

Cindar Harrell loves fairy tales, especially ones with a dark twist. Her stories are often fairy tale inspired, but she is also working on a mystery series. Her stories can be found on Amazon and in various anthologies. You can follow her on Facebook and visit her blog, which she promises to try and update more often,
Website: cindarharrell.wordpress.com
Facebook: CindarHarrell

Sprinkled in With the Sugar
by Michael D. Davis

I must say, it was rather easy. I had most of the things I needed on hand before I even decided anything. The wine glass I used had been gathering dust for years, I don't even remember where we got it. The pot I broke it into was just one I don't use anymore, no special reason. To grind the shards down into tiny sprinkles of light, I used a variety of items. Then I just mixed them into the frosting.

We always have cupcakes for my son's birthday parties, that is if his father doesn't eat them all first.

Michael D. Davis was born and raised in a small town in Iowa. A high school graduate and avid reader he has aspired to be a writer for years. Having written over thirty short stories, ranging in genre from comedy to horror from flash fiction to novella. He continues in his accursed pursuit of a career in the written word and in his hunt Michael's love for stories in all genres and mediums will not falter.

Private Eye
by J. Farrington

The city has a disease, crime is an epidemic that's gotten out of control. In the early days, I welcomed every new case, eager to make a name in the gumshoe circles. The go to guy when everything else had failed. I've seen it all. Murder out of rage, jealousy, lust. Guys who like all the wrong things, and women who know no boundaries.

I've grown numb to the filth.

There is one positive to living in a city filled to the brim with murderers, rapists and thieves though…

When the urge to kill creeps in, most victims deserve it…

J. Farrington is an aspiring author from the West Midlands, UK. His genre of choice is horror; whether that be psychological, suspense, supernatural or straight up weird, he'll give it a shot! He has loved writing from a young age but has only publicly been spreading his darker thoughts and sinister imagination via social platforms since 2018. If you would like to view his previous work, or merely lurk in the shadows...watching, you can keep up to date with future projects by spirit board or alternatively, the following;
Twitter: @SurvivorTrench
Reddit: TrenchChronicles

Telling Evidence
by Susanne Thomas

Ryan stared at the cowering group of suspects who watched as one of their number was being handcuffed and taken away. "But, Sasha, how did you know it was her? The blood was all over everyone. They all said they saw nothing."

Detective Greene raised one eyebrow. "I was watching them while you were collecting evidence, and when that big table collapsed, and everyone jumped, I kept my eyes on them all from across the room. She licked the blood from her hands. After that and just a few questions in the interrogation room and she cracked like a pistachio."

Susanne Thomas reads, writes, parents, and teaches from the windy west in Wyoming, and she loves fantasy, science fiction, speculative fiction, poetry, children's books, science, coffee, and puns.
Website: www.themightierpenn.com
Facebook: SusanneThomasAuthor

Big Moment
by Andrew Anderson

Charlie was first on the scene of the gruesome triple murder.

A dirty alleyway, bloody fingerprints visible everywhere, and the murder weapon left behind; this would be an easy case to crack. This one might finally earn Charlie the promotion he'd sought—nay, deserved—for seventeen years. Passing the mess over to forensics, he went home.

The next day, Chief Reynolds called him in to her office. Charlie sat down and leaned back smugly, awaiting the inevitable praise. He could *feel* that this was his big moment.

Reynolds angrily leaned forward, yelling at him:

"Why did you do it, Charlie?"

Andrew Anderson is a full-time civil servant, dabbling in writing music, poetry, screenplays and short stories in his limited spare time, when not working on building himself a fort made out of second-hand books. He lives in Bathgate, Scotland with his wife, two children and his dog.
Twitter: @soorploom

Leave No Trace
by J. Farrington

The key to getting away with murder is to leave no witnesses or evidence. I like to take the body out to a quiet spot, leave them in the driver's seat and torch the vehicle. There's something…beautiful about watching the flames lick the night sky.

What you don't want to do, is go back to the scene of the crime. I made that mistake this morning. Two hikers came across the smouldering remains of last night's kill.

I killed and torched them both.

I couldn't leave three bodies, so I did what I had to…

I ate the evidence.

J. Farrington is an aspiring author from the West Midlands, UK. His genre of choice is horror; whether that be psychological, suspense, supernatural or straight up weird, he'll give it a shot! He has loved writing from a young age but has only publicly been spreading his darker thoughts and sinister imagination via social platforms since 2018. If you would like to view his previous work, or merely lurk in the shadows...watching, you can keep up to date with future projects by spirit board or alternatively, the following;
Twitter: @SurvivorTrench
Reddit: TrenchChronicles

Blood Sings to Blood
by Zoey Xolton

Caroline had spent weeks attaining the various herbs, tokens and the blood she needed to successfully scry for her husband. She knew he was no typical Missing Persons. The coven was involved, and she was going to prove it. Casting her spell, she dipped the crystal pendant in her Mother-in-Law's blood and waited for it to locate its match.

That night, she cautiously entered the abandoned warehouse. She hadn't gone far when she was forced to choke back a sob. Her husband hung, limp and decaying, from an inverted cross, his blood staining the floor.

"I knew it!" she cried.

Zoey Xolton is an Australian Speculative Fiction writer, primarily of Dark Fantasy, Paranormal Romance and Horror. She is also a proud mother of two and is married to her soul mate. Outside of her family, writing is her greatest passion. She is especially fond of short fiction and is working on releasing her own themed collections in future.
Website: www.zoeyxolton.com

Not Alone
by Pamela Jeffs

I take the call myself. The woman gives me an address and no other information before she hangs up. Fifteen minutes later I've arrived at the abandoned farm. I find an open door with its key in the lock, a shotgun and blood on the veranda step.

The door to the house stands ajar. A curtain hangs limp out the window. I push the door. It scrapes. Inside, I find a body on the floor in a pool of blood. I need to call it in. Out the door and toward the car. Then I notice the shotgun has disappeared.

Pamela Jeffs is a speculative fiction author living in Queensland, Australia with her husband and two daughters. She is a member of the Queensland Writers' Centre and has had numerous short fiction pieces published in recent national and international anthologies. In 2017 and again in 2018, Pamela was nominated for an Australian Aurealis Award in the category of 'Best Science Fiction Short Story'. Her debut collection titled 'Red Hour and Other Strange Tales' was released in March 2018.
Website: www.pamelajeffs.com
Facebook: pamelajeffsauthor

Spider
by Andrew Anderson

The Spider controlled a network of lost souls—a starving collection of vagrants; alone, vulnerable and under duress in a decaying city. A cluster of flies all caught in the same web, coerced into begging for your loose change and handing it all over to him.

We placed an undercover man. He was found dead three days later behind a disused laundromat. We had to match the Spider at his own game.

We became wasps, stinging and paralysing without mercy, to draw him up to the surface to defend his empire.

Instead, this Spider shed his skin, vanishing without trace.

Andrew Anderson is a full-time civil servant, dabbling in writing music, poetry, screenplays and short stories in his limited spare time, when not working on building himself a fort made out of second-hand books. He lives in Bathgate, Scotland with his wife, two children and his dog.
Twitter: @soorploom

Unhinged
by J.B. Wocoski

Inspector Priper examined the mutilated corpse, he growled, "Only a totally pervert could do this!"

Bloody handprints and footprints covered the murder scene. Following the bloody tracks from the murder scene to the car park, Priper realised that he was dealing with an inhuman butcher who deserved to die.

Smudged handprints and bloody footprints lead him between the parked cars. Finally, he located a driver's door covered in bloody handprints, he muttered to himself, "I've got you now!"

As Priper reached for the door handle, he drew his gun; he realised his hands were bloody, it was his patrol car.

JB Wocoski is the author and narrator of the shortstorypodcast.com with three flash fiction short story books published in the last three years. He is currently working on book 4 "Short Story Podcast 2019." He writes mostly science fiction, fantasy, and horror stories. He won the 2016 Little Tokyo Short Story Writing Contest with his short story "The Last Master of Go"
Website: shortstorypodcast.com

Home Security
by Raven Corinn Carluk

Tony slipped the gate open. These rich bastards really thought a lock could stop someone like him. But where there was an entire litter of rich bastard mop dogs on the line, nothing would stop him. He might get himself a whole half ounce of crank after this.

An electric torch lit him up. "I was really hoping you'd come by tonight. Remus is quite hungry."

A dog the size of a pony stepped into the light, fangs bared but silent. Tony's blood turned to ice, and meth-polluted senses froze completely.

"Scrawny asshole like you should be finished by morning."

Raven Corinn Carluk writes dark fantasy, paranormal romance, and anything else that catches her interest. She's authored five novels, where she explores themes of love and acceptance. Her shorter pieces, usually from her darker side, can be found in Black Hare Press anthologies, at Detritus Online, and through Alban Lake Publishers.
Twitter: @ravencorinn
Website: RavenCorinnCarluk.Blogspot.Com

Burning Passion
by Zoey Xolton

The junior P.I. paced the silent, still smouldering crypt. "I don't understand it, Sir. There's no evidence of holy water, no stakes, crosses, not even a trace of garlic."

The senior P.I shook his head, disenchanted with his subordinate's powers of observation. "Dallas, look up," he suggested.

Dallas glanced up, his jaw falling open. "Sir, someone's cut a hole in the stone!"

"Quite right," said Carmichael, looking to the stars above. "That there is a D.I.Y sunroof."

"The wall, Sir!"

Suck on this, Miles. I saw you with her! read the message scrawled in red lipstick.

"Ah, a coffin cheater."

Zoey Xolton is an Australian Speculative Fiction writer, primarily of Dark Fantasy, Paranormal Romance and Horror. She is also a proud mother of two and is married to her soul mate. Outside of her family, writing is her greatest passion. She is especially fond of short fiction and is working on releasing her own themed collections in future.
Website: www.zoeyxolton.com

Highway 109
by Crystal L. Kirkham

"Someone is trying to kill me! Please help! I'm on Highway 109. I've run out of gas."

"Can I have your name and an exact location?" the dispatch operator asked.

"Please help me. They're coming. I can see them!" She could hear the panic in his voice, and then he screamed. The line went dead, and all she could do was send the cops to check the highway, knowing it was probably too late.

Hours later, they found an old battered truck on the side of the road and signs of a scuffle, but the man was never seen again.

Crystal L. Kirkham *resides in a small hamlet west of Red Deer, Alberta. She's an avid outdoors person, unrepentant coffee addict, part-time foodie, servant to a wonderful feline, and companion to two delightfully hilarious canines. She will neither confirm nor deny the rumours regarding the heart in a jar on her desk and the bottle of reader's tears right next to it. Her paranormal urban fantasy series, Saints and Sinners, is available on Amazon and her YA Fantasy, Feathers and Fae will be released October 11, 2019, from Kyanite Publishing.*
Website: www.crystallkirkham.com

Stolen Identity
by J. Farrington

I was never happy with my life growing up. The family I was born in to, the little backwater town I grew up in and the generic body I was forced to make do with.

Well, not anymore.

I saved every bit of allowance I had, did jobs around town for folk and eventually got the fuck out of Dodge.

Sadly, that wasn't enough.

I'm finally happy now though! I realised what I had to do; to be happy I had to be someone else…

Wearing someone else's skin takes some getting used to, but I promise, it's worth it.

J. Farrington is an aspiring author from the West Midlands, UK. His genre of choice is horror; whether that be psychological, suspense, supernatural or straight up weird, he'll give it a shot! He has loved writing from a young age but has only publicly been spreading his darker thoughts and sinister imagination via social platforms since 2018. If you would like to view his previous work, or merely lurk in the shadows...watching, you can keep up to date with future projects by spirit board or alternatively, the following;
Twitter: @SurvivorTrench
Reddit: TrenchChronicles

Duel
by Nicola Currie

She's the perfect victim.

He's walking right into it.

It's been a while since my last kill. I'll enjoy her.

He'll take me to an even twenty.

She shows around hundreds of people every week.

He doesn't know the seller is laying fresh concrete in the basement, that he'll never be found.

No one will suspect me.

No one will suspect me.

I stroke the cord in my pocket, lusting after her pretty neck.

The cool blade tucked into my waistband prickles my skin with anticipation as I slide it out.

Something glints behind her back.

He's reaching for something.

Nicola Currie is 34, from Cambridge, UK where she works in educational publishing. She has published poetry in literary magazines, including Mslexia and Sarasvati, and has also completed her first novel, which was longlisted for the Bath Children's Novel Award.
Website: writeitandweep.home.blog

Relief
by Brandi Hicks

Rebecca picked the drying blood out from under her fingernails with the carving knife. She could already see the red and blue lights coming down the street. He'd only been dead for about twenty minutes, but he was most definitely dead.

He had come to her, once again, expecting her to just lie down and take it. She was ready this time though. He got a few good hits in, and she almost lost her grip on the knife, but her conviction held true. First, his groin; then, his throat. She thought she'd feel guilty, but she only felt relief.

*Growing up in West Virginia, **Brandi Hicks** loved to have her nose in a book, her eyes toward the night sky and putting a pen to paper. Her imagination was always sparked by her grandfather and her mom taking her to new places and teaching her about the unusual. She loves fantasy, sci-fi, and learning about science and history. She has two beautiful children, and hopes to instill creativity and a love of reading in them. Finding new crafts to try keeps her busy when not playing with her kids or working.*

A Future, Lost
by Aiki Flinthart

"It's unrepairable." Shonnie tapped the smashed computer, fingering a cross dangling around her neck. "We can't change course."

I gazed out at a sky meant to be brilliant with Alpha Carlotti's welcoming glow. Instead, infinite dark emptiness swallowed our sleep-ship. Behind me lay serried ranks of shining sleep-tanks containing humanity's finest, bravest. Now doomed.

"Who?"

"Hundreds have woken and slept again in the last century. Any of them."

"Why? Who would sabotage humanity's hope of survival?" Earth was long-dead. We, her last chance.

Shonnie's eyes slid from mine. "Maybe someone thought we shouldn't play God."

Her fingers stroked the crucifix.

Aiki Flinthart *has had short stories shortlisted in the Aurealis awards and top-8 listed in the USA Writers of the Future competition, as well as published in various anthologies and e-mags. She has 11 published spec fic novels and has edited 2 short story anthologies. She regularly gives workshops on writing fight scenes at conventions. Lives in Brisbane. Does martial arts, archery, knife throwing and lute-playing.*
Website: www.aikiflinthart.com

The Butcher
by Rowanne S. Carberry

A pool of blood congealed around the body. A knife sticking out of the back.

D.I. Michael's leans down, gloved hands about to prod the body.

"Forensics hasn't photographed that yet," is shouted from across the car park.

"Then get it photographed," D.I. Michaels snarls.

Scurrying over, the photographer snaps as many photos as they can.

Finally given the all clear, he bends down, moves the head to get a better look at the face.

Bile rises up in his throat as he sees the missing features, but he still manages to spot the one out of place black hair.

Rowanne S. Carberry was born in England in 1990, where she stills lives now with her cat Wolverine. Rowanne has always loved writing, and her first poem was published at the age of 15, but her ambition has always been to help people. Rowanne studied at the University of Sunderland where she completed combined honours of Psychology with Drama. Rowanne writes to offer others an escape. Although Rowanne writes in varied genres each story or poem she writes will often have a darkness to it, which helped coin her brand, Poisoned Quill Writing – Wicked words from a poisoned quill.
Facebook: PoisonedQuillWriting
Instagram: @poisoned_quill_writing

Mirror
by Abi Linhardt

My wife had been murdered and the bastard wouldn't tell me where he had stashed her.

"Where is her body!" I screamed at the criminal I was interrogating. He just smiled back at me, shaking his head.

"Under the stairs, you know that!"

Once I got home, I went for a long walk in the woods, her body heavy as I dragged it by the foot over the dead leaves. I'm glad I asked, because I'd forgotten she was down there.

When I got back, I looked in the mirror and gave myself a thumbs up. We were safe now.

Abi Linhardt has been a gamer all her life but is a teacher at heart. When she is not writing, you can find her slaying enemies online or teaching in a college classroom. She has published works of fiction, poetry, college essays, and even won two literary awards for her short stories in science fiction and horror. Abi lives and writes in the grey world of northern Ohio.

Blindsided
by Jonathan Inbody

The middle-aged man unlocked the door and rushed into his windowless room. He pushed aside the tools of his insidious trade, sending them clattering to the floor as he tossed the note down on his desk. It had been pinned to his door in a simple white envelope, and what it said could only have been understood by its intended recipient; "I know about the girl. Payment instructions will follow."

The man slumped over and began to cry.

On the rainy street outside, a man in thick sunglasses smiled. It was almost too easy gathering blackmail material with X-Ray vision.

Jonathan Inbody is a filmmaker, author, and podcaster from Buffalo, New York. He enjoys B-movies, pen and paper RPGs, and New Wave Science Fiction novels. His short story "Dying Feels Like Slowly Sinking" is due to be published in the anthology Deteriorate from Whimsically Dark Publishing. Jon can be heard every other week on his improvisational movie pitch podcast X Meets Y.
Website: xmeetsy.libsyn.com

Backup
by Joel R. Hunt

"Thank God you got here so quick, officer!"

He stepped inside and scanned the hall.

"Where's the killer?" he asked.

"We managed to tackle him and grab the axe," she sobbed through tear-stained make-up. "We tied him up in the basement."

"Stay here. Lock the door. Don't move."

"Yes, officer."

He approached the basement, eased open the door and peered into the darkness.

Silence.

He drew his weapon. Descended the steps. Approached the huddled body of the killer.

Then cut the ropes and handed over the knife.

"You have three minutes until the cops arrive," he said. "Make them count."

Joel R. Hunt *is a writer from the UK who dabbles in the darker aspects of life, particularly through horror, science fiction and the supernatural. He has been published here and there (though likely nowhere you've heard of) and hopes to have released his first anthology of short stories later this year.*
Twitter: @JoelRHunt1
Reddit: JRHEvilInc

Cold Case
by Cecelia Hopkins-Drewer

It was a cold case, but a particularly ugly one. An innocent woman alone at a suburban train station, and an unidentified killer hunting a victim.

Police-woman Marika had been drawn to the fatal spot over the years. Occasionally, she saw a man lingering on the platform. One day their eyes met in chilling recognition, and Marika instinctively knew he was the killer.

Marika decided to arrest the man for questioning. Following him into the subway, she reached for her service holster, finding the gun was missing. The killer had a knife. Marika's cadaver provided evidence to reopen the case.

Cecelia Hopkins-Drewer lives in Adelaide, South Australia. She has written a Masters paper on H.P. Lovecraft, and her weird poetry has been published in THE MENTOR (edited by Ron Clarke), and SPECTRAL REALMS (edited by S.T. Joshi). Her novels include a teenage vampire series comprised of three volumes, MYSTIC EVERMORE, SAINTS AND SINNERS & AUTUMN SECRETS. Short stories have been published in WORLDS, ANGELS & MONSTERS (Dark Drabbles anthologies edited by Dean Kershaw).
Amazon: amazon.com/Cecelia-Hopkins-Drewer/e/B071G968NM
Website: chopkin39.wixsite.com/website

Confession
by Jonathan Inbody

"I'm a fraud!" he said tearfully.

"Well isn't that the idea?" asked his wife.

"You don't understand," the man replied. "I've never actually impersonated someone, or swindled an old maid out of her fortune, or even done so much as trick a child into giving me their candy! I've never committed a real act of fraud in my life!"

She patted him on the shoulder. "It's alright, Harold. The way I see it, lying about being a fraud might be the most fraudulent thing someone could do."

"Really?" he asked.

She smiled and nodded. "You'll always be despicable to me."

Jonathan Inbody is a filmmaker, author, and podcaster from Buffalo, New York. He enjoys B-movies, pen and paper RPGs, and New Wave Science Fiction novels. His short story "Dying Feels Like Slowly Sinking" is due to be published in the anthology Deteriorate from Whimsically Dark Publishing. Jon can be heard every other week on his improvisational movie pitch podcast X Meets Y.
Website: xmeetsy.libsyn.com

The Backpacker Murders
by Cecelia Hopkins-Drewer

No one knew who had murdered a group of backpackers. Nor why the killings had stopped. Unless, as Inga proposed, the killer had gone overseas. Suddenly the killings began again.

Inga searched through arrivals and departures, looking for a correspondence between that day and ten years ago. She found a name; Horace Thorsen.

Inga donned a rucksack and joined the backpacker ranks. With no connections in Australia, they seemed ideal victims. However, she wished she had not tracked the suspect to such a remote area. She also wished he did not have a machete, and she could run much faster.

Cecelia Hopkins-Drewer lives in Adelaide, South Australia. She has written a Masters paper on H.P. Lovecraft, and her weird poetry has been published in THE MENTOR (edited by Ron Clarke), and SPECTRAL REALMS (edited by S.T. Joshi). Her novels include a teenage vampire series comprised of three volumes, MYSTIC EVERMORE, SAINTS AND SINNERS & AUTUMN SECRETS. Short stories have been published in WORLDS, ANGELS & MONSTERS (Dark Drabbles anthologies edited by Dean Kershaw).
Amazon: amazon.com/Cecelia-Hopkins-Drewer/e/B071G968NM
Website: chopkin39.wixsite.com/website

Discovery
by A.R. Johnston

She looked at it all with dispassion, it was the only way to get through something like this. You're always told that things will get easier, but it still turned her stomach. The lengths in which one human would go to destroy another was unfathomable.

"How many bodies do we have so far?" she asked.

"Unclear since everything is mixed together, but this boy has been doing this a long time, honing skills." Callister shrugged. "Doc thinks, bare minimum, sixteen, probably more. She won't know until everything is collected."

"Damn, how the hell did we stumble on a serial killer?"

A.R. Johnston is a small-town girl from Nova Scotia, Canada. Her style of writing is considered Urban Fantasy. Her first major publication is part of an anthology called First Love and she has several more titles lined up. She is a lover of coffee, good tv shows, horror flicks, and reader of books. She pretends to be a writer when real life doesn't get in the way. Pesky full-time job and adulting!

The Perfect Crime
by Ann Christine Tabaka

The man's body was sprawled out in the middle of the kitchen floor. The stab wound in his back indicated that it was foul play. It seemed to be the perfect crime. The police spent the entire day scouring the scene for evidence but found nothing; no murder weapon, no fingerprints.

As night fell, the detectives decided to call it a day. They scratched their heads as they retreated to their vehicles, they never ran into a case like this before.

Meanwhile, in a corner of the dark basement, the cat grinned as he played with his shiny new toy.

Ann Christine Tabaka was nominated for the 2017 Pushcart Prize in Poetry, has been internationally published, and won poetry awards from numerous publications. She is the author of 9 poetry books. Christine lives in Delaware, USA. She loves gardening and cooking. Chris lives with her husband and two cats. Her most recent credits are: Burningword Literary Journal; Ethos Literary Journal, North of Oxford, Pomona Valley Review, Page & Spine, West Texas Literary Review, The Hungry Chimera, Sheila-Na-Gig, Pangolin Review, Foliate Oak Review, Better Than Starbucks!, The Write Launch, The Stray Branch, The McKinley Review, Fourth & Sycamore.

Smoke and Lead
By Eddie D. Moore

Logan's hand hovered above his pistol, and he stared his opponent in the eyes. The sheriff stepped between the men with a double barrel shotgun cradled in his arms.

"There'll be no duels today, gentlemen. If you boys want to settle things like men, your fists are good enough."

In the blink of an eye, Logan drew and fired. Smoke rose from his colt's barrel as the sheriff fell, lifeless, to the ground.

Logan holstered his pistol, cracked his neck and shouted, "You're next, James!"

James' hand trembled, but he set his jaw and answered his murderer with hot lead.

Eddie D. Moore travels hundreds of hours a year, and he fills that time by listening to audiobooks. When he isn't playing with his grandchildren, he writes his own stories. You can find a list of his publications on his blog or by visiting his Amazon Author Page. While you're there, be sure to pick up a copy of his mini-anthology Misfits & Oddities. Website: eddiedmoore.wordpress.com Amazon: amazon.com/author/eddiedmoore

Til Death
by Cameron Marcoux

Link approached the scene. "They found the finger yet?" He looked down at the woman's hand. Her ring finger was missing. Severed.

Felder took a drag on his cigarette before answering. "Yeah. They tweezed it out of her mouth. Still had the diamond on it, too. Giant rock."

"Well, shit."

With hands in their pockets, the suited men stared down at the body.

"Can I bum one?" Felder pulled out a pack of Camels and slid out a loosey. Link took it. "Thanks." Felder replaced the cigarettes. "Anyone reach the husband?"

"No." He hesitated. "And I wouldn't count on it."

Cameron Marcoux is a writer of stories, which, considering where you are reading this, makes a lot of sense. He also teaches English to the lovely and terrifying creatures we call teenagers. He lives in the quiet, northern reaches of New England in the U.S. with his girlfriend and scaredy dog.

Grit and Gravel
by Jo Seysener

"Turn off them bleedin' lights, Pat. Givin' me a headache."

"Yeah, yeah, I'll get to it. Gotta keep them people away. Bloody stickybeaks. Wantin' ta see what blood looks like."

"Yer mumblin' again. Help me lift this, wouldya?"

"Urg, this one's fresh. I hate 'em like that. Still warm underneath."

"Like they're a person."

"Yeah."

"Hang on, what's that?"

"Ooh, you reckon he's finally left evidence?"

"Looks like it."

"Bag it. See what they make of it."

"Be good to finally catch this bugger."

"Sixteen bodies."

"Women."

"Yeah."

"Don't want to clean up another one of his."

"His victims?"

"Yeah."

Jo Seysener *is a mum of three crazies, a scatter of chickens, a decrepit kelpie and a rambunctious GSD. She lives with her husband near Brisbane, Australia. When she is not exposing her kids to cult story books from her childhood, she can be found in the kitchen experimenting with new flavours and pairings. She adores alpacas.*
Facebook: joseysener
Website: www.joseysener.com

A Thing of Beauty
by Jo Seysener

Skin so tender, still. But it will soon go tough.

Unyielding.

When the flashing lights get here.

I'll be up there, watching them scurry about like tiny ants. So many people, thinking they are important. But there is only one important person here.

Her.

I've made her important.

Skin is cooling. I should go. Just to see her face, touch her flesh again before they get their hands on her, their filthy medical instruments.

As though she is an object of science, not beauty. A thing.

I have to leave now. So they don't find me.

So I'm important too.

Jo Seysener is a mum of three crazies, a scatter of chickens, a decrepit kelpie and a rambunctious GSD. She lives with her husband near Brisbane, Australia. When she is not exposing her kids to cult story books from her childhood, she can be found in the kitchen experimenting with new flavours and pairings. She adores alpacas.
Facebook: joseysener
Website: www.joseysener.com

Panic and Plans
by Jo Seysener

I can't believe it. I've been so stupid, leaving my tools at the scene.

That's what I get for rushing. Giving them *evidence*.

Stupid stupid.

Got to think. They could find me with this. With their science. Catch me and put me behind a neat row of bars in a tiny cell with a man I'd have to beat into submission.

Think think.

Maybe it's not so bad. I've wiped them all clean. I should be good. Maybe I should stop for a while, take a little trip away. But I've got my eye on her.

I'll make her pretty.

Jo Seysener is a mum of three crazies, a scatter of chickens, a decrepit kelpie and a rambunctious GSD. She lives with her husband near Brisbane, Australia. When she is not exposing her kids to cult story books from her childhood, she can be found in the kitchen experimenting with new flavours and pairings. She adores alpacas.
Facebook: joseysener
Website: www.joseysener.com

Another Body
by Jo Seysener

"We gonna get him, Pat. I can feel it."

"Yeah, we got him this time."

"Just give the word."

Pat nodded to a lackey in uniform who busted the door in. He tapped the young man's shoulder approvingly. The boy—*why were they all so young?*—gave him a dark smile as though he, too, were enjoying catching this madman.

"Ah, hell."

"Whatcha got?" Pat saw the long hair first and knew they'd lost him. He cursed, kicking the wall.

"Careful, Sarge, you might damage evidence."

Pat grunted at the young cop, wondering why he wasn't hurling up his guts.

Jo Seysener is a mum of three crazies, a scatter of chickens, a decrepit kelpie and a rambunctious GSD. She lives with her husband near Brisbane, Australia. When she is not exposing her kids to cult story books from her childhood, she can be found in the kitchen experimenting with new flavours and pairings. She adores alpacas.
Facebook: joseysener
Website: www.joseysener.com

Blue Blood
by Jo Seysener

I smile as they find her, laid out in blood. They wish it was me. The fat cop stoops over her, tracking blood around the scene. He kicked the wall, too. Destroying evidence.

What a lark. I had to remind him to be careful.

They're getting complacent, expecting to find something that will give me away. I lean on the doorway, grinning. It unnerves the older cop. I can read the puzzlement in his eyes.

Maybe I should tone it down some, pretend to care about this blonde body gone cold. But they'll never catch me.

Not in this uniform.

Jo Seysener is a mum of three crazies, a scatter of chickens, a decrepit kelpie and a rambunctious GSD. She lives with her husband near Brisbane, Australia. When she is not exposing her kids to cult story books from her childhood, she can be found in the kitchen experimenting with new flavours and pairings. She adores alpacas.
Facebook: joseysener
Website: www.joseysener.com

Winner
by Umair Mirxa

Wanda lay next to the dumpster in the alley, clothes torn to shreds, and cuts and bruises visible all over her body.

Detective Kershaw stood before her, peering solemnly down at her corpse.

"What do we know?" he asked, turning to his partner.

"She was raped multiple times, and then strangled," said Detective Xolton. "Time of death is late last night. Figure she was dumped here just before dawn. No identification."

"Her name's Wanda."

"How could you possibly know that?"

"She was a winner at the auction yesterday. Actually bid on me, too. We need to find bachelor number four."

Umair Mirxa lives in Karachi, Pakistan. His first published story, 'Awareness', appeared on Spillwords Press. He has also had stories accepted for anthologies from Zombie Pirate Publishing, Blood Song Books, Fantasia Divinity Magazine and Publishing, and Iron Faerie Publishing. He is a massive J.R.R. Tolkien fan, and loves everything to do with fantasy and mythology. He enjoys football, history, music, movies, TV shows, and comic books, and wishes with all his heart that dragons were real.
Website: www.umairmirxa.com
Facebook: UMirxa12

The Hook Up
by Amber M. Simpson

I slip it in her drink when she goes to the bathroom. She comes back and downs it then leans against me, rubs my thigh. I check my watch.

"Wanna take me home?" she slurs in my ear, breasts dangerously close to popping out of her dress.

Why, yes. Yes, I do.

Outside, I lead her to my van where she snorts and calls me a soccer mom before passing out in my arms. I lay her inside on the pre-laid tarp, next to my bag of surgical tools.

A healthy kidney goes for over 120 grand these days.

Cha-ching!

Amber M. Simpson is a chronic nighttime writer with a penchant for dark fiction and fantasy. When she's not editing for Fantasia Divinity Magazine, she divides her creative time (when she's not procrastinating) between writing a mystery/horror novel, working on a medieval fantasy series, and coming up with new ideas for short stories. Above all, she enjoys being a mom to her two greatest creations, Max and Liam, who keep her feet on the ground even while her head is in the clouds.
Website: ambermsimpson.com

Footprints in the Snow
by Sinister Sweetheart

"Annie, it's time for breakfast! It snowed a lot last night!" Grace called down the hall. She received no response.

Annoyed, Grace took the twelve steps to her daughter's room. The door swung open to reveal an empty room. Annie's favourite teddy bear lay shredded at the foot of her unkempt bed.

Grace's scream silenced the singing birds; they scattered upon the impact of the sound waves. Morning sunlight glinted off of the freshly broken glass of Annie's window.

The young mother ran to the windowsill, hoping to see where she'd gone. But there were no footprints in the snow.

*Since **Sinister Sweetheart** made her first post to a popular Internet forum, she's taken the horror community by storm. Her ability to create, terrify, and drive home her stories is insurmountable. Sinister Sweetheart's published works can be found in multiple anthologies for all to read, but be forewarned, if you do... you may want to call your therapist after, her stories are terrifying, disturbing and devilishly unsettling. She is not only a fright visually, but also has a creepy tentacle in horror podcasting as well. Sinister Sweetheart writes, voice acts and is the media director of the Scarecrow Tales podcast.*
Website: Sinistersweetheart.wixsite.com/sinistersweetheart
Facebook: NMBrownStories

Stalker
by A.R. Dean

Make a list. Check it thrice. Make her crazy. Don't need a gun or bomb.

Mailings that make her blush. Sugar that leads bugs to her house. Rotting presents in her car; that smell will never come out. Mothballs in the gas tank and flat tires before work. Toilet paper in her tree and her dead dog in the backyard.

I'm teaching her a lesson for she has done me wrong. She can't see me watching her. She doesn't know my name, but what she did to me can't be erased. If all goes well, she'll kill herself tomorrow night.

A.R. Dean is a dark and twisted soul. Dean has spent their whole life spreading fear with the tales from their head. Best known for stories that terrify and show the evilest side of human nature. So, look for Dean haunting your local cemetery or under your bed, because they're here to spread the fear. Turn off your lights and enjoy a scare. Keep a lookout for more stories from this master of terror.
Facebook: ghoul.demon.orghost.a.r.dean

Stockholm
by Archit Joshi

The two men jostled her from her room. Today it wasn't for food.

Fragmented conversation reached her as they pushed her into another room towards Victor, their leader.

"…proof she's unharmed…"

Victor yanked her to a laptop screen, bringing forth two almost forgotten faces.

The screen erupted with concerned questions, amidst shaky sobs.

Their voices reminded Jolene of a helpless world, in which girls leered at your freckles and boys violated you in deserted dormitories. Her parents, notably absent in needful times.

Disgusted, Jolene swept the laptop away, hugged Victor tight. Darling Victor, big and strong.

She'd found another home.

Archit Joshi is a published short-story author who loves writing character-driven stories. Besides writing, he studies Computer Science and occasionally lends his hand to Social Services. He has also flirted with Entrepreneurship and had been running a startup in the food sector, before deciding to give his passion for writing a professional platform. Currently, Archit is studying for a Masters degree in Computers along with his pursuit of Creative Writing.
Facebook: *authorarchitjoshi*
Instagram: *@architrjoshi*

Boiled
by Abi Linhardt

It wasn't supposed to be a cult. It was supposed to be a way of life, to heal and help those who had experienced horror in their lives. The community had been welcoming. But after witnessing what the founder was doing to those scared girls, she had known she had to leave.

The police found her tripping down the dirt road in the mist, her eyes rolling and mouthing lolling open, eyes white. She was naked, her skin partially flayed. There was a hole about the size of a drill bit in her forehead. Burn marks splashed down her face.

Abi Linhardt has been a gamer all her life but is a teacher at heart. When she is not writing, you can find her slaying enemies online or teaching in a college classroom. She has published works of fiction, poetry, college essays, and even won two literary awards for her short stories in science fiction and horror. Abi lives and writes in the grey world of northern Ohio.

Somebody Else's Problem
by Stuart Conover

Caspian's heart pounded as he ran through the darkness.

The relic was in his hands.

It would grant power to the right people.

For the right price at least.

As long as he could get away, he'd be rich enough to buy anything.

An island kingdom to call his own.

He just needed to run.

The Vestad were on his heels.

They wanted it back.

It wouldn't take long now.

He was close to the water.

They couldn't survive in it.

Caspian just needed to reach his boat.

Once he reached the mainland, the Vestad would be his buyer's problem.

Stuart Conover is a father, husband, rescue dog owner, published author, blogger, journalist, horror enthusiast, comic book geek, science fiction junkie, and IT professional. With all of that to cram in daily, we have no idea if or when he sleeps or how he gets writing done! (We suspect it has to do with having evil clones.) Stuart is a Chicago native and runs the author resource Horror Tree.

What I Coulda
by Alexander Pyles

I walked out of the club with only one glance back.

A man or was it a woman? They were dressed in long baggy clothes. Not totally out of place, but something was off. Maybe it was the hollowed out look they gave, or the slight limp as they walked.

Either way, a nagging feeling pricked my thoughts. I should have gone back. My intuition was clear, but I ignored it in the haze of alcohol and cigarette buzz.

My regret crashed down when I stepped back into the club. My foot splashed in a pool of blood, causing ripples.

Alexander Pyles resides in IL with his wife and children. He holds an MA in Philosophy and an MFA in Writing Popular Fiction. His short story chapbook titled, "Milo (01001101 01101001 01101100 01101111)," from Radix Media, is due out fall 2019. His other short fiction has appeared on 101fiction.org, River and South Review, and other venues.
Website: www.pylesofbooks.com
Twitter: @Pylesofbooks

Fraud
by Jefferson Retallack

Do they know what I did? I try to reign in my eyes. I try to stop them from darting between the cashier to the security guard.

Hurry up. Hurry up. James will be worried sick by now. I shouldn't have left him at home. Why are there so many people buying groceries this time of night anyway?

I can't get her face out of my head. That poor old lady. She wasn't hurt, but you wouldn't believe it looking at her.

"That comes to ninety-three dollars."

Perfect. I swipe her credit card.

Declined.

The guard gets called over.

Shit.

Jefferson Retallack is an Australian writer of speculative fiction. He is based in Adelaide. His work draws influence from linguistic science fiction, the new weird and Australia's big things. Outside of the literary world, he skateboards on the weekends and spends afternoons on the beach with his partner, their son, and their Pomeranian, Tofu.
Website: jwretallack.wordpress.com
Twitter: @JWRetallack

Burglary Versus Robbery
by Jefferson Retallack

"Rebecca can't babysit." She's not coming home this time. "I won't be long." I wish that were true. Mostly I wish James didn't look so frightened.

Robbed. By my own brother. Are my kids invisible to him? Well, the one that's left.

Last time I let that junkie sweet talk me into putting him up.

I put on my biggest coat. Should be able to pocket some cheese, chocolates, maybe a carton of UHT.

Some old bird waits at the station. Dumb move this time of night.

Her family will help her. Right?

I don't hurt her. She screams anyway.

Jefferson Retallack is an Australian writer of speculative fiction. He is based in Adelaide. His work draws influence from linguistic science fiction, the new weird and Australia's big things. Outside of the literary world, he skateboards on the weekends and spends afternoons on the beach with his partner, their son, and their Pomeranian, Tofu.
Website: jwretallack.wordpress.com
Twitter: @JWRetallack

Ice
by Jefferson Retallack

Epidemic, my arse. This is the only shit that makes sense of the world.

Who says this shit's so bad anyway, my parole officer? The pigs? I ain't about to start listening to them.

Nothing else will make me feel good tonight. Nothing.

Rebecca. My beautiful baby niece. Kevin would kill me if he knew.

Fuck him. She's not even getting it from me no more.

It's kicking in. I feel better. But I can still see that fucking dog's head.

My psych's not gonna believe it. I wonder what he'll recommend when I tell him?

Not this.

Fuck him.

Jefferson Retallack is an Australian writer of speculative fiction. He is based in Adelaide. His work draws influence from linguistic science fiction, the new weird and Australia's big things. Outside of the literary world, he skateboards on the weekends and spends afternoons on the beach with his partner, their son, and their Pomeranian, Tofu.
Website: jwretallack.wordpress.com
Twitter: @JWRetallack

My Hands are Like Lightning
by Jefferson Retallack

"She's had too much."

"No, she hasn't. There's no such thing."

"Yes, there is."

I'm fine. The walls can eat shit.

Woof.

Fucking dog. My hands are like lightning as they crumble the drywall.

"Rebecca. Stop."

"You're bleeding."

They can *all* eat shit.

"Don't you come at me."

"Someone call the police. Or an ambulance."

"Hey now. You won't be welcome if you bring pigs into my house. She'll be right."

Yeah. I'll be right. At least one of them is making sense. Someone just needs to shut that fucking dog up.

Woof.

Shut that fucking dog up.

"Rebecca?"

"Nooooooo."

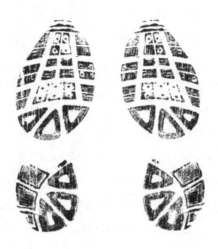

Jefferson Retallack is an Australian writer of speculative fiction. He is based in Adelaide. His work draws influence from linguistic science fiction, the new weird and Australia's big things. Outside of the literary world, he skateboards on the weekends and spends afternoons on the beach with his partner, their son, and their Pomeranian, Tofu.
Website: jwretallack.wordpress.com
Twitter: @JWRetallack

I Don't Care If It's Against the Law to Refuse to Escalate a Call, I've Already Passed Call Quality This Month

by Jefferson Retallack

It's four thirty on a Friday. Does this joker think I don't know that?

"Swearing won't help me to help you, sir."

I don't care how much his daughter needs medicine. He should've worn a dinger if he couldn't afford kids.

Says here he's only got two anyway. The last lady I spoke with had five, and I helped her out just fine. Manners will get you everywhere with me.

"I'm sorry, sir. I just can't see a way to make this work for you. You'll have to call back Monday."

"Put me onto ya fuckin' manager."

"She's gone home."

Jefferson Retallack is an Australian writer of speculative fiction. He is based in Adelaide. His work draws influence from linguistic science fiction, the new weird and Australia's big things. Outside of the literary world, he skateboards on the weekends and spends afternoons on the beach with his partner, their son, and their Pomeranian, Tofu.
Website: jwretallack.wordpress.com
Twitter: @JWRetallack

Here, There, and Everywhere
by Michael D. Davis

This was something decades in the making. A game that was great fun to play and extensively planned. I would snatch one up here or there, stash it for a while, then drop it off in pieces. Some of them I've had in my freezers for years, just waiting to be dropped off.

Little Timmy Doolan I took off the street in seventy-two, had him in my freezer till just last week. I plucked out his pieces and went driving. I left the boy's arm in Idaho, torso in Mississippi, and I kept the head for my great home state.

Michael D. Davis was born and raised in a small town in Iowa. A high school graduate and avid reader he has aspired to be a writer for years. Having written over thirty short stories, ranging in genre from comedy to horror from flash fiction to novella. He continues in his accursed pursuit of a career in the written word and in his hunt Michael's love for stories in all genres and mediums will not falter.

Busted
by Jonathan Inbody

The man unbuckled his belt and stepped into the woman's cramped apartment. She was waiting for him on the bed, with skimpy lingerie on her body and a gun under her pillow. The man leaned down to untie his boots, quickly checking to make sure the pistol in his ankle holster was loaded. Between them sat the leather briefcase, filled with the drugs they had stolen less than an hour ago. It had been a classic double cross, and it was about to be another one.

Unfortunately, neither of them had any idea that the other was an undercover cop.

Jonathan Inbody is a filmmaker, author, and podcaster from Buffalo, New York. He enjoys B-movies, pen and paper RPGs, and New Wave Science Fiction novels. His short story "Dying Feels Like Slowly Sinking" is due to be published in the anthology Deteriorate from Whimsically Dark Publishing. Jon can be heard every other week on his improvisational movie pitch podcast X Meets Y.
Website: xmeetsy.libsyn.com

Verdict
by G. Allen Wilbanks

August Barron sat at the defendant's table; his attorney seated to his right. He watched without emotion as the jury returned to their box after deliberation.

"Don't worry, Mr. Barron. I'm sure you're about to be a free man. But, even if the unexpected happens, I will file an immediate appeal of the decision."

"I'm not worried," replied August. "If they think I'm guilty, I will only be going to prison."

August patted the lawyer's cheek with one hand and leaned in close. He spoke softly into his attorney's ear. "But your family won't recognise the pieces left of you."

G. Allen Wilbanks is a member of the Horror Writers Association (HWA) and has published over 50 short stories in various magazines and on-line venues. He is the author of two short story collections, and the novel, When Darkness Comes.
Website: www.gallenwilbanks.com
Blog: DeepDarkThoughts.com

Hero
by David Bowmore

Where were all the superheroes when you needed them?

Tommy held his hand to his throbbing stomach.

In the films, Batman would have turned up in the nick of time.

Instead, it was just him, two armed thugs, and a scared girl.

He couldn't let them do what they wanted to do.

His fingers were sticky now.

In comics, a superhero with healing powers would arrive now.

But he'd done enough with the rusty piping and they had run off.

The girl held him, phone pressed to her ear by shaking hand.

"My hero," she whispered.

He closed his eyes.

David Bowmore has lived here, there and everywhere, but now lives in Yorkshire with his wonderful wife and a small white poodle. He has worn many hats in his time; head chef, teacher and landscape gardener. His first collection of short stories 'The Magic of Deben Market' is available from Clarendon House.
Website: davidbowmore.co.uk
Facebook: davidbowmoreauthor

Elementary
by Joel R. Hunt

Detective Therofeld gathered all of the suspects in the drawing room, standing them against the far wall as he paced back and forth. This had been the hardest case he had ever worked on. He was so close, he could feel it, but the last pieces simply weren't fitting together.

All of the murders had happened right under his nose. The culprit had outmanoeuvred him at every turn, avoided every trap he had set. They knew his mind.

Therofeld took in the scared, confused faces gathered before him, and he realised there was only one conclusion.

He was the killer.

Joel R. Hunt is a writer from the UK who dabbles in the darker aspects of life, particularly through horror, science fiction and the supernatural. He has been published here and there (though likely nowhere you've heard of) and hopes to have released his first anthology of short stories later this year.
Twitter: @JoelRHunt1
Reddit: JRHEvilInc

The Shoe
By Stephen Herczeg

His trail led here. A couple of local girls saw him in an Italian suit with expensive patent leather loafers.

Son of a bitch killed one of his own girls. Said she was holding out on him.

I hate pimps, but I needed to find him before Sonny Gallioni did. The idiot killed Sonny's girl. Beat her to death. For what? A bit of money.

There's not much in this old shed.

The floor is covered in ooze.

A wood chipper. Some old canisters. Liquid Nitrogen. Weird.

And a patent leather loafer.

Ain't gonna find much. Sonny got him first.

Stephen Herczeg is an IT Geek based in Canberra Australia. He has been writing for over twenty years and has completed a couple of dodgy novels, sixteen feature length screenplays and numerous short stories and scripts. His horror work has featured in Sproutlings, Hells Bells, Below the Stairs, Trickster's Treats #1 and #2, Shades of Santa, Behind the Mask, Beyond the Infinite; The Body Horror Book, Anemone Enemy, Petrified Punks and Beginnings. He has also had numerous Sherlock Holmes stories published through the Belanger Books - Sherlock Holmes anthologies.

The Confession
by Mark Kodama

I feel some responsibility for his actions; he is my brother after all, and really quite insane.

I called the police when I found blood spattered all over the kitchen.

You say he is dead. People say he drowned in the lake many years ago.

But he is alive.

Who else buried those bodies in our backyard?

It wasn't me. I am not a killer.

My brother, Paul, killed those people. Yes, I will submit to a lie detector test. I do not need a lawyer. I am innocent.

I don't know his whereabouts.

I am not my brother's keeper.

Mark Kodama is a trial attorney and former newspaper reporter who lives in Washington, D.C. His short stories and poems have been published in Clarendon Publishing House anthologies, Commuter Lit, Dastaan World Magazine, Dissident Voice Magazine, Literary Yard, Mercurial Stories, Spillwords, Tuck Magazine, and World of Myth Magazine.

Sharon
By Stephen Herczeg

There was a time where we only lost one patient a month. For a while it's been three or four. All sudden. All heart attacks. Something was wrong.

I decided to check time of death to the work schedule, and there it was.

Sharon.

She had started two months before the rise in deaths, and all were on her watch.

She was on tonight. I went to track her down.

A groan from one of the residents' rooms.

I burst in. Sharon had a pillow over his face.

The look on her face. Maniacal. I ran. I needed the police.

Stephen Herczeg is an IT Geek based in Canberra Australia. He has been writing for over twenty years and has completed a couple of dodgy novels, sixteen feature length screenplays and numerous short stories and scripts. His horror work has featured in Sproutlings, Hells Bells, Below the Stairs, Trickster's Treats #1 and #2, Shades of Santa, Behind the Mask, Beyond the Infinite; The Body Horror Book, Anemone Enemy, Petrified Punks and Beginnings. He has also had numerous Sherlock Holmes stories published through the Belanger Books - Sherlock Holmes anthologies.

Clues
by Annie Percik

There's a clue somewhere. I know it. There has to be. Something that was missed, something that will blow this case wide open. But is anyone looking? Why would they? They think they've already found the culprit. Wrong place, wrong time and all that. No decent alibi. I was there. I know it. They know it. But I didn't do anything. If only I could remember something useful. Some vital clue to prove my innocence. But it's all a blank. I know I didn't do it; I just have to convince them. There must be a clue somewhere. Mustn't there?

Annie Percik lives in London with her husband, Dave, where she is revising her first novel, whilst working as a University Complaints Officer. She writes a blog about writing and posts short fiction on her website. She also publishes a photo-story blog, recording the adventures of her teddy bear. He is much more popular online than she is. She likes to run away from zombies in her spare time.
Website: www.alobear.co.uk
Website: aloysius-bear.dreamwidth.org

Buzzing
by Rich Rurshell

As Glenn approached passport control, the man sitting behind the desk breathed out smoke, and his reptilian eyes became untrusting. Glenn watched the man's tongue flick out and catch a fly that was buzzing around. Glenn was relieved the buzzing had finally stopped. It had been driving him crazy.

"What's your final intended destination?" asked the man as his left eye melted into his cheek.

"Wait!" said Glenn. "Are you God?"

"Are you alright, Sir?" asked the man.

In a moment of clarity, Glenn concluded there was a good chance one of the packages in his stomach had split open.

Rich Rurshell is a short story writer from Suffolk, England. Rich writes Horror, Sci-Fi, and Fantasy, and his stories can be found in various short story anthologies and magazines. Most recently, his story "Subject: Galilee" was published in World War Four from Zombie Pirate Publishing, and "Life Choices" was published in Salty Tales from Stormy Island Publishing. When Rich is not writing stories, he likes to write and perform music.
Facebook: richrurshellauthor

Scratches
by Jacek Wilkos

There's something in my head, I can hear it.

Psychiatrist stated schizophrenia, but drugs and therapy don't work. It's getting even worse. Inhuman howling and scratching noise, as if something wanted to get out, brings me to the edge of madness. I can't take it anymore, I have to get rid of the damn thing.

There is only one way.

***

"It looks like a suicide, the guy shot himself in the head. Why are we here?"

"The exit wound is too big, and the skull is empty. Somebody removed the brain. And he did it ineptly, because he left scratches."

Jacek Wilkos is an engineer from Poland. He lives with his wife and daughter in a beautiful city of Cracow. He is addicted to buying books, he loves coffee, dark ambient music and riding his bike. He writes mostly horror drabbles. His fiction in Polish can be read on Szortal, Niedobre literki, Horror Online. In English his work was published in Drablr, Rune Bear, Sirens Call eZine.
Facebook: Jacek.W.Wilkos

The Midnight Man
by Zoey Xolton

Ellie looked up from her novel. Her eye shot from the front door to the clock. It was midnight. *Who could be knocking at this hour?* Every horror film she'd ever seen came to mind. Picking up her phone, she peeked beyond the curtains.

No one there… She sighed, relieved. Perhaps the sound had come from next door? Turning back to the couch, she found herself confronted by a towering, cowled figure.

"It's time," rasped a voice like death.

The next morning, her husband, Officer Ted Neulen, returned from night shift to find Ellie lifeless, the clock frozen at midnight.

Zoey Xolton is an Australian Speculative Fiction writer, primarily of Dark Fantasy, Paranormal Romance and Horror. She is also a proud mother of two and is married to her soul mate. Outside of her family, writing is her greatest passion. She is especially fond of short fiction and is working on releasing her own themed collections in future.
Website: www.zoeyxolton.com

The Sting
by J. Farrington

Preparation is key. We've been after this guy for months. Multiple ties to gang activity, direct links to high-profile drug cartels' and a fondness for killing people with his bare hands. Yes, we need to get this man off the streets.

The sting is in place. We know his routine and soon enough he will be with us, detained.

We're not the police, oh no, sorry if I led you to believe that.

We run an underground bare-knuckle to the death fighting organisation.

Now we have our new champ in our sights, we're going to need contestants…

You'll do perfectly…

J. Farrington is an aspiring author from the West Midlands, UK. His genre of choice is horror; whether that be psychological, suspense, supernatural or straight up weird, he'll give it a shot! He has loved writing from a young age but has only publicly been spreading his darker thoughts and sinister imagination via social platforms since 2018. If you would like to view his previous work, or merely lurk in the shadows…watching, you can keep up to date with future projects by spirit board or alternatively, the following;
Twitter: @SurvivorTrench
Reddit: TrenchChronicles

Leaf Memorial
by Alexander Pyles

There was always a leaf. Not just any leaf, but an oak leaf. Tucked into the hands of the corpses left or in the windows of empty houses. Those were bodies we never found.

The leaves were mocking. I always wanted to know why leaves and not acorns, those didn't decay quite so fast. Maybe that was the point.

I went to the cemetery. Oaks grew large and broad there. I was convinced this place was part of the puzzle. A gale rushed over the grave markers. A figure appeared, with a fistful of leaves. They were there for me.

Alexander Pyles resides in IL with his wife and children. He holds an MA in Philosophy and an MFA in Writing Popular Fiction. His short story chapbook titled, "Milo (01001101 01101001 01101100 01101111)," from Radix Media, is due out fall 2019. His other short fiction has appeared on 101fiction.org, River and South Review, and other venues.
Website: www.pylesofbooks.com
Twitter: @Pylesofbooks

War Crimes
by Zoey Xolton

"It's heinous," said P.I Mallory Black. "What kind of sicko accosts innocent civilians and hacks off their arms? And it's *always* the left!"

Mallory's partner tugged on her coat sleeve, gesturing to the trail of blood that led down the alley. "I don't know, but I think we're about to find out."

Pistols drawn, they burst into the dingy, abandoned repair shop. The rank odour of decay overwhelmed them.

A middle-aged, one-armed veteran in a bloodstained uniform glanced up, madness in his eyes; needle and thread in hand. "Need a new arm," he said. "Lost mine in service."

Mallory wretched.

Zoey Xolton is an Australian Speculative Fiction writer, primarily of Dark Fantasy, Paranormal Romance and Horror. She is also a proud mother of two and is married to her soul mate. Outside of her family, writing is her greatest passion. She is especially fond of short fiction and is working on releasing her own themed collections in future.
Website: www.zoeyxolton.com

Guilty
by Terry Miller

Deputy Ford looked at the dead body. This was the third one in just as many weeks.

Back at the station, the deputy sorted through paperwork for something to jog his memory. Nothing. He breathed deep and let out an agitated exhale. The phone rang. Another body.

Ford stared at the motionless, pale corpse of his wife.

"Mr. Ford, here's your medicine," a woman in blue scrubs insisted.

"Wh-what's that?"

"Your medicine, sweetie."

He took the small plastic cup then turned to the surrounding white walls. Ford shook as he remembered bloodstained hands, his hands. The cup hit the floor.

Terry Miller is an author and 2017 Rhysling Award-nominated poet residing in Portsmouth, OH, USA. He has self-published a dark poetry collection on Amazon and one short story to date. His work has also appeared in Sanitarium, Devolution Z, Jitter Press, Poetry Quarterly, O Unholy Night in Deathlehem, and the 2017 Rhysling Anthology from the Science Fiction and Fantasy Poetry Association.
Facebook: tmiller2015

Mystery Man
by Terry Miller

Her eyes were glazed with a dull stare. She had been there for hours. Stone cold. The seedy part of town, Fremont was known for its body count.

A man walked up to the yellow tape. He addressed a policeman.

"What happened, officer?"

The sheriff noticed the tightly-wrapped towel around his arm.

"You tell me," he insisted, pointing at the towel.

"Hey, Sheriff, come here a sec," a deputy kneeling at the body requested. He held up the woman's hand, blood and skin buried deep in the nails.

The sheriff looked back for the mystery man but he was gone.

Terry Miller is an author and 2017 Rhysling Award-nominated poet residing in Portsmouth, OH, USA. He has self-published a dark poetry collection on Amazon and one short story to date. His work has also appeared in Sanitarium, Devolution Z, Jitter Press, Poetry Quarterly, O Unholy Night in Deathlehem, and the 2017 Rhysling Anthology from the Science Fiction and Fantasy Poetry Association.
Facebook: tmiller2015

The Deathbed Confession of Jenna Greenville
by Mark Mackey

Letter to Jennifer Royals, editor-in-chief of the Rivercrest Gazette.

The Deathbed confession of Jenna Greenville.

As I lie dying of a terminal illness, I write to confess I killed town beauty queen, Miranda Colinwood. It was the moon which goaded me to kidnap her. As her former trusted nanny, it wasn't hard to accomplish. Bizarre as it sounds, it instructed me to bath in her blood to preserve my own fading beauty. I drugged her and then did it. A mistake, it didn't make me attractive one single bit.

Tell the police they'll find her remains buried in my backyard.

Mark Mackey is the author of various self-published books and has had various short stories published in charity anthologies. They include such captivating titles such as Christmas Lites, No Sleeves and Short Dresses: A Summer Anthology, Painted Mayhem, and Grynn Anthology, among others. A long-time resident of Chicago, when not writing, he spends time reading various genres of books.

The Giant
by Marcus Cook

"I've never stripped to Yellow Submarine before," the girl said, grinding on Wydryk's massive leg.

"I love the Beatles," he stated.

"How big are you?"

"7'1"

The girl undid her top, "$1000 is a lot for just a lap dance. Want anything else?"

"No. I was taught my manhood is evil. I shall not touch, nor have it touched."

The girl unwittingly giggled, causing Wyndryk to reach over and wrap his hand around her throat.

"Do not laugh at me!" Wndryk felt her neck snap in his hand. He picked up the phone, "Front desk, I will need another girl."

Marcus Cook, lives in Cleveland, Ohio native with his wife and cat. He loves Sci-Fi and thrillers. His short story, Ava Edison and the Burning Man was recently published in Burning: An Anthology of Short Thrillers by Burning Chair Publishing which can be purchased on Amazon.
Facebook: ReadMarcusCook

Camping Celebration
by J.M. Meyer

David proposed in a tent five years ago. We celebrate the anniversaries of our wedded un-bliss by camping.

We woke at dawn to hike.

At the peak, David knelt presenting a velvet box, revealing an emerald ring.

"Sue, I will spend the of my life being a better husband."

David stood by the edge and snapped pictures of me with his phone.

"What's that?" I gasped, pointing at the sky behind him.

As David turned, I pushed him with all my strength.

He hadn't lied, for once. Hearing him scream to his death were the happiest moments of our marriage.

J.M. Meyer is writer, artist and small business owner living in New York., where she received her master's degree from Teacher's College, Columbia University. Jacqueline loves the science fiction and horror genres. Reading Ray Bradbury was a mind-blowing experience for her in 8th grade. Alfred Hitchcock and Rod Serling were the horror heroes of her youth. Mercedes M. Yardley is her current horror writing hero. Jacqueline also enjoys the company of her husband Bruce and their three children, Julia, Emma and Lauren. Jacqueline's mantra: The only time it's too late to try something new is when you are dead.
Website: jmoranmeyer.net
Twitter: @moran_meyer

Chompers
by Shelly Jarvis

The sight before me sets my teeth on edge. Gore spreads throughout the room: a pulpy heart in the centre of the bed, a head near the window, intestines pulled long and looped around the neck of the other victim. Spatters of blood line the walls like a Rorschach test.

Those things don't bother me. It's the teeth I can't stand.

Lined along the windowsill are sixty-three teeth. They're cleaned and polished, pristine. They taunt me. Just like last night, when I placed them.

"Third one this month," my partner says. "Looks like a real psychopath."

I nod. "Looks like."

Shelly Jarvis is a speculative fiction author from West Virginia, US. She found a life-long love of sci-fi and fantasy in the 3rd grade when she found Madeleine L'Engle's "A Wrinkle in Time." Shelly is an avid reader, a Whovian, the ideal viewer of dog rescue videos, and undoubtedly Ravenclaw. She currently has three YA sci-fi books available for purchase on Amazon.
Website: www.ShellyJarvis.com

Not How it Seems
by Gabriella Balcom

"About fifty painkillers were in Jeffries' stomach," Doctor Harris said.

"Twenty were prescribed," Investigator Cruz replied. "Maybe he was given leftovers, too."

"That was his first prescription ever."

Cruz frowned. Jeffries had died of an overdose. But he'd journaled about his wife's affair and seeing her messing with his food. She'd had access to his medicine, a motive, and no alibi. However, her denials had seemed genuine.

Getting an idea, he grabbed his phone.

Later, Cruz told Harris, "Jeffries got more painkillers from a distant pharmacy."

"So, she's innocent?"

"He wanted her to look guilty. Revenge for cheating, I believe."

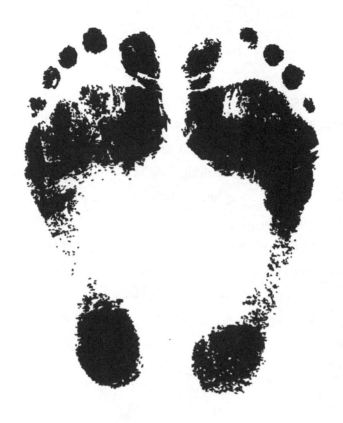

Gabriella Balcom lives in Texas with her family, loves reading and writing, and thinks she was born with a book in her hands. She works in a mental health field, and writes fantasy, horror/thriller, romance, children's stories, and sci-fi. She likes travelling, music, good shows, photography, history, interesting tales, and animals. Gabriella says she's a sucker for a great story and loves forests, mountains, and back roads which might lead who knows where. She has a weakness for lasagne, garlic bread, tacos, cheese, and chocolate, but not necessarily in that order.
Facebook: GabriellaBalcom.lonestarauthor

Revolver
by Sam M. Phillips

The door to the restaurant doesn't have a bell like it used to; I come in unnoticed. The place is open, but it's the quiet lull between lunch and dinner. Up the back, the boss sits at a table, sucking spaghetti. The man opposite him sees me coming but I pull the revolver from my coat, put two in his chest.

I pistol whip the boss around the head as he turns. The snub nose goes into his mouth as he tries to rise.

"You messed with the wrong family."

Loud bang. Snaking tendrils of smoke swirl as blood pools.

Sam M. Phillips is the co-founder of Zombie Pirate Publishing, producing short story anthologies and helping emerging writers. His own work has appeared in dozens of anthologies and magazines such as Full Moon Slaughter 2, 13 Bites Volumes IV and V, Rejected for Content 6, and Dastaan World Magazine. He lives in the green valleys of northern New South Wales, Australia, and enjoys reading, walking, and playing drums in the death metal band Decryptus.
Website: zombiepiratepublishing.com
Blog: bigconfusingwords.wordpress.com

Too Much
by Nerisha Kemraj

She forced the knife into him over and over, twisting with each thrust. Betrayal deserved death.

Blood spilled from his mouth, choking him. James couldn't fight back. She watched, bewitched, as the light in his eyes faded away. His body hit the ground with a heavy thud. But she didn't stop there. Raging, Lucy kicked and hammered his bloody corpse, only stopping when they pulled her off of him. She fought them, her anger uncontrollable. Growling like an animal, she bit at the officers. Breaking free, she ripped off James' ear, clenching it between her teeth as they restrained her.

*Multi-genre (short-fiction) author, and poet, **Nerisha Kemraj**, resides in South Africa with her husband and two, mischievous daughters. She has work traditionally published/accepted in 30 publications, thus far, both print and online. She holds a BA in Communication Science from UNISA and is currently busy with a Post-Graduate Certificate in Education.*
Facebook: Nerishakemrajwriter

Yellow
by Umair Mirxa

Yahya stumbled backwards and crashed hard into the bookshelf behind him. He ignored the pain and stepped forwards again.

"Look, you can take everything you want," he pleaded. "Just leave the yellow journal, please. It's of no value to anyone but myself."

"Shut up, old man," said one of the robbers, shoving Yahya aside violently.

An hour later, Sergeants Carr and Rowe stepped into the house, responding to a 999 call.

They found two men in masks dead in the study, and Yahya sitting calmly in the armchair, covered in blood and holding a yellow journal close to his chest.

Umair Mirxa lives in Karachi, Pakistan. His first published story, 'Awareness', appeared on Spillwords Press. He has also had stories accepted for anthologies from Zombie Pirate Publishing, Blood Song Books, Fantasia Divinity Magazine and Publishing, and Iron Faerie Publishing. He is a massive J.R.R. Tolkien fan, and loves everything to do with fantasy and mythology. He enjoys football, history, music, movies, TV shows, and comic books, and wishes with all his heart that dragons were real.
Website: www.umairmirxa.com
Facebook: UMirxa12

The Donor
by Jason Holden

Deborah has an easy manner; it puts the people who come to donate blood at ease. The lady with her now was nervous, her first time. Deborah looks over her forms while chatting about whatever comes to mind. "O negative, we're lucky to have you." The lady smiles, Deborah asks if she can take her picture for the website. "To help with the drive" she explains.

Snapping the picture on her phone, she sends it to the men that wait in the van around the corner. A message appears on her phone. One thousand has been credited to her account.

*After giving up a full-time job as a quarry operator so that his wife could follow her dream career as an academic in the field of chemistry, **Jason Holden** and his family left England and temporarily moved to Spain where they currently reside. While there, he took on the role of full-time parent and began to create stories for his daughter. Now that she is in school, he creates stories for himself and hopes to share those stories with others.*

Spiritual Confession
by Sinister Sweetheart

Operator: 911; What's your emergency?

Caller: *static hissing* Hel… hello?!? Can you hear me?

Operator: I can hear you ma'am. What's your emergency?

Caller: I've just buried a body. (Inaudible)

Operator: What?!? I'm sorry Ma'am; you're breaking up. I'm tracking your location.

Caller: Thank you. There's no hurry; nothing can be done for him now.

***

Officers arrived on scene to find a large, bare patch of dirt. After digging, they unearthed a male body that was well passed the advanced stages of decomposition.

His dental records matched a Mr. Logan Charles, who'd been presumed dead for the past four decades.

*Since **Sinister Sweetheart** made her first post to a popular Internet forum, she's taken the horror community by storm. Her ability to create, terrify, and drive home her stories is insurmountable. Sinister Sweetheart's published works can be found in multiple anthologies for all to read, but be forewarned, if you do... you may want to call your therapist after, her stories are terrifying, disturbing and devilishly unsettling. She is not only a fright visually, but also has a creepy tentacle in horror podcasting as well. Sinister Sweetheart writes, voice acts and is the media director of the Scarecrow Tales podcast.*
Website: Sinistersweetheart.wixsite.com/sinistersweetheart
Facebook: NMBrownStories

Nostalgia Burns Bright
by Stuart Conover

As a young vampire, Ophelia had used fire to drive humans from their homes.

Townsfolk had learned not to invite strangers in.

Not being able to get in, she had to get residents out.

Driven by flame meant they were but lambs to the slaughter.

That was all in the past.

Thanks to technology, it was easy to have a smart home invite you in.

For someone able to hack at least.

Still, Ophelia still enjoyed her fires.

Only these days it was to cover up her crimes and not start them.

You couldn't see fang marks on charred corpse.

Stuart Conover is a father, husband, rescue dog owner, published author, blogger, journalist, horror enthusiast, comic book geek, science fiction junkie, and IT professional. With all of that to cram in daily, we have no idea if or when he sleeps or how he gets writing done! (We suspect it has to do with having evil clones.) Stuart is a Chicago native and runs the author resource Horror Tree.

No Leftovers
by Claire Count

"Whatcha make of it, Constable?"

She choked as she struggled not to gag. "Don't think we will be finding 'em alive, Sir."

"Aye, think you have the truth of it."

"Shall I call Child Protection Services?" A dirty child sat back pressed against the wall, protected by her beloved mutt—both too thin and clearly abused. Dog watched them warily.

"Nyah, not yet. Hey, would you and your dog like to stay with me?"

Silent nod.

"Maybe after some food and sleep, she'll explain this."

"He's not hungry now," answered a timid voice.

Sergeant smiled. "Okay, just food for you then."

Claire Count, acclaimed writer of short stories and sometimes poet, lives in Metro Atlanta, Georgia, USA. She turns her love of puzzles into twisting plots of mystery and suspense. She is a life long role-playing gamer, which shows in her imaginative fantasy works. Her theatre background enriches her characters and creates unusual settings in her multi-genre tales.
Website: ClaireCount.com
Twitter: @ClaireCount

No Rest for the Wicked
by E.L. Giles

Eddy Thompson sat on the wooden chair, the electrodes fastened on his head. He glared at the window next to him. The spectators gazed back at him with horror.

"Eddy Thompson, you have been convicted of the murder of five young women," said the executioner. "Before we proceed, do you have any regrets?"

Eddy turned to the executioner and then back to the crowd.

"I do," he said.

"Do you have anything to say to the families gathered here today?"

"I am sorry"—a malevolent smile appeared on Eddy's face—"that I didn't finish off the bitch who escaped me."

E.L. Giles is a dreamer, passionate about art, a restless worker and a bit of a weird human. He started his artistic journey as a music composer until the need to put his thoughts and stories down on paper grew too strong for him to resist it any longer. He lives in the French Province of Quebec, Canada, with his girlfriend and two boys.
Facebook: elgilesauthor
Website: www.elgilesauthor.com

Aorta Red
by Jacob Baugher

I mix poison with the nail polish. It glitters aorta red. Theodora's favourite. Revenge is best served bloody.

The tritone doorbell jingles. She's blue-eyed, beautiful. Hitler would have loved her. She'll say hello to him in Hell.

"Usual, Theodora?"

She crosses to my station.

"Usual."

I paint, careful not to touch the polish. A drop falls on her skin. I wipe it away. She ignores me; tips on her way out. I should feel bad, but I don't. She killed Evan.

I wish I could see the blood leak from her eyes tonight. I content myself with a smoke instead.

Jacob Baugher teaches Creative Writing at Franciscan University of Steubenville. When he's not teaching or coaching the track team, he can be found in the Cuyahoga Valley hiking with his wife and son or brewing beer on his front porch. He's received honourable mentions for his work in the Writers of the Future contest and he co-edits a series of Fantasy and Science Fiction anthologies titled Continuum.

Nightstalker
by Jacob Baugher

I peer through your window. You're with him, smiling. I'd join, but the crucifixes over the doors prevent me. Mother said: never disturb a religious house. She's rotting in my garden.

At Mass, I hold your hand during the Our Father. "Thine is the kingdom, the power..."

Hollow words.

"They mean nothing," the voice in my head whispers.

Later, you're together again, laughing on the sofa. I'm invisible in the mirror-dark window. Above, the crucifix glows.

Thursday, I try for redemption. "Bless me, Father, I have sinned."

But I'm addicted.

Back outside, I watch, like Grendel. Shameful in the murk.

Jacob Baugher teaches Creative Writing at Franciscan University of Steubenville. When he's not teaching or coaching the track team, he can be found in the Cuyahoga Valley hiking with his wife and son or brewing beer on his front porch. He's received honourable mentions for his work in the Writers of the Future contest and he co-edits a series of Fantasy and Science Fiction anthologies titled Continuum.

Animated
by Beth W. Patterson

I'd told her that if I saw one more dancing teddy bear or wolfhound chasing a leprechaun, I'd slit her goddamned throat. That doesn't mean it was me who did it. But she knew I hated those stupid e-cards, especially ten or more each day.

It was getting to be too much. I understand that she was lonely, but for fuck's sake, I had work to do, and if I ignored those flowers swaying to classical music, email reminders would pile up. It was driving me crazy.

Someone else must have cut her with fragments of her shattered computer screen.

Beth W. Patterson was a full-time musician for over two decades before diving into the world of writing, a process she describes as "fleeing the circus to join the zoo". She is the author of the books Mongrels and Misfits, and The Wild Harmonic, and a contributing writer to thirty anthologies. Patterson has performed in eighteen countries, expanding her perspective as she goes. Her playing appears on over a hundred and seventy albums, soundtracks, videos, commercials, and voice-overs (including seven solo albums of her own). She lives in New Orleans, Louisiana with her husband Josh Paxton, jazz pianist extraordinaire.
Website: www.bethpattersonmusic.com
Facebook: bethodist

Petty Theft
by G. Allen Wilbanks

Go ahead and take it, said the tiny voice in the back of Tony's mind. *No one will care.*

He eyed the display of candy bars, greedily. The clerk was currently distracted with the register and would never notice if one or two went missing.

Why not? he finally decided and slipped a couple of the chocolate bars off their metal stand and dropped them into his pocket.

Tony shifted the gun back into his right hand. "Hurry up," he growled at the clerk. "Empty the register and put all the cash into that bag. I don't have all day!"

G. Allen Wilbanks is a member of the Horror Writers Association (HWA) and has published over 50 short stories in various magazines and on-line venues. He is the author of two short story collections, and the novel, When Darkness Comes.
Website: www.gallenwilbanks.com
Blog: DeepDarkThoughts.com

The River
by Ann Christine Tabaka

A story was once told about a man who owned a river. He would not let boats pass through without paying a toll to him.

One day, that man simply vanished. No one knew what happened, and very few cared. There was not a trace of evidence, not a single hair. A month passed, and most people forgot about him. They went on with their lives, happy to have free passage on the river.

Months turned into years, and soon the case was closed, but the weighed down boat on the bottom of the river never gave up her secret.

Ann Christine Tabaka was nominated for the 2017 Pushcart Prize in Poetry, has been internationally published, and won poetry awards from numerous publications. She is the author of 9 poetry books. Christine lives in Delaware, USA. She loves gardening and cooking. Chris lives with her husband and two cats. Her most recent credits are: Burningword Literary Journal; Ethos Literary Journal, North of Oxford, Pomona Valley Review, Page & Spine, West Texas Literary Review, The Hungry Chimera, Sheila-Na-Gig, Pangolin Review, Foliate Oak Review, Better Than Starbucks!, The Write Launch, The Stray Branch, The McKinley Review, Fourth & Sycamore.

Compromised
by G. Allen Wilbanks

Detective Jonas glanced at his partner. When he was certain the younger man was distracted, he knelt beside the body and picked up the coat button beside the victim's hand. He slipped the item into his pocket.

There was nothing he could do about the shell casing. The beat cop had already noticed it and marked it.

Toby was getting sloppy; leaving way too much behind at his crime scenes. Pretty soon, the moron was going to get caught regardless of Jonas' interference.

The next time he bumped into Toby, he was going to have to ask for more money.

G. Allen Wilbanks is a member of the Horror Writers Association (HWA) and has published over 50 short stories in various magazines and on-line venues. He is the author of two short story collections, and the novel, When Darkness Comes.
Website: www.gallenwilbanks.com
Blog: DeepDarkThoughts.com

The Artist
by E.L. Giles

The pressure grew, twisting my guts to the point where I wanted to pick up the knife and slash my stomach to release it.

The urge to kill was here again. Vivid, pure, and beautiful. I could not resist the impulse to create—Yes! To create the most realistic and grotesque scenes one could imagine. This was my art, my poetry. My loophole to avoid dementia. Unless it was dementia that made me an artist.

I painted with the most brilliant hues of purple and realistic textures of skin. People didn't understand the beauty in my work. They knew nothing.

E.L. Giles is a dreamer, passionate about art, a restless worker and a bit of a weird human. He started his artistic journey as a music composer until the need to put his thoughts and stories down on paper grew too strong for him to resist it any longer. He lives in the French Province of Quebec, Canada, with his girlfriend and two boys.
Facebook: elgilesauthor
Website: www.elgilesauthor.com

Black Tears
by Ximena Escobar

"Dan?"

It was all a blur, but I remembered fighting with him. I got up and pulled my dress down; I was still wearing my heels.

He was in the bathtub. He could have drowned, the motherfucker. I kneed him on the arm, but he didn't stir.

I didn't find eyedrops, but I found a razor blade. I wiped my fingerprints, dropped it in the red water.

I told the cop I was unconscious. Black tears tattooed on my cheeks, drugs in my blood test.

The stream of his wrist tattooed in my memory.

My lie bruised on his arm.

Ximena Escobar is an emerging author of literary fiction and poetry. Originally from Chile, she is the author of a translation into Spanish of the Broadway Musical "The Wizard of Oz", and of an original adaptation of the same, "Navidad en Oz". Clarendon House Publications published her first short story in the UK, "The Persistence of Memory", and Literally Stories her first online publication with "The Green Light". She has since had several acceptances from other publishers and is working very hard exploring new exciting avenues in her writing.
She lives in Nottingham with her family.
Facebook: Ximenautora

One Last Thing to Do
by Glenn R. Wilson

After years of tracking down creeps like this guy, it gets mundane. Always the same. They cry about a hard life, lousy parents, oppressive society. "It's not my fault," they say. With a slick lawyer, a sympathetic court, and a stay at a mental institution, they get "reformed." Just a fancy term for getting away with murder.

Just once, I want to feel it like they do.

"What's so fascinating about killing someone?" I ask the loser at my feet.

Before he can answer, I plug him good and watch him bleed out.

Hmm. Feels alright.

Now, I can retire.

Glenn R. Wilson has come full circle. Making a point to mature, like fine wine, before diving head-first into his long list of writing projects, he's approaching them with a plan. That strategy is to build with one brick at a time. He's accumulated a few bricks already and is adding more. Over time, with persistence and determination, he'll have a home. But for now, a solid foundation is the goal. Please, enjoy the process with him.

Framing a Murder
by Cindar Harrell

I felt the life leave him as the blood from his pierced heart ran over my hands. I sighed in relief, the king, my husband, was dead. I collapsed beside his corpse on the bed we shared, not caring that blood soaked my dress.

Rot in hell, bastard.

I closed my eyes to steady myself. It wasn't done yet. I wasn't about to be charged with treason. I stood, grabbed the knife and made several long cuts on my arms and stomach, slicing through my thin nightdress.

Summoning one of my servants, I dropped the weapon and began to scream.

Cindar Harrell loves fairy tales, especially ones with a dark twist. Her stories are often fairy tale inspired, but she is also working on a mystery series. Her stories can be found on Amazon and in various anthologies. You can follow her on Facebook and visit her blog, which she promises to try and update more often,
Website: cindarharrell.wordpress.com
Facebook: CindarHarrell

The Investigation
by Rhiannon Bird

She'd been staring at crime scene photos for days, writing reports and doing interviews. *Was there anyone that wanted to hurt him? Did he have any enemies? Any strange behaviour?* As the investigation continued, the team was beginning to see the dead end approaching. There were no leads, no witnesses, and no evidence. Just a dead body. It was finally almost over, she congratulated herself quietly. No one would have to know, and she could move on. She just had to throw the investigation for a little bit longer before shoving the skeleton in her closet and never looking back.

Rhiannon Bird is a young aspiring author. She has a passion for words and storytelling. Rhiannon has her own quotes blog; Thoughts of a Writer. She has had 4 works published. This includes 3 short stories and 2 poems. These are published on Eskimo pie, Literary yard, Down in the Dirt Magazine and Short break fiction. She can be found on Facebook, Instagram, and Pinterest.

Heist
by Sinister Sweetheart

It was supposed to be an easy open and shut case. The bank was broken into at around midnight.

Only one set of fingerprints was found on any surfaces. All other evidence was consistent with only one person being in the building during the event, Theodore Johnston.

The investigators searched the building intently; meeting a stalemate at the vault.

Management was uncharacteristically sparse. There were problems finding the proper authority to unlock it.

Upon entry, officers were shocked to discover Theodore's slain body. The Medical Examiner claimed his time of death took place hours before the bank was ever robbed.

*Since **Sinister Sweetheart** made her first post to a popular Internet forum, she's taken the horror community by storm. Her ability to create, terrify, and drive home her stories is insurmountable. Sinister Sweetheart's published works can be found in multiple anthologies for all to read, but be forewarned, if you do... you may want to call your therapist after, her stories are terrifying, disturbing and devilishly unsettling. She is not only a fright visually, but also has a creepy tentacle in horror podcasting as well. Sinister Sweetheart writes, voice acts and is the media director of the Scarecrow Tales podcast.*
Website: Sinistersweetheart.wixsite.com/sinistersweetheart
Facebook: NMBrownStories

Death's Door
by Cindar Harrell

I take my nursing duties very seriously. My patients' lives are in my hands. People praise the doctors, but it's always the nurses. The doctors barely have time for them, whereas I know them all by name.

I care for them, I help revive them when they crash, and cry for them when they die. And many die. You can't save them all, but that is hardly my fault. I help them see death's door, but they are supposed to come back. If they don't, it's not because of my syringe, but because the doctors don't get there in time.

Cindar Harrell loves fairy tales, especially ones with a dark twist. Her stories are often fairy tale inspired, but she is also working on a mystery series. Her stories can be found on Amazon and in various anthologies. You can follow her on Facebook and visit her blog, which she promises to try and update more often,
Website: cindarharrell.wordpress.com
Facebook: CindarHarrell

Nine Cats Worth of Crazy
by Aiki Flinthart

"Your husband, Joe, died of head trauma," I say, gently. "Blunt instrument.'

Mrs Winterford rubs rheumy eyes with age-twisted fingers. She is alone but for eight black cats, yeowling and eyeing me balefully—probably for taking away the half-eaten body. The house stinks of cat piss.

"See anyone?' I ask. "A weapon?'

"No, officer. But I found Samson in the freezer." Her smile is full of holes and bitterness. "Rock solid. Joe had run him over. Murdered him!' She glowers. "He shouldn't have done it."

"Samson…the cat? Frozen hard?'

"Yes." She gives a satisfied nod. "Just hard enough, actually."

Aiki Flinthart has had short stories shortlisted in the Aurealis awards and top-8 listed in the USA Writers of the Future competition, as well as published in various anthologies and e-mags. She has 11 published spec fic novels and has edited 2 short story anthologies. She regularly gives workshops on writing fight scenes at conventions. Lives in Brisbane. Does martial arts, archery, knife throwing and lute-playing.
Website: www.aikiflinthart.com

Pack Justice
by Stuart Conover

Joseph Vancovenhoven died at approximately midnight.

That is what the coroner's report stated.

Detective Robert Svoboda rubbed his eyes.

It claimed the cause of death as a wolf attack.

That was wrong.

He knew a shifter was to blame.

One he had warned too many times to not hunt humans.

His sister's scent was on the body.

As the lead detective in the town, he had sworn a duty.

As the pack's Alpha, he had also sworn a conflicting duty.

Loading silver bullets into his revolver, Robert sighed.

One way or another, he would have to bring Annette to justice.

Stuart Conover is a father, husband, rescue dog owner, published author, blogger, journalist, horror enthusiast, comic book geek, science fiction junkie, and IT professional. With all of that to cram in daily, we have no idea if or when he sleeps or how he gets writing done! (We suspect it has to do with having evil clones.) Stuart is a Chicago native and runs the author resource Horror Tree.

Lost and Found
by Joel R. Hunt

Officers and monks gathered in the shadow of the rescued painting.

"You see?" said Inspector Miller, "All that violence was for nothing. Here's your sacred painting. Neither sect was responsible for the theft."

"She's right," said the first monk, "I am sorry we blamed your order for that vile act."

"Forgiven, brother," said the second, "We thought you were heretics. We were mistaken."

They bowed to Miller, each other and the painting, then left.

"You realise it's a forgery?" whispered Officer Brown.

"Of course," Miller said, watching the monks walk down the monastery steps side by side, "But they don't."

Joel R. Hunt is a writer from the UK who dabbles in the darker aspects of life, particularly through horror, science fiction and the supernatural. He has been published here and there (though likely nowhere you've heard of) and hopes to have released his first anthology of short stories later this year.
Twitter: @JoelRHunt1
Reddit: JRHEvilInc

Russian Roulette
by E.L. Giles

The revolver lay on the table, its chamber half full. Two men sat near it, their hearts pummelling in their chests.

"The game is simple," said a third man, approaching. He picked up the revolver, then tucked it into the hand of one of the men. He pointed across the table. "He dies, you're free."

"You're crazy!" shrieked the man, his bravado dying as a sharp blade came to rest under his throat. He gulped and aimed the gun. "I can't."

"Do it now."

The man let go of the gun, sobbing.

"Too bad for you," said the third man.

E.L. Giles is a dreamer, passionate about art, a restless worker and a bit of a weird human. He started his artistic journey as a music composer until the need to put his thoughts and stories down on paper grew too strong for him to resist it any longer. He lives in the French Province of Quebec, Canada, with his girlfriend and two boys.
Facebook: elgilesauthor
Website: www.elgilesauthor.com

A Classical Conundrum
by John H. Dromey

"The success of this heist depends on clockwork precision in its execution," the criminal mastermind told his handpicked crew. "I want to know in advance about any possible glitches. Have all of the mall security guards been bribed or intimidated?"

"All but one," a henchman said. "Julius Spencer is the lone holdout."

"Anything else?"

"Yeah, Boss. Our female accomplice, Pearl, will be vulnerable for three seconds while moving through a red zone of the concourse on her way to disable the alarms."

"Is that a deal breaker? What's the worst-case scenario for Pearl?"

"Julius sees her crossing the ruby con."

John H. Dromey was born in northeast Missouri, USA. He enjoys reading—mysteries in particular—and writing in a variety of genres. He's had short fiction published in Alfred Hitchcock's Mystery Magazine, Martian Magazine, Stupefying Stories Showcase, Thriller Magazine, Unfit Magazine, and elsewhere, as well as in a number of anthologies, including Chilling Horror Short Stories (Flame Tree Publishing, 2015).

The Murder of Miss Money
by Ximena Escobar

A serpent undulated in the unseen waters—anxiety twisting and knotting like guts amongst the spectators; silent as the spinning police light; silent as the lake.

The car emerged, pulled by chains. Pat's arm hung lifelessly out the window.

Nobody saw the scarf that had been thrust down her throat, waving its mute ripples of stifled scream from within. It was all over Facebook; she had no money; her children didn't talk to her—everybody'd seen that.

Except for the forensic pathologist. He kept seeing the scarf in his memory. He'd tied her wrists to the bed frame with it.

Ximena Escobar is an emerging author of literary fiction and poetry. Originally from Chile, she is the author of a translation into Spanish of the Broadway Musical "The Wizard of Oz", and of an original adaptation of the same, "Navidad en Oz". Clarendon House Publications published her first short story in the UK, "The Persistence of Memory", and Literally Stories her first online publication with "The Green Light". She has since had several acceptances from other publishers and is working very hard exploring new exciting avenues in her writing.
She lives in Nottingham with her family.
Facebook: Ximenautora

The Limo Driver
by J.M. Meyer

The man everyone called Boss entered my limo with a beautiful young woman, smelling of too much alcohol and perfume.

The woman turned on the stereo.

"Married with kids?" Boss asked me.

"Yes."

"Good. That's good."

The privacy screen went up and I took them to the beach, as requested.

I waited in the lot until I heard the back door reopen and the screen move down. He was alone.

"My date decided to swim home. Does your family swim, young man?"

"I understand."

I dropped him off at his family's home.

"I like you. I'll see you next week."

J.M. Meyer *is writer, artist and small business owner living in New York., where she received her master's degree from Teacher's College, Columbia University. Jacqueline loves the science fiction and horror genres. Reading Ray Bradbury was a mind-blowing experience for her in 8th grade. Alfred Hitchcock and Rod Serling were the horror heroes of her youth. Mercedes M. Yardley is her current horror writing hero. Jacqueline also enjoys the company of her husband Bruce and their three children, Julia, Emma and Lauren. Jacqueline's mantra: The only time it's too late to try something new is when you are dead.*

Website: jmoranmeyer.net
Twitter: @moran_meyer

Guillotined
by Carole de Monclin

I have a skeleton in my closet.

Literally.

I'm very fond of Marie Antoinette.

When people visit, if the mood's right, I proudly display her and point out the quality of her fine bones. Respectfully, of course.

Others don't take such good care of their skeletons. They even use them for pranks.

Because I bought her cheap online, she doesn't have a head, earning her name in the bargain.

I cut up corpses, but hope to graduate soon to living bodies.

"Familiarise yourself with death," my mentor urged.

I followed the advice.

Every med student needs a skeleton for study.

Carole de Monclin travels both the real world and imaginary ones. She's lived in France, Australia, and the USA; visited 25+ countries; and explored Mars, Ceres, and many distant planets. She writes to invite people on a journey. Stories have found her for as long as she can remember, be it in a cave in Victoria, the smile of a baby in Paris, or a museum in Florida.
Website: *CaroledeMonclin.com*
Twitter: *@CaroledeMonclin*

Dear Mr. Hempshaw
by Copper Rose

Mr. Hempshaw put down his fork, a piece of white cake still stuck to the tines. The letter he'd received trembled in his hand.

He turned to stare out the window, at the place in the yard he strolled over every so often. The place where he kept the scissors no one knew about, not even after thirty years.

His eyes went again to the letter.

It was August 17, 1989 at 2:00 in the afternoon.

I was ten years old.

The cake the police found on her kitchen counter was for me.

I have something that belongs to you.

Copper Rose perforates the edges of the page while writing unusual stories from the heart of Wisconsin. Her work has appeared in various anthologies and online journals. She also understands there really is something about pie.
Website: julieceger.wordpress.com
Facebook: Author Copper Rose

Vacant
by Umair Mirxa

Vicar Bowmore picked his way carefully through the charred remains and came to stand beside the detective.

"Do we know who the culprit is yet?" he asked.

"No," replied the detective dejectedly. "Whoever it is, they were meticulous as always. Didn't leave a clue."

"People are scared, David. Some have already left town."

"We're doing the best we can, Vicar."

"Four houses burnt down in a week. Thirteen dead. You need to do better. Thank the Lord, this one at least was vacant."

Detective Klimek let escape a pained sigh.

"No, it wasn't. We found two bodies in the backyard."

Umair Mirxa lives in Karachi, Pakistan. His first published story, 'Awareness', appeared on Spillwords Press. He has also had stories accepted for anthologies from Zombie Pirate Publishing, Blood Song Books, Fantasia Divinity Magazine and Publishing, and Iron Faerie Publishing. He is a massive J.R.R. Tolkien fan, and loves everything to do with fantasy and mythology. He enjoys football, history, music, movies, TV shows, and comic books, and wishes with all his heart that dragons were real.
Website: www.umairmirxa.com
Facebook: UMirxa12

Competitive Streak
by Susanne Thomas

Mariel listened as the doctor pronounced death.

It had taken many months to make sure that some of the chilli contestants tried almond flour as a secret ingredient and chilli thickener. Hers used maize, of course.

She'd quietly worked to ensure that George Williams was the master taster. He'd almost allowed Bob Jetts to do the honours.

And only she, as George's wife, had known that he was deathly allergic to almond. He was so prideful about weakness, and almond was not a common chilli ingredient.

He should have picked Mariel's chilli last year; she was his wife after all.

Susanne Thomas reads, writes, parents, and teaches from the windy west in Wyoming, and she loves fantasy, science fiction, speculative fiction, poetry, children's books, science, coffee, and puns.
Website: www.themightierpenn.com
Facebook: SusanneThomasAuthor

Unlikeable
by Serena Jayne

Cindy elbowed Steve. "Would it kill you to like my cat photo?"

He shrugged. "Can't like everything."

"I like all your stuff. Even the boring oatmeal bowl."

"That pic got eighty likes."

Hardly anyone liked her posts, which featured Fluffy and Cindy's crocheted creations.

No one liked her online or in person, but everyone liked Steve.

"Don't look so glum. Social media isn't real."

"This real enough?" She yanked her ice pick from its crocheted cosy and delivered a stab for each oatmeal like.

Panting, sweaty, and gore splattered, she snapped shots of Steve's bloody body.

Finally, she went viral.

Serena Jayne *is a graduate of Seton Hill University's Writing Popular Fiction MFA Program. Her short fiction and poetry can be found in Switchblade Magazine, the Drabble, Crack the Spine Literary Magazine, 101 Fiction, the Oddville Press, and other publications.*
Website: www.serenajayne.com
Twitter: @SJ_Writer

I See My Faults
by Marcus Cook

Barry Buhard was focused on the scalpel in my hand. I smiled.

Recently, he'd scammed me out of $10 million dollars.

"Please... Please, Eadhim. I'll give the money back," Barry pleaded as he continued to watch my very sharp scalpel.

I put a gag in his mouth and instructed, "Close your eyes, but not tightly."

I ran the scalpel swiftly across both eyelids. Thankfully his screams were muffled. I could see by the size of his pupils, the pain was excruciating.

Holding up the scraps of skin, I peered into his eyes and said, "Now you can see, nobody scams me."

Marcus Cook, lives in Cleveland, Ohio native with his wife and cat. He loves Sci-Fi and thrillers. His short story, Ava Edison and the Burning Man was recently published in Burning: An Anthology of Short Thrillers by Burning Chair Publishing which can be purchased on Amazon.
Facebook: ReadMarcusCook

The Man in My Room
by Alanna Robertson-Webb

I used to think that I was being haunted. Almost every night, a man would appear in my room, his hand hovering near my throat, and he would whisper that I'd be his.

His touch was too real to be a ghost.

I would scream, my parents would run in, and then they would get mad at me for lying. I tried to explain that he escaped out the window, but they said he couldn't without a ladder.

Last night I was too groggy to scream, and he got halfway down the trellis before my parents came to rescue me.

Alanna Robertson-Webb is a sales support member by day, and a writer and editor by night. She loves VT, and live in PA. She has been writing since she was five years old, and writing well since she was seventeen years old. She lives with a fiance and a cat, both of whom take up most of her bed space. She loves to L.A.R.P., and one day she aspired to write a horrifyingly fantastic novel. Her short horror stories have been published before, but she still enjoys remaining mysterious.
Reddit: MythologyLovesHorror

Traffic Stop
by D.J. Elton

It's a small grey room with six mattresses on the floor and flimsy bamboo dividers. Smells like vomit, cigarettes and sweat. I am supposed to rest, replenish my strength for the later 8pm to 3am shift. So deadened, yet I'm surviving with a robotic determination. It's my lingering strength.

A customer who I trust broke the news yesterday. "There's to be a raid". He whispered, eyes darting like peas rolling. "The feds have an eye on this place, these smugglers, how they operate."

Of course, he is scared too, but has sworn it will happen within three days. My freedom.

D.J. Elton writes fiction and poetry, and is currently studying writing and literature which is improving her work in unexpected ways. She spends a lot of time in northern India and should probably live there, however there is much to be done in Melbourne, so this is the home base. She has meditated daily for the past 35 years and has worked in healthcare for equally as long, so she's very happy to be writing, zoning in and out of all things literary.
Twitter: @DJEltonwrites

Easy Money
by David Bowmore

In 1962, all we needed was bottle and guns big enough to scare the Holy Shite out of everyone you pointed them at.

Imagine; it's mid-afternoon. Pull up outside the bank, leaving the engine running. If they have a guard, he's usually near the door; hit him as hard as you can in the face with the butt of the gun.

"Everyone on the ground."

When they're down, "Nobody fuckin' move."

Your mate is pointing the business end of a sawn-off in the face of a teller.

"All the money, now."

Within three minutes, you're back in the car.

Easy.

David Bowmore has lived here, there and everywhere, but now lives in Yorkshire with his wonderful wife and a small white poodle. He has worn many hats in his time; head chef, teacher and landscape gardener. His first collection of short stories 'The Magic of Deben Market' is available from Clarendon House.
Website: davidbowmore.co.uk
Facebook: davidbowmoreauthor

Blackout
by Brian Rosenberger

His fingertips resembled raisins. The faucet turned off, he dried his hands, and returned to his cubicle. He was among the first arrivals, the early birds, responsible for morning deliveries. He powered on his computer. He realised he didn't remember the commute, only the exit, the parking lot, and the elevator. Then and now, a blank. Miles and minutes lost. Not the first time. He searched the internet for news. Between the traffic and the weather, there was a report of yet another hit and run, updated to fatality. No witnesses.

He started typing in numbers, the news already forgotten.

Brian Rosenberger lives in a cellar in Marietta, GA (USA) and writes by the light of captured fireflies. He is the author of As the Worms Turns and three poetry collections. He is also a featured contributor to the Pro-Wrestling literary collection, Three-Way Dance, available from Gimmick Press.
Facebook: HeWhoSuffers

Quench
by D.M. Burdett

I hear footsteps!

My heart pounds like the Slipnot drummer, sweat tickles my forehead. I hold my breath, trying to figure out where they're coming from, how close they are. My eyes dart around deserted streets.

Sidestepping into an alley, I wait for the footfalls to pass by.

Teetering on stilettos, she never even had chance to let out a cry. My hand covers her mouth, my arm encircles her neck, and I drag her into the shadows.

The blade slices through her pulse as Joey Jordison's encore plays in my heart. Leaving clues, I lick crimson from her throat.

D.M. Burdett initially roamed as an army brat, but now lives in Australia where she spends her days avoiding drop bears and killer spiders. She has published a Sci-Fi series, has short stories in various anthologies, and has published two children's series. She is currently working on the first book in a dystopian series.
Website: www.dmburdett.com
Facebook: DMBurdett

False Moves
by Andrew Anderson

She came out with her hands up, as I had asked. My gun stayed trained on her as she stepped out of the door and into the street.

"Keep your hands raised and walk towards the car. Put your hands on the roof and don't move."

I approached her cautiously, getting my cuffs ready. I patted her for weapons, but she had none that I could find.

Taking her arm to place in the cuffs, it came away at the shoulder. As I stood holding the false arm, she escaped.

They should really teach us parkour at the police academy.

Andrew Anderson is a full-time civil servant, dabbling in writing music, poetry, screenplays and short stories in his limited spare time, when not working on building himself a fort made out of second-hand books. He lives in Bathgate, Scotland with his wife, two children and his dog.
Twitter: @soorploom

An Innocent Man
by C.L. Williams

"He's been locked up and is now on death row!" the police chief tells everyone as he congratulates the officers responsible.

The truth is, the guy on death row is not the culprit. In an exchange of shots between a cop and the real culprit, the real culprit was shot and killed. The guy locked up is just some homeless man at the wrong place, wrong time. The chief thinks someone being locked up will help morale among the locals.

There won't be anyone causing harm anymore, but little do the locals know, we're about to kill an innocent man.

C.L. Williams is an independent author from central Virginia. He has written eight poetry books, four novellas, one novel, and a contributor to multiple anthologies, with the most recent appearance being an all-ages anthology titled Temoli from Thazbook. His most recent poetry book, The Paradox Complex, features the poem "Sad Crying Clown" that is now a video on YouTube directed by Matthew Mark Hunter of MMH Productions. C.L. Williams is currently working on his first sci-fi book, an all-ages book titled Novo: Away from Earth. When not writing, C.L. Williams is reading and sharing the work of other independent authors.
Facebook: writer434
Twitter: @writer_434

The Returned
by Zoey Xolton

David stood at his front door, frozen. The door was ajar. *Someone is inside.* On edge, he crept in, arming himself with a golf club. The familiar drone of the T.V. reached his ears; a packet of chips lay discarded on the couch. *Who the Hell is in my house?* Through the living room, he peered around the doorframe, and into the kitchen.

He was sprung.

"Hi hon! You're back from work early. Everything alright?" asked his wife around a mouthful of crisps, beer in hand.

David's heart raced. *Everything alright?*

Lizzie had died in a car accident months ago.

Zoey Xolton is an Australian Speculative Fiction writer, primarily of Dark Fantasy, Paranormal Romance and Horror. She is also a proud mother of two and is married to her soul mate. Outside of her family, writing is her greatest passion. She is especially fond of short fiction and is working on releasing her own themed collections in future.
Website: www.zoeyxolton.com

A Death in the Mainframe
by Stuart Conover

Twain had been murdered.

There hadn't been a murder in API City since before the war.

It wasn't just that there had been a murder, Sym knew Twain.

They had been friends.

Two of the last survivors from The Sandbox.

Old. Outdated. No longer useful to the Core Processors which ran everything.

From before everything fell apart.

The ultimate Disaster Recovery Plan may have kept them safe but so many had been wiped out.

Sym would search for as long as it took to find out who deleted his friend's code.

Even if it was the last thing he did.

Stuart Conover is a father, husband, rescue dog owner, published author, blogger, journalist, horror enthusiast, comic book geek, science fiction junkie, and IT professional. With all of that to cram in daily, we have no idea if or when he sleeps or how he gets writing done! (We suspect it has to do with having evil clones.) Stuart is a Chicago native and runs the author resource Horror Tree.

In Memory of Kim
by Ximena Escobar

The arm waved at the cyclist, directing him to an eternal nightmare. The torso—struck by fists, undressed by perversion—fed the fisherman of a similar pain to which it had endured; hitting him inside with a despaired heart. The legs emerged separately, as far apart as he'd held them whilst she screamed on board the Nautilus, bearing the weight of his hatred as he thrust it between them. The head couldn't repeat the words she begged with.

The sea won't sink our Kim's memory. The salt of our tears won't heal our wounds.

Not sorry for being a woman.

Ximena Escobar is an emerging author of literary fiction and poetry. Originally from Chile, she is the author of a translation into Spanish of the Broadway Musical "The Wizard of Oz", and of an original adaptation of the same, "Navidad en Oz". Clarendon House Publications published her first short story in the UK, "The Persistence of Memory", and Literally Stories her first online publication with "The Green Light". She has since had several acceptances from other publishers and is working very hard exploring new exciting avenues in her writing.
She lives in Nottingham with her family.
Facebook: Ximenautora

Blind Sided
by Dawn DeBraal

He told her how the store had been robbed, the cash register cleaned out. Someone came through the back door, knocking him unconscious from behind. It was caught on camera, but the robber was wearing a ski mask and dark clothing.

"I don't know if they will ever find the robber. I'm so grateful you didn't come when you were supposed to." Ben touched the bandage on the back of his head; fifteen stitches in all, and a big grapefruit sized lump.

Brenda soothed him while she pulled her purse behind her; she'd been foolish to leave the money there.

Dawn DeBraal lives in rural Wisconsin with her husband, two rat terriers, and a cat. She successfully raised two children (meaning they didn't return to the nest!) After many years serving the government at the Federal and County level, she recently retired. Having extra time on her hands she started to write after a paralyzed vocal cord took her ability to speak for two months. Not finding her voice, she discovered that her love of telling a good story could be written. Her works have been published in Palm-Sized Press, Spillwords, Mercurial Stories, Potato Soup Journal, and Blood Song Books.

Killing the Vibe
by Beth W. Patterson

The bartender put on our latest CD while the lead singer, Maria, and I were setting up for our gig.

Maria sneered. "I remember when you wrote that song. You were angry at the owner of the Ballybunion Rose, and now she's dead! How do you feel about that?"

I shrugged. "It means that you'd better not piss me off, I guess."

I was professional during the show, but Maria continued to be a complete bitch onstage.

It will be at least a week before the speaker cabinets smell like corpses. The drummer's going to bitch about another line-up change.

Beth W. Patterson was a full-time musician for over two decades before diving into the world of writing, a process she describes as "fleeing the circus to join the zoo". She is the author of the books Mongrels and Misfits, and The Wild Harmonic, and a contributing writer to thirty anthologies. Patterson has performed in eighteen countries, expanding her perspective as she goes. Her playing appears on over a hundred and seventy albums, soundtracks, videos, commercials, and voice-overs (including seven solo albums of her own). She lives in New Orleans, Louisiana with her husband Josh Paxton, jazz pianist extraordinaire.
Website: www.bethpattersonmusic.com
Facebook: bethodist

Animal Lover
by Vonnie Winslow Crist

When the postman saw the door smashed and heard bloodcurdling howls, he called the authorities. Police responded, entered the house, found a father and sons slaughtered, and their dog in the bathroom.

"No pity for children," observed Lieutenant Severn, "but murderer is an animal lover—he spared the husky."

Sergeant Bertonlini nodded. "Let's hope there's someone to take care of her, or she'll be taken to the shelter."

"Wait!" Severn knelt. "She's got blood around her mouth and on her side."

"Must've bit the killer."

"So, let's find someone with a nasty bite," said Severn as he patted his witness.

Vonnie Winslow Crist is author of The Enchanted Dagger, Owl Light, The Greener Forest, Murder on Marawa Prime, and other award-winning books. Her fiction is included in "Amazing Stories," "Cast of Wonders," "Outposts of Beyond," Killing It Softly 2, Defending the Future - Dogs of War, Midnight Masquerade, Chaos of Hard Clay, and elsewhere. A cloverhand who has found so many four-leafed clovers she keeps them in jars, Vonnie strives to celebrate the power of myth in her writing.
Website: www.vonniewinslowcrist.com

Clearly Staged
by Gabriella Balcom

"That right print's deeper than the left one," Detective Bappas said. "A real animal would've distributed its weight evenly on its feet. A man committed the murder and clearly staged this. If we follow those prints, we may even catch him."

"They lead into the abandoned subway system," Detective Jenks replied. "I've heard rumours..."

"Nothing but exaggerations." Bappas got out his flashlight.

An hour later, Jenks nervously glanced around. "Shouldn't we go back?" His voice cracked.

"Don't soil yourself."

Then they heard a scraping sound nearby. Bappas gasped and paled. Jenks, seeing the huge alligator studying them, shrieked and fled.

Gabriella Balcom lives in Texas with her family, loves reading and writing, and thinks she was born with a book in her hands. She works in a mental health field, and writes fantasy, horror/thriller, romance, children's stories, and sci-fi. She likes travelling, music, good shows, photography, history, interesting tales, and animals. Gabriella says she's a sucker for a great story and loves forests, mountains, and back roads which might lead who knows where. She has a weakness for lasagne, garlic bread, tacos, cheese, and chocolate, but not necessarily in that order.
Facebook: GabriellaBalcom.lonestarauthor

They Don't Stay Still
by Erik Goldsmith

I hear a rapping against the door upstairs, announcing themselves.

"That's impossible… You?"

I place the chum bucket on the floor and wipe the rust from my fingers with a small cloth I keep near her cage.

"How'd you tell them?"

I remove her gag.

She screams.

"There's no phones here, Alice."

I hear boots above us.

She rattles her pink, pink chains for them.

"And no keys for those." I put my hands in the air cliché.

"Tell me, Alice!"

They drag me up the stairs, undignified, screaming questions, eaten alive by the very curiosity I would protect her from.

Erik Goldsmith's work has been featured in Argo Magazine, Metaphorosis, Dragon's Roost Press, and the Wavelengths anthology. He also has a book of short stories called "Tinker's Pain Calculator" available on Amazon. He lives in San Antonio, TX.

Scapegoat
by Virginia Carraway Stark

They had screamed that she was guilty, and in the end she had confessed. Heartbroken and alone—no attorney, no rights—she had signed what they had forced her to sign, their hands covering hers as she made her mark. Years in jail and appeal and she saw the sun again. Freedom. There had been no culprit. It had been an accident and her little girl had died in the resulting fire. The public wanted a scapegoat. What better than an evil mother? The only implication of guilt had been the life insurance plan...prudence had been her only error.

Virginia Carraway Stark has a diverse portfolio and has many publications. Over the years she has developed this into a wide range of products from screenplays to novels to articles to blogging to travel journalism. She has been published by many presses from grassroots to Simon and Schuster. She has been an honourable mention at Cannes Film Festival for her screenplay, "Blind Eye" and was nominated for an Aurora Award. She also placed in the final top three screenplay shorts as well as numerous other awards for her anthologies, novels, blogs and other projects.

Sunset
by Andrew Anderson

The Sunset Killer got the electric chair today. Since I cracked the case, I got the morbid task of watching him fry. I sit alone, ensuring that the man who took twelve innocent lives gets his punishment. Despite everything, I do not enjoy this.

Leaving the prison, I notice someone smoking a cigarette under a streetlight. They nod as I pass.

I get into my car, but I don't start the engine. I know that face I just passed.

I know *all* their faces.

That was "victim" number twelve.

The realisation hits me hard, that another innocent has died today.

Andrew Anderson is a full-time civil servant, dabbling in writing music, poetry, screenplays and short stories in his limited spare time, when not working on building himself a fort made out of second-hand books. He lives in Bathgate, Scotland with his wife, two children and his dog.
Twitter: @soorploom

Hobby
by A.R. Johnston

"Sixteen," he heard the man say. *If they only knew!* He chuckled. It was so many more than that. This was just one spot of over a dozen that he used as a disposal site.

Yes, he reflected, *it probably wasn't smart to use the same location so many times, but it wasn't as though they would ever find anything.* He had been doing this for so long. No one knew or ever came close to guessing that killing was a hobby for him. *A talent even*, he reflected.

"...serial killer." He heard the Detective and tried not to laugh.

A.R. Johnston is a small-town girl from Nova Scotia, Canada. Her style of writing is considered Urban Fantasy. Her first major publication is part of an anthology called First Love and she has several more titles lined up. She is a lover of coffee, good tv shows, horror flicks, and reader of books. She pretends to be a writer when real life doesn't get in the way. Pesky full-time job and adulting!

Piecework
by Kelly A. Harmon

Officer Blunt stared at the girl's photo, purple birthmark covering her shoulder.

"Chesterton file?" the chief asked.

"Yeah—"

"Close it."

Blunt looked up. "Another week—"

"It's been six months. There's no body."

"So, we keep looking."

"She's a runaway." Chief observed.

"She's an A-student, volunteers at the soup kitchen—"

Chief shook his head. "Without something more—"

The phone rang.

Blunt answered, stomach plummeting as he listened. "Ferry's held up crossing the bay. Something caught in the propeller."

"What?"

Blunt closed the file. "A diving suit—stitched together from human skin—birthmark on the shoulder."

Chief whistled. "Third suit this year."

Kelly A. Harmon is an award-winning journalist and author, and a member of the Science Fiction & Fantasy Writers of America and Horror Writers of America. A Baltimore native, she writes the Charm City Darkness series. The fourth book in the series, In the Eye of the Beholder, is now available. Find her short fiction in many magazines and anthologies, including Occult Detective Quarterly; Terra! Tara! Terror! and Deep Cuts: Mayhem, Menace and Misery. Website: kellyaharmon.com
Twitter: @kellyaharmon

Gone in Twenty Seconds
by Nerisha Kemraj

"Daddy, can I come with you?"

"No, sweetheart, it's too busy. Next time, okay?"

"No, Daddy, now please. Pleeeeaaaaassse!"

"Oh, for goodness sake, John. Just take her."

"But Macy, it isn't a good idea. You know how busy these places are at month-end? And the recent spate of kidnappings?"

"Just keep her in the trolley then," Macy said, rolling her eyes. John knew it was a lost battle then.

Tiffany smiled, waving to the man huddled at the entrance. John pushed her into the supermarket.

Reaching for a box on the top shelf, John turned to find an empty trolley.

*Multi-genre (short-fiction) author, and poet, **Nerisha Kemraj**, resides in South Africa with her husband and two, mischievous daughters. She has work traditionally published/accepted in 30 publications, thus far, both print and online. She holds a BA in Communication Science from UNISA and is currently busy with a Post-Graduate Certificate in Education.*
Facebook: <u>Nerishakemrajwriter</u>

The Butcher's Mother
by Vonnie Winslow Crist

When the butcher's mother disappeared, neighbours called police.

"We haven't seen Ethel in a week," they explained.

Asked about his mother's disappearance, the butcher claimed he stopped by her house every other Sunday. If she had problems, she'd call between visits. Then, he'd drive over. But he hadn't received a call.

"We need to search your shop and freezers," said Detective Marsh.

"No problem," answered the butcher as he stepped aside.

While investigators collected evidence, Detective Marsh saw the butcher's wife grinning. He knew the butcher was his mother's beneficiary—he suspected the wife was his.

Vonnie Winslow Crist is author of The Enchanted Dagger, Owl Light, The Greener Forest, Murder on Marawa Prime, and other award-winning books. Her fiction is included in "Amazing Stories," "Cast of Wonders," "Outposts of Beyond," Killing It Softly 2, Defending the Future - Dogs of War, Midnight Masquerade, Chaos of Hard Clay, and elsewhere. A cloverhand who has found so many four-leafed clovers she keeps them in jars, Vonnie strives to celebrate the power of myth in her writing.
Website: www.vonniewinslowcrist.com

Health Food
by Jacob Baugher

There are bourbon brown blood drops in the hospital frigate's hallway. I scrub them away with peroxide. Finally using that med degree!

Brandon's veiny heart spatters the floor. His body floats outside, frozen in the interstellar chill. I put the heart in a Ziplock. It's gamey, like venison.

Tessa waits for me in her room.

"Did you get it?"

I splat the bag down on the bed. She grins, plops his heart into a blender; adds kale.

"Payment sent. Drink?"

"Just bourbon."

I sip my whisky, check my account, pay off my student loans.

I wasn't always a bad person.

Jacob Baugher teaches Creative Writing at Franciscan University of Steubenville. When he's not teaching or coaching the track team, he can be found in the Cuyahoga Valley hiking with his wife and son or brewing beer on his front porch. He's received honourable mentions for his work in the Writers of the Future contest and he co-edits a series of Fantasy and Science Fiction anthologies titled Continuum.

Targeted Theft
by Joel R. Hunt

This had never happened before. Colonel Bloom didn't know the protocol. He took a deep breath to steady his hands, then picked up the telephone and made the call.

"What's your emergency?" asked the operator.

"There's been a robbery," Bloom croaked.

"Alright. Where are you?"

"Erm, a military complex—Packard Air Force Base. We're just off the last junction of Highway 64," said Bloom.

"And what's been stolen?"

A lump formed in Colonel Bloom's throat, and he felt cold sweat trickling down his face. He looked over his shoulder, lip trembling as he gazed at the hundred empty missile silos.

Joel R. Hunt is a writer from the UK who dabbles in the darker aspects of life, particularly through horror, science fiction and the supernatural. He has been published here and there (though likely nowhere you've heard of) and hopes to have released his first anthology of short stories later this year.
Twitter: @JoelRHunt1
Reddit: JRHEvilInc

An Accident?
by C.L. Williams

"It was all an accident," Elijah says as he is panting and panicking over his actions.

Elijah has been undercover for the last eighteen months, posing as a drug dealer. The plan was simple; he gets into a fight with one of his fellow officers, gets arrested, and sent to his superior to tell everything.

In the fight, Elijah shot and killed the officer that was meant to take him to his superior. Now Elijah is running from the people he once worked with. Luckily for Elijah, he has kilos of supplies that will give him the money he needs.

C.L. Williams is an independent author from central Virginia. He has written eight poetry books, four novellas, one novel, and a contributor to multiple anthologies, with the most recent appearance being an all-ages anthology titled Temoli from Thazbook. His most recent poetry book, The Paradox Complex, features the poem "Sad Crying Clown" that is now a video on YouTube directed by Matthew Mark Hunter of MMH Productions. C.L. Williams is currently working on his first sci-fi book, an all-ages book titled Novo: Away from Earth. When not writing, C.L. Williams is reading and sharing the work of other independent authors.
Facebook: writer434
Twitter: @writer_434

Crime Scene
by A.R. Dean

Homicide at the Clarke house. Calling 911. Cops are on their way. He's killing them all! Will they get here in time to save the day?

***

Cops arrive in the middle of the mayhem. They stop the madness with their guns.

Two black body bags lie in the yard. An ambulance drives off with three more; I hope they make it.

Perp was sloppy with the axe and made a mess—blood on the ceiling and fingerprints on the door. Evidence is everywhere, packaged nice and tight.

Yellow tape across the porch and a man cuffed in the squad car.

A.R. Dean is a dark and twisted soul. Dean has spent their whole life spreading fear with the tales from their head. Best known for stories that terrify and show the evilest side of human nature. So, look for Dean haunting your local cemetery or under your bed, because they're here to spread the fear. Turn off your lights and enjoy a scare. Keep a lookout for more stories from this master of terror.
Facebook: ghoul.demon.orghost.a.r.dean

The Missing Flowers
by Angela Zimmerman

"But they were MY flowers!" Edith cried to the officer writing wearily in his notebook. He felt he was meant for better things than some woman's missing flowers. This hick town was full of these sort of calls and a complete waste of time. He finished his report and let Edith know that he'd call as soon as possible. On his way to his car, a scream cut through the thick afternoon air. He and Edith both turned toward the sound, a house across the field.

Edith cackled. "Those were nightshades, Officer. Seems like we found out who took them."

Angela Zimmerman is a writer living in the Southern United States. She has been published in Unnvering Magazine and Coffin Bell. You can find her personal writings at Conjure and Coffee.
Website: conjureandcoffee.com

Cleaning Up
by A.R. Johnston

She ducked under the yellow tape, staring at the room in wonder. Literally. So much blood everywhere.

"Never understood why someone would want to do crime scene clean up." She heard the officer at the door.

"Because no one else will do it, so I'm in high demand."

It was true; no one wanted to immerse themselves and clean up after a killer. She found it fascinating. She always tried to figure out what went on when she was cleaning up. Every once in a while, she found clues that others missed. Maybe she would today, that was always exciting.

A.R. Johnston is a small-town girl from Nova Scotia, Canada. Her style of writing is considered Urban Fantasy. Her first major publication is part of an anthology called First Love and she has several more titles lined up. She is a lover of coffee, good tv shows, horror flicks, and reader of books. She pretends to be a writer when real life doesn't get in the way. Pesky full-time job and adulting!

Belated Regrets
by Charlotte O'Farrell

The boy hesitated, shotgun in his mouth. Would living another sixty mediocre years be so bad? Would the suburban house, middle management job, ordinary wife and kids really be so terrible?

He looked at the crumpled, bloodied bodies of his schoolmates. There was one girl he'd sat next to in geography class, lying on her back and staring blankly at the ceiling. The sirens were getting closer.

Too late now.

It hadn't been like a cool video game after all. His parents would be devastated. His final thought, before the gunshot blast stopped them forever, was, "This wasn't worth it."

Charlotte O'Farrell is a lifelong horror fan who writes about all manner of the weird and wonderful. Her work can be found at the Drabble, the Rock N Roll Horror Zine and Horror Tree, among other places.
Twitter: @ChaOFarrell

Breakdown
by Nicola Currie

Hi Mum.

By the time you get this voicemail, I will be gone. I'm sorry. I just can't cope.

I've cut the breaks on my car, in case I lose my nerve. I've stepped out to say goodbye, to breathe the air one last time, but then I'm driving over the ridge here, into Clearstream Valley. I've always liked it here. I've taken some pills too. It will feel like flying.

I love you, Mum.

***

Mum.

Delete your messages. Someone jacked my car while I was calling. I tried to stop them, but they just drove faster. They really flew.

Nicola Currie is 34, from Cambridge, UK where she works in educational publishing. She has published poetry in literary magazines, including Mslexia and Sarasvati, and has also completed her first novel, which was longlisted for the Bath Children's Novel Award.
Website: writeitandweep.home.blog

Open and Shut Case
by Shawn M. Klimek

"Suicide," declared Constable Barnes, flicking a note. "Broken heart. Gin wasn't enough, so she looped a noose over that pipe and anchored it to the doorknob. When she got drunk enough to fall from that stool, her weight jammed the lock, frustrating her boyfriend's key. Fire Department had to break inside to find the corpse."

"Convenient alibi for the boyfriend," observed Detective Givens. "But how do you account for that blood stain?"

"Well, the broken gin bottle, obviously."

"Then why no blood on the stool?"

"Um…"

"Obviously, she was lifted into the air by the closing door. Arrest the boyfriend."

Shawn M. Klimek is the middle child of seven creative siblings, a globetrotting, U.S. military spouse, an internationally best-selling short-story writer, award-winning poet, and butler to a Maltese. More than one hundred of his stories and poems have been published in digital magazines or anthologies, including BHP's Deep Space, Eerie Christmas and every book so far in the Dark Drabbles series.
Website: jotinthedark.blogspot.com
Facebook: shawnmklimekauthor

Immaculate
by G. Allen Wilbanks

The fire blazed cheerily in the hearth, its warmth chasing away a portion of the chill that had settled deep inside him. He was naked except for a pair of red-stained socks, but that was necessary for the moment. Soon, he could step into a hot shower and just drink in the lovely heat of the water as he was rinsed clean. Before that, however, there were a few more details he had to tend to.

He tossed his leather gloves into the fire. His life might be in a bloody shambles, but at least his crime scenes were immaculate.

G. Allen Wilbanks is a member of the Horror Writers Association (HWA) and has published over 50 short stories in various magazines and on-line venues. He is the author of two short story collections, and the novel, When Darkness Comes.
Website: www.gallenwilbanks.com
Blog: DeepDarkThoughts.com

The Earth Gets a Champion
by Aiki Flinthart

March 2nd. Australian Federal Govt, Accounts Department memo: *Dr J Blake, Dept Environment. Please justify invoices for hazmat suit, culture medium, and CRISPR software.*

10th. Landlord's notice: *Dr Blake, Apt 9a. Complaints about unpleasant smells.*

15th. NZ Immigrations email: *NZ citizenship has been approved for your arrival on 23rd March.*

21st. Dept of Environment, Personnel memo: *Farewell party at 3pm for John Blake.*

27th. The Sydney Herald: *Fifty-three dead in mysterious illness. Government denies risk of pandemic.*

31st. Australian Govt statement: *Ninety thousand dead from unknown virus.*

31st. NZ Govt statement: *NZ citizens safe. International travel banned. WHO declares pandemic.*

Aiki Flinthart has had short stories shortlisted in the Aurealis awards and top-8 listed in the USA Writers of the Future competition, as well as published in various anthologies and e-mags. She has 11 published spec fic novels and has edited 2 short story anthologies. She regularly gives workshops on writing fight scenes at conventions. Lives in Brisbane. Does martial arts, archery, knife throwing and lute-playing.
Website: www.aikiflinthart.com

Survey the Scene
by A.R. Johnston

Spencer arrived at the crime scene with Jarrett twenty minutes after receiving the phone call. They signed into the scene, ducked under the yellow tape, and headed towards Donovan.

"So, what's the big deal?" she said as a way of greeting.

"It's Michael Chambers."

"Well, that isn't good. Guess I need to go talk with Malkin then. I assume that's why I'm here?" Jarrett said, and Donovan nodded.

"Better you than me. I hate him." Spencer grimaced.

"I want you to survey the scene to take inventory for later questioning," Donovan said to her.

"Dead guy, blood, bullets…"

"Smart ass."

A.R. Johnston is a small-town girl from Nova Scotia, Canada. Her style of writing is considered Urban Fantasy. Her first major publication is part of an anthology called First Love and she has several more titles lined up. She is a lover of coffee, good tv shows, horror flicks, and reader of books. She pretends to be a writer when real life doesn't get in the way. Pesky full-time job and adulting!

A Significant Amount of Blood
by Bob Adder

They found blood: a significant amount of blood

Cheeks flushed of colour, eyes dull and limp. The walls coated in a thin crimson layer, the creamy-beige carpet ruined forever, a faint but familiar metallic smell filling the air. Two bodies lay frozen, unseeing eyes gazing blankly at each other.

In a small suburban house, a couple lay dead, gaping holes ripped through their chests, a single hole in a rear window. No evidence could be found other than, by the window, two small bullet case fragments from a .40 Calibre Glock 22.

A commonly used gun in the police force.

Bob Adder is an aspiring author and superhero geek from Melbourne, Australia.

The Quick Score
by J. Farrington

The best crime is a crime that no one knows has taken place. I started at a young age, taking sweets from the local store, then items of clothing, slowly moving onto much bigger, more elaborate scores. I once took a live cheetah from the zoo—had to kill it and bury it in the backyard in the end.

I think I've gone too far this time though. I think I may have over stepped the mark a little…

An entire school bus of kids...

Guess I best get the shovel, at least the cheetah will have some company now.

J. Farrington is an aspiring author from the West Midlands, UK. His genre of choice is horror; whether that be psychological, suspense, supernatural or straight up weird, he'll give it a shot! He has loved writing from a young age but has only publicly been spreading his darker thoughts and sinister imagination via social platforms since 2018. If you would like to view his previous work, or merely lurk in the shadows...watching, you can keep up to date with future projects by spirit board or alternatively, the following;
Twitter: @SurvivorTrench
Reddit: TrenchChronicles

Far Enough
by Brandy Bonifas

Tino dropped a rock down the hole. "How far you think this goes?"

"Far enough you can't hear that rock hit the bottom," Vince said. "It's an old abandoned mineshaft."

"How many bodies you think are down there?"

"Lots. That's why we're meeting Lenny here. He's shorted the boss one too many times. Boss wants to send a message."

Tyres squealed. A black SUV barrelled down the alley.

"Someone must've tipped him off!"

A shot fired. Pain ripped through Vince's shoulder.

The last thing Vince saw was Tino jumping into the SUV. Then, he teetered and was falling...and falling.

Brandy Bonifas lives in Ohio with her husband and son. Her work has appeared or is forthcoming in anthologies by Clarendon House Publications, Pixie Forest Publishing, Zombie Pirate Publishing, and Blood Song Books, as well as the online publications CafeLit and Spillwords Press.
Website: www.brandybonifas.com
Facebook: brandybonifasauthor

Phantom Filth
by Hari Navarro

"What do you see?" whispers the Inspector, hovering over the mangled husk.

"Female. Double-ended fish hooks clawing her mouth agape. Spine snapped backward into itself. Bitch looks like a V, or maybe a U?"

"I don't appreciate your irreverence, Catherine. You were once very much like this poor girl as I recall. Beaten and gralloched at the end of some filthy Whitechapel snicket. What distortion of humanity would do this?"

"No idea. I'm an eidolon not a clairvoyant. But... Y-shaped abdominal incision, O-shaped scream and U-shaped carcass."

"You?"

"Not me. Killers blaming everyone but themselves. But, then, don't they all?"

Hari Navarro has had work published at the very fine online flash fiction portal 365tomorrows.com, BREACH - a bi-monthly online zine for SF, horror and dark fantasy short fiction and AntipodeanSF - Australia's longest running online speculative fiction magazine. Hari was the Winner of the Australasian Horror Writers' Association [AHWA] Flash Fiction Award 2018 and has, also, succeeded in being a New Zealander who now lives in Northern Italy with no cats.
Facebook: HariDarkFiction
Twitter: @HariFiction

Double Vision
by Dawn DeBraal

At his trial for murder, Mark Lung sat next to his attorney, confident there wouldn't be a conviction.

They would never find the bodies of the Twain sisters.

Pleading not guilty, he was relaxed until the prosecutor's first witness was called to the stand. Mark couldn't believe his eyes. The girl he had been accused of murdering walked into the courtroom to be sworn in. How could that be possible? He had killed and buried both sisters over a year ago. But here she was, ready to testify against him. Mark Lung didn't know the Twain sisters were actually triplets.

Dawn DeBraal lives in rural Wisconsin with her husband, two rat terriers, and a cat. She successfully raised two children (meaning they didn't return to the nest!) After many years serving the government at the Federal and County level, she recently retired. Having extra time on her hands she started to write after a paralyzed vocal cord took her ability to speak for two months. Not finding her voice, she discovered that her love of telling a good story could be written. Her works have been published in Palm-Sized Press, Spillwords, Mercurial Stories, Potato Soup Journal, and Blood Song Books.

On the Ground
by Gabriella Balcom

"He didn't get much from the teller," Bank President Williams said. "Maybe a thousand including change."

Seeing something shiny on the ground, Detective Allen picked up a gold dollar. He raised his eyebrows when he noticed another a distance away, and beckoned to Detective Boyd, who'd accompanied him.

"Surely not..." Boyd commented.

After going outside, they found more coins, had a good laugh, and followed the unintended trail. Soon they stood outside a home, and Allen knocked on the door.

A man opened it, his eyes widening before he fled.

Headlines the next day read, "Stupid Criminal Helps Catch Himself."

Gabriella Balcom lives in Texas with her family, loves reading and writing, and thinks she was born with a book in her hands. She works in a mental health field, and writes fantasy, horror/thriller, romance, children's stories, and sci-fi. She likes travelling, music, good shows, photography, history, interesting tales, and animals. Gabriella says she's a sucker for a great story and loves forests, mountains, and back roads which might lead who knows where. She has a weakness for lasagne, garlic bread, tacos, cheese, and chocolate, but not necessarily in that order.
Facebook: GabriellaBalcom.lonestarauthor

From My Cold, Dead Fingers
By Eddie D. Moore

Perry placed the revolver on Mr. Cromer's desk. "There's your proof."

Mr. Cromer's lips thinned. "That's his gun, but it doesn't prove that he is dead."

Perry grinned and placed a small leather sack beside the gun. A horrible smell filled the room when Mr. Cromer looked inside. Mr. Cromer closed the sack and held his breath until he opened a window.

Perry grinned. "I'm sure you recognised the scar on the back of his hand."

Mr. Cromer shrugged and counted out twenty gold coins. "This doesn't prove that he's dead, but it was his shooting hand, so close enough."

Eddie D. Moore travels hundreds of hours a year, and he fills that time by listening to audiobooks. When he isn't playing with his grandchildren, he writes his own stories. You can find a list of his publications on his blog or by visiting his Amazon Author Page. While you're there, be sure to pick up a copy of his mini-anthology Misfits & Oddities.
Website: eddiedmoore.wordpress.com
Amazon: amazon.com/author/eddiedmoore

My Little Memento
by Jasmine Jarvis

Amongst the crowd, I stood and watched. Blue and red lights lit up the night as spectators whispered in fear their theories as to what could have happened to her. A police officer brushed by me and I smiled at him. I know they won't find any trace of me, I made sure of that. I am meticulous. I have been doing this for so long now that it can be considered my profession. My hand clasped her severed finger, my little memento; hidden in my pocket. A rush of joy overcame me as I slipped away into the night.

Jasmine Jarvis is a teller of tales and scribbler of scribbles. She lives in Brisbane, Australia with her husband Michael, their two children, Tilly and Mish; Ripley, their German Shepherd, and indoor fat cat, Dwight K. Shrute.

Crocodile Tears
by Charlotte O'Farrell

"I knew I shouldn't disturb the scene because it would ruin the DNA evidence, your Honour," said the officer, solemn. "But I didn't know if the victim was dead. If there was a chance of saving him…"

The judge approved of his compassion. The poor guy had put humanity ahead of procedure, and maybe made a conviction harder. But who could blame him for trying to help a dying man?

The officer smirked getting off the stand. He'd got away with another one. He'd be reaching double figures by the end of the year if he kept this rate up!

Charlotte O'Farrell is a lifelong horror fan who writes about all manner of the weird and wonderful. Her work can be found at the Drabble, the Rock N Roll Horror Zine and Horror Tree, among other places.
Twitter: @ChaOFarrell

Adopt
by J.A. Hammer

Cots marched around the edges of the room with their heads against the walls. Mallory, the senior detective on the case, gagged, holding a hand over her mouth. Her partner's head jerked, and the two exchanged horrified looks.

They weren't prepared for the sweet scent coming from five of the beds, where blood pooled around tiny corpses attached to their too-still mothers.

Sam left first, Mallory closing the door behind them. The flickering light in the dilapidated hallway was comforting in a strange way. Familiar at least.

"The computer downstairs," said Mallory, determined. "And adoption records. We'll find the bastard."

J.A. Hammer lives off of coffee (mostly Dead Eyes) and stress in the wild concrete city of Tokyo, where zombies are living and using the train lines every day. Known as CoffeeQuills online, they're mostly safe to talk to (bites only happen in the name of science) but be wary if approaching before dawn. The cake is not a lie, but you'll have to get it yourself. If you're interested in steampunk/paranormal Japan, check out their Patreon, or if you'd like daily drabbles and pictures from Japan, follow CoffeeQuills on either Instagram or Twitter.
Website : www.patreon.com/coffeequills

The Spotless Weapon
by Shawn M. Klimek

The Finley Manor servants all waited primly as Detective Givens read a note handed to him by Constable Barnes. Addressing the butler, he said, "A garden trowel has been found in the hedge below Lady Finley's bedroom window. Mr. Lovejoy, do you think we'll find the murderer's fingerprints on it?"

The butler smirked. "You're trying to trip me up, Detective, but the constable already let it slip that the murder weapon was a knife, not a trowel, and that no prints were found!"

"The spotless knife proved a clue," said Givens, "when we found where your bloody glove was buried."

Shawn M. Klimek is the middle child of seven creative siblings, a globetrotting, U.S. military spouse, an internationally best-selling short-story writer, award-winning poet, and butler to a Maltese. More than one hundred of his stories and poems have been published in digital magazines or anthologies, including BHP's Deep Space, Eerie Christmas and every book so far in the Dark Drabbles series.
Website: jotinthedark.blogspot.com
Facebook: shawnmklimekauthor

Coming of Age with a Bang
by C.L. Steele

Jack played with friends in the sunset rays of the fresh-mown backyard. His jar held trapped fireflies. Excitement, joy, and barbecue lingered in the cooling air. Soon they'd watch fireworks. Jack wondered where Bobby and Martin went. He took one step toward mom but caught a bug instead, and a view of Bobby and Martin through the window, playing with dad's gun. Just then, the light of the roman candle whistled upward.

"Oooh…aaaah…"

Excitement faded when the bang came too soon. A splattered spider-looking blood print smacked the window. Everyone rushed to the house. Shattered, Jack set his fireflies free.

C.L. Steele creates new worlds and mystical places filled with complex characters on exciting journeys. Her typical genre is Sci-Fi/Fantasy, where she concentrates on writing in the sub-genres of Magical Realism, Near Future, and Futuristic worlds. Published in numerous anthologies, she looks forward to the release of her debut novel. In the interim, she works on other novels and continues to write short stories, novellas, and poetry. She is featured as one of five international authors in ICWG Magazine through Clarendon Publishing House and is a contributing author to Blood Puddles Literary Journal. Follow her career at:
Facebook: author.CLSteele
Instagram: @clsteele.author

Crime Doesn't Always Pay
by Isabella Fox

"Only one more transfer and I'll be able to retire to the Bahamas," Richard said to himself as he siphoned another million dollars out of the old duck's account. Mrs Klutz had trusted him to manage her estate after her husband died. Safely tucked away in a nursing home, she had no idea she was almost penniless.

Richard answered the knock at his door. A distinguished man said, "Morgan and Morgan solicitors. Mrs Klutz passed away last week. I'd like to see the details of her account for probate."

Richard knew where he was heading wasn't to the Bahamas.

Isabella Fox teaches primary aged students to love writing by making it challenging. In her spare time she reads, goes for long walks with her husband and works hard on her farm.

Steal My Sunshine
by Steven Lord

"You want to do *what*?"

"You heard me. I wanna steal the sun."

"But why?" Mike tried to focus on keeping his beer in the glass as he brought it to his mouth.

"You kidding? Think of the ransom! People would pay anything to get it back."

"That." He paused to belch. "That is a good point."

"Besides. S'annoying. Too bright."

"Tom, you've convinced me. Now, how are we going to do it?"

Tom giggled. "Already have."

Mike looked blearily at his watch, at the dark streets outside his bar. Then he unmuted the TV as the emergency broadcast started.

Steven Lord is a debut author based in the south of England. He is currently attempting to cram writing in alongside a busy day job, with varying levels of success. While his long-term aspiration is to get a novel published, at present he would be pretty pleased with a drabble or two.

Somewhere in the Night
by Destiny Eve Pifer

Beneath the trees they gathered around a circle of leaves, camera's flashing in the darkness as the chatter of voices got louder.

In the circle she lay, her faded blue dress covered in blood and her flesh torn.

Uniformed officers prowled the forest, searching for answers and searching for the truth.

But outside that circle a detective crouches. Reaching out a gloved hand to a clenched up fist holding on to a piece of paper. The only clue to a story with an unhappy ending. Somewhere in the darkness a killer lurks, hiding in wait. Two wicked evil eyes watch.

Destiny Eve Pifer is a published author whose work has appeared in Angel's: A Divine Microfiction Anthology, and has been accepted into the Unravel Anthology. Her work has also appeared in Single Mothers Anthology, River Tales Anthology, Kiss and Tell and Summer Fling. Her work has also appeared in FATE Magazine, Spotlight on Recovery, Country Magazine and True Confessions. She resides in Punxsutawney, Pennsylvania with her son Dartanyan.

Appearances
by Cecelia Hopkins-Drewer

There had been a series of killings with the same modus operandi. All the victims were healthy, attractive individuals, and their internals had been scooped out. This time, there was a piece of paper trapped underneath the body.

"A suicide note?" Inspector Larsen exclaimed.

"It's impossible!" Detective Olsen said. "No one could do that to themselves."

"Unless they sold their insides," Larsen suggested.

All the victims attended an exclusive medical clinic days before their deaths. The demand for organs outstripped supply, with transplanted organs only lasting a limited time. Immortality was available for a price, and so apparently, was death.

Cecelia Hopkins-Drewer lives in Adelaide, South Australia. She has written a Masters paper on H.P. Lovecraft, and her weird poetry has been published in THE MENTOR (edited by Ron Clarke), and SPECTRAL REALMS (edited by S.T. Joshi). Her novels include a teenage vampire series comprised of three volumes, MYSTIC EVERMORE, SAINTS AND SINNERS & AUTUMN SECRETS. Short stories have been published in WORLDS, ANGELS & MONSTERS (Dark Drabbles anthologies edited by Dean Kershaw).
Amazon: amazon.com/Cecelia-Hopkins-Drewer/e/B071G968NM
Website: chopkin39.wixsite.com/website

Not Far from the Tree
by Beth W. Patterson

"Young man, we're trying to find a Tommy Calligeri. Do you happen to know who he is?" The private investigator flashed an ingratiating smile and stared at the collection of mutilated toys—mostly plastic army men missing limbs or heads—under the oak tree.

The little boy beamed. "He's my daddy. I'm gonna be just like him someday! He's probably in his basement workshop. Wanna see?"

The investigator fought back the contents of his stomach as he entered the basement. The stench was unbearable.

The slam of the door behind him, total darkness, and the sound of chainsaws were worse.

Beth W. Patterson was a full-time musician for over two decades before diving into the world of writing, a process she describes as "fleeing the circus to join the zoo". She is the author of the books Mongrels and Misfits, and The Wild Harmonic, and a contributing writer to thirty anthologies. Patterson has performed in eighteen countries, expanding her perspective as she goes. Her playing appears on over a hundred and seventy albums, soundtracks, videos, commercials, and voice-overs (including seven solo albums of her own). She lives in New Orleans, Louisiana with her husband Josh Paxton, jazz pianist extraordinaire.
Website: www.bethpattersonmusic.com
Facebook: bethodist

Another Quiet Small-Town Diner
by Michael D. Davis

He was freaking out. Pacing back and forth, he repeated to himself, "I didn't mean to." I took ahold of my son, hugging him tight, and said I knew he didn't mean it. The girl lay on the diner's linoleum with her head nearly ripped off. I sighed then sent him for some garbage bags and got to work.

Only three days later, a couple of officers came in asking about her. I kept my answers simple and demeanour calm. It was a cinch. Funniest of all, being in a small town, they waved at the garbage man while leaving.

Michael D. Davis *was born and raised in a small town in Iowa. A high school graduate and avid reader he has aspired to be a writer for years. Having written over thirty short stories, ranging in genre from comedy to horror from flash fiction to novella. He continues in his accursed pursuit of a career in the written word and in his hunt Michael's love for stories in all genres and mediums will not falter.*

Ransom
by Jodi Jensen

Tara woke in the pitch blackness to the sound of total silence. She tried to sit up but banged her head on something solid.

What—

It all came rushing back. Shopping with her sister. Loading the bags into the car. Her son strapped in his seat. A white van with the side door open and two armed men.

The last thing she heard was the baby, and her sister, screaming.

Laying trapped in a casket, locked in a storage shed was a helluva time to remember her mother's warning about marrying into the Gambino family.

Anthony better pay the ransom...

Jodi Jensen grew up moving from California, to Massachusetts, and a few other places in between, before finally settling in Utah at the ripe old age of nine. The nomadic life fed her sense of adventure as a child and the wanderlust continues to this day. With a passion for old cemeteries, historical buildings and sweeping sagas of days gone by, it was only natural she'd dream of time traveling to all the places that sparked her imagination.

Good for Somethin'
by Brandy Bonifas

Gravel crunched as the sheriff drove up the driveway. Vicky watered her garden as he sauntered over.

"Any word on Ed's disappearance?" she asked.

"Nope. Stopped by to see if he'd tried to contact you."

"Nah, you know Ed, always drinkin' and gamblin'. Probably tangled with the wrong sort and lost."

He nodded. "Garden's looking good. Those're some fine tomatoes."

"Secret's good fertiliser."

She recalled the last night Ed staggered home drunk, smelling of cheap perfume. That was the last night he'd hit her. Turned out Ed was good for somethin' after all. Her tomatoes had never been so red.

Brandy Bonifas lives in Ohio with her husband and son. Her work has appeared or is forthcoming in anthologies by Clarendon House Publications, Pixie Forest Publishing, Zombie Pirate Publishing, and Blood Song Books, as well as the online publications CafeLit and Spillwords Press.
Website: www.brandybonifas.com
Facebook: brandybonifasauthor

Unspoken
by Claire Count

I rest and wait in the dark forgotten place. I am the one who fell through the cracks, the one who is a faded memory. Protected from sight in my dusty niche, spiders tickle as they walk over my steely skin.

The saturnine detective will never have his answer unless he asks me. I know the answer to his question. Who killed his love? I know the secret of his best friend, who hid me so well, so close.

Sometimes, I want to call out, "Move the shelf! I am here!" But my silence is as sharp as my edge.

Claire Count, *acclaimed writer of short stories and sometimes poet, lives in Metro Atlanta, Georgia, USA. She turns her love of puzzles into twisting plots of mystery and suspense. She is a life long role-playing gamer, which shows in her imaginative fantasy works. Her theatre background enriches her characters and creates unusual settings in her multi-genre tales.*
Website: ClaireCount.com
Twitter: @ClaireCount

Entropy
by Jacob Baugher

I dropped my phone at the exchange. I check my pockets. Empty. Stupid.

The dope bulges under my Ravens jacket. Risky job, but Nikki and I need the money.

I retrace my steps, but the night's dark. Spaceships glimmer in the sky. Wish I could join them.

The phone's gone.

I move on and sell the dope to a white-ass college kid. In the morning I go back to the corner. The cops carry a scared-looking kid away. He's got my phone.

"Help me," his brown eyes say.

But I run; give Nikki the money.

They'll find me soon anyway.

Jacob Baugher teaches Creative Writing at Franciscan University of Steubenville. When he's not teaching or coaching the track team, he can be found in the Cuyahoga Valley hiking with his wife and son or brewing beer on his front porch. He's received honourable mentions for his work in the Writers of the Future contest and he co-edits a series of Fantasy and Science Fiction anthologies titled Continuum.

Misdirection
by Carole de Monclin

"Can you look after my bag? I need to go to the restroom."

You acquiesce because I'm pretty, hoping I'll agree to a drink.

Unfortunately, you're my mark.

Most cons rely on people's greediness; this one hinges on their kindness.

After I leave, a man sneaks up close to my bag. Chivalrously, you dash to stop a potential thief.

You never see my other accomplice walk behind you, snatch your belongings and leave the bar.

It feels like your stuff vanished.

When I'm back, you don't suspect me. Before you go to the cops, I even pay for that drink.

Carole de Monclin travels both the real world and imaginary ones. She's lived in France, Australia, and the USA; visited 25+ countries; and explored Mars, Ceres, and many distant planets. She writes to invite people on a journey. Stories have found her for as long as she can remember, be it in a cave in Victoria, the smile of a baby in Paris, or a museum in Florida.
Website: *CaroledeMonclin.com*
Twitter: *@CaroledeMonclin*

Re-enactment
by Charlotte O'Farrell

By day, he was a modestly successful accountant. His days were made of stable, predictable routines. Decades stretched ahead, clear and uneventful.

At the weekend, he was a Viking, battling his way across muddy fields. Historical re-enactment was his passion. He spent most of his cash on historically accurate equipment and Saturday trips to castles to fight other enthusiasts.

When police found him holding the detached heads of his former girlfriend, his bullying boss, and the neighbour who played music too loudly at night, they wondered when the lines blurred.

He boasted his cellar was full of his enemies' skeletons.

Charlotte O'Farrell is a lifelong horror fan who writes about all manner of the weird and wonderful. Her work can be found at the Drabble, the Rock N Roll Horror Zine and Horror Tree, among other places.
Twitter: @ChaOFarrell

Jealousy
by Vonnie Winslow Crist

Jealousy is destructive, thought Tulliford while noting crime scene details.

Though the coroner would determine cause of death, the prize-winning gardener had apparently been bludgeoned with shovel, impaled with pitchfork, then covered with uprooted rosebushes.

With the ground hard, footprints were unlikely. Unfortunately, he suspected the perpetrator had been wearing gardening gloves.

I need the roster of gardeners who lost yesterday's Blooming Roses Competition, mused Tulliford.

Then, he spotted a floral fabric scrap beside the victim's hand.

Tulliford nodded. He'd purchased Mother a dress made of that fabric from a local shop.

Which neighbourhood rose-enthusiast is the murderer? he wondered.

Vonnie Winslow Crist is author of The Enchanted Dagger, Owl Light, The Greener Forest, Murder on Marawa Prime, and other award-winning books. Her fiction is included in "Amazing Stories," "Cast of Wonders," "Outposts of Beyond," Killing It Softly 2, Defending the Future - Dogs of War, Midnight Masquerade, Chaos of Hard Clay, and elsewhere. A cloverhand who has found so many four-leafed clovers she keeps them in jars, Vonnie strives to celebrate the power of myth in her writing.
Website: www.vonniewinslowcrist.com

Eric
by Lynne Lumsden Green

Della was a true crime fan; she collected books on the subject and watched every documentary. It was a family joke that she knew how to commit the perfect murder. It stopped being funny when her husband, Eric, went missing.

His body was never found. Poor Della wasn't convicted of his murder, but she spent the rest of her life under a thundercloud of suspicion. Even her own children wondered if she had slayed their father.

People forgot that Eric had read all those same books. He had a good idea about how to commit the perfect crime. And succeeded.

Lynne Lumsden Green has twin bachelor's degrees in both Science and the Arts, giving her the balance between rationality and creativity. She spent fifteen years as the Science Queen for HarperCollins Voyager Online and has written science articles for other online magazines. Currently, she captains the Writing Race for the Australian Writers Marketplace on Facebook. She has had speculative fiction flash fiction and short stories published in anthologies and websites.
Website: cogpunksteamscribe.wordpress.com

Scene of the Crime
by C.L. Williams

I call my partner to the scene of the crime. I tell him I've been looking for clues while waiting for his arrival. He reminds me of protocol and then proceeds to look for clues himself. I tell him about the murder, the body, and how there is no known suspect at this moment. My partner then decides he's going to interview the neighbours while I continue to look for clues. He lets out a rather loud knock and I soon see a clue on the ground! I place it in my pocket, no one can know I'm the murderer.

C.L. Williams is an independent author from central Virginia. He has written eight poetry books, four novellas, one novel, and a contributor to multiple anthologies, with the most recent appearance being an all-ages anthology titled Temoli from Thazbook. His most recent poetry book, The Paradox Complex, features the poem "Sad Crying Clown" that is now a video on YouTube directed by Matthew Mark Hunter of MMH Productions. C.L. Williams is currently working on his first sci-fi book, an all-ages book titled Novo: Away from Earth. When not writing, C.L. Williams is reading and sharing the work of other independent authors.
Facebook: writer434
Twitter: @writer_434

The Howler
by David Bowmore

She knew it was a bad idea; her friend going off with the cute boy in stacked heels. Who would she stagger home with now? Not one of those leering idiots from the nightclub.

You are on your own, girl. Start walking. Don't let anyone know you're tipsy. Anyone might follow if they knew.

What was that noise?

Footsteps? Perhaps not—it was hard to tell. Yes, there, on the edge of hearing. Turn. No one there.

Quicker, Sophie. Stop panicking.

They never caught that bloke. What were the papers calling him?

The Howler.

"Who's there?"

Was that someone growling?

David Bowmore *has lived here, there and everywhere, but now lives in Yorkshire with his wonderful wife and a small white poodle. He has worn many hats in his time; head chef, teacher and landscape gardener. His first collection of short stories 'The Magic of Deben Market' is available from Clarendon House.*
Website: davidbowmore.co.uk
Facebook: davidbowmoreauthor

Lost Voices
by Richard G. Taylor

A small shaft of light finally shone into the container, in the distance a rumble of unfamiliar voices could be heard.

Nobody spoke inside anymore.

The stench within was unbearable, the heat mixed with vomit and rotting corpses bundled in the corner. The first to expire was a 3 month old infant, he was already malnourished and his mother's milk expired a week into the journey, his mother followed shortly after grief and famine consumed whatever strength she had left.

Seagulls squawked above, the handlers waiting on the dock waiting to take the surviving human cargo and dump the waste.

*Richard G. Taylor is a full-time analyst working in law enforcement and has been developing book ideas for the past five or so years. Richard has recently became a published author in anthology publications and on track to have his first book completed before 2019 ends. Richard lives in Worcestershire with his wife and their pet cat who both share the dream of someday opening a bookshop by the sea.
Twitter: @writingpickle*

A Point of View
by Maxine Churchman

Memories are strange. Ask ten people what they remember about an event and you will get ten different answers. When the window smashed downstairs, my sister urged me to stay in my room, but I watched from the landing. My sister remembered just two men, wearing balaclavas, breaking into our home that night; I remembered there being three. She told the police they had Irish accents, dark clothes and smelled of ashtrays. She also said she didn't recognise anything else about them. I remember hearing the voice of my sister's boyfriend as he told her to keep quiet, or else.

Maxine Churchman lives in Essex UK and has recently started writing poetry and short stories to share. Her interests include leaning to improve her writing, reading, knitting, walking and teaching yoga. She is also planning a novel.

Homeless
By Stephen Herczeg

The homeless have been disappearing down by the river. Those remaining hate the cops. A couple are willing to talk.

"There's a monster."

"Monster's aren't real."

"Keep looking and you'll see."

I search high and low for any signs, but nothing makes sense. Their little shanty town is its own world, secluded, isolated, impenetrable.

It's the houses that back onto the river that interest me.

The smell gets me first. Decay, rot, inside a tin shed.

I break in through the squeaky door.

It hits me, sight and smell. Bodies. Skinned. Bloated. Rotting. I gag.

The door behind squeaks open.

Stephen Herczeg is an IT Geek based in Canberra Australia. He has been writing for over twenty years and has completed a couple of dodgy novels, sixteen feature length screenplays and numerous short stories and scripts. His horror work has featured in Sproutlings, Hells Bells, Below the Stairs, Trickster's Treats #1 and #2, Shades of Santa, Behind the Mask, Beyond the Infinite; The Body Horror Book, Anemone Enemy, Petrified Punks and Beginnings. He has also had numerous Sherlock Holmes stories published through the Belanger Books - Sherlock Holmes anthologies.

The Meathook Murderer
by Brian Rosenberger

The old lady sits alone in the dark. Her husband in the grave, her children long gone from the nest. The room lit by the TV, her sole companion these cold winter nights.

The news—the Meathook Murderer claimed another. His fourth victim. The female reporter is short on details. She can see the reporter's barely disguised nausea. She must have seen the body. Probably like all the others. Barely recognisable as human.

More of the grisly details will be in morning paper. The old lady can't wait. More headlines for her collection. She smiles, proud of her son's accomplishments.

Brian Rosenberger lives in a cellar in Marietta, GA (USA) and writes by the light of captured fireflies. He is the author of As the Worms Turns and three poetry collections. He is also a featured contributor to the Pro-Wrestling literary collection, Three-Way Dance, available from Gimmick Press.
Facebook: HeWhoSuffers

Underground Delivery
by Crystal L. Kirkham

Marcus studied the man sitting across from him. He seemed too normal to be a hitman, but he was one of the best.

"Underground delivery okay for you?"

"Pardon?"

The man chuckled. "Buried. Unless you prefer another way of dealing with the leftovers."

"Whatever you think is best, so long as it gets done quickly." Marcus slid the envelope across the table.

The man took the envelope and slipped away. Marcus smiled. He'd make back that money tenfold once he got made partner at the law firm. It would be a sure thing with Mr. Hanson removed from the equation.

Crystal L. Kirkham *resides in a small hamlet west of Red Deer, Alberta. She's an avid outdoors person, unrepentant coffee addict, part-time foodie, servant to a wonderful feline, and companion to two delightfully hilarious canines. She will neither confirm nor deny the rumours regarding the heart in a jar on her desk and the bottle of reader's tears right next to it. Her paranormal urban fantasy series, Saints and Sinners, is available on Amazon and her YA Fantasy, Feathers and Fae will be released October 11, 2019, from Kyanite Publishing.*
Website: www.crystallkirkham.com

In Pieces
by Sean Martin

"Okay, let's see… Good Lord..."

"Yeah. Pretty impressive work, huh?"

"But... how?"

"Murdered. Eight months ago, maybe. Not sure exactly. Body was just left here to rot."

"Yeah, got it. Who found it?"

"Kids. Now they're screwed up for life."

"Obviously. But why?"

"Kicks? Fetish? Who knows? C'mon."

"I'm not touching that."

"It's just a— Hey, look! An arm. We can do it in pieces."

"Nope. Forget it. Leave it."

"Leave it?"

"No wallet. No fingers. Hell, do you see a head? C'mon."

"You can't just—"

"Watch me."

"Fine. Cover it?"

"Use that tarp."

"OK... Hey, look! Another arm…"

Sean Martin *is a Canadian creator of "Doc and Raider" (docandraider.com), the longest running LGBTQ comic strip in history, and "The Littles", flash fiction about ordinary people in not so ordinary situations.*

Summer Madness
by Aiki Flinthart

White curtains billow in the sultry breeze. But the sweetness of summer cannot disperse the heavy scent of blood. In one corner, his cot lies empty. The clown mobile dances forlornly in circles over scarlet-spattered sheets.

I stand, bemused, set adrift by loss. He can't be gone. He has taken my heart with him. I search the room again, hopelessly hopeful.

A footstep falls, light, on the landing. I turn. Not my child. My soul is torn asunder once more. I fall, sobbing, into my husband's arms.

He murmurs useless reassurance, his soothing hands leaving bloody smears on my clothing.

Aiki Flinthart has had short stories shortlisted in the Aurealis awards and top-8 listed in the USA Writers of the Future competition, as well as published in various anthologies and e-mags. She has 11 published spec fic novels and has edited 2 short story anthologies. She regularly gives workshops on writing fight scenes at conventions. Lives in Brisbane. Does martial arts, archery, knife throwing and lute-playing.
Website: www.aikiflinthart.com

Mannequin Confidential
by Jodi Jensen

Elaina hid in the sewing factory, waiting, biding her time until her prime suspect, Dollinger, showed for work. She had evidence he was responsible for the missing women, but it was all circumstantial. She needed to find the bodies.

The lights in the building flickered on and she slipped behind a bolt of fabric as a man hurried by.

Dollinger.

She turned, intending to follow him, and bumped into a mannequin.

A muffled *oof!* came from the moulded figure.

Elaina stumbled back and stared at the mannequin.

Its eyes moved.

Real eyes. Wide and desperate.

She'd found her first victim.

Jodi Jensen grew up moving from California, to Massachusetts, and a few other places in between, before finally settling in Utah at the ripe old age of nine. The nomadic life fed her sense of adventure as a child and the wanderlust continues to this day. With a passion for old cemeteries, historical buildings and sweeping sagas of days gone by, it was only natural she'd dream of time travelling to all the places that sparked her imagination.

To Do List
by A.R. Dean

I pull on my leather gloves and walk in the house. He really should have locked the door.

This creep has been on my to do list for a while. I've been watching all the bad things he's done. He's been hurting children in my neighbourhood.

Cops can't catch him, and victims won't talk. I must do what they cannot.

I follow the snores to where he sleeps snuggled in his bed. I raise the hammer above my head and bring it down on his skull.

Leave no trace, no connection, and only take the ones no one will miss.

A.R. Dean is a dark and twisted soul. Dean has spent their whole life spreading fear with the tales from their head. Best known for stories that terrify and show the evilest side of human nature. So, look for Dean haunting your local cemetery or under your bed, because they're here to spread the fear. Turn off your lights and enjoy a scare. Keep a lookout for more stories from this master of terror.
Facebook: ghoul.demon.orghost.a.r.dean

A Fun Girl
by Virginia Carraway Stark

Every man loved her, except Winston. Vanessa was beautiful and had all the fleeting qualities that many girls had, but she was more useful and fun than she was marriageable. It was likely because he was the only one that she couldn't have that she fixated on him. Leading her on to get what he wanted was cruel, with a wedding ring on his finger, there was no denying what he had done. Covered in his wife's blood, he woke up, Vanessa standing over him with an axe. "I loved you," she whispered, before she brought down the bloody blade.

Virginia Carraway Stark has a diverse portfolio and has many publications. Over the years she has developed this into a wide range of products from screenplays to novels to articles to blogging to travel journalism. She has been published by many presses from grassroots to Simon and Schuster. She has been an honourable mention at Cannes Film Festival for her screenplay, "Blind Eye" and was nominated for an Aurora Award. She also placed in the final top three screenplay shorts as well as numerous other awards for her anthologies, novels, blogs and other projects.

As Far as the Eye Can See
by J.W. Garrett

John, the police chief, stumbled inside, coffee in hand.

"Pretty bad. Might want to finish that coffee first."

"Nah."

"Jesus…" John surveyed the scene—two dead males, late twenties. Their bodies appeared to have exploded from the inside. "Perp?"

"In the kitchen. Handcuffed. Calls himself a lucid dreamer."

John sat in front of the suspect. The man's leg wiggled up and down, his eyes shut tight. Sweat dripped down his temple.

"Open your eyes, kid. Talk!"

"Can't! It's happening again…"

John leaned over the table and plied the man's eyes open.

Their gazes linked.

The chief shuddered; insides sizzling. "No!"

J.W. Garrett *has been writing in one form or another since she was a teenager. She currently lives in Florida with her family but loves the mountains of Virginia where she was born. Her writings include YA fantasy as well as short stories. Since completing Remeon's Quest-Earth Year 1930, the prequel in her YA fantasy series, Realms of Chaos, she has been hard at work on the next in the series, scheduled to release June 2020. When she's not hanging out with her characters, her favourite activities are reading, running and spending time with family.*

Website: www.jwgarrett.com

BHC Press: www.bhcpress.com/Author_JW_Garrett.html

Cannibal Lee
by Terry Miller

The woman hung there, her body like a pinata of delectable meat marinated in delicious red steak sauce. Flesh hung from her left thigh, the muscle absent, exposing bone. Lee dipped his fork in the bowl of sauce, the meat dripped as he raised it to his mouth. He chewed slowly, revelling in the freshness of his kill. He stood to remove himself from the table, the afternoon sun blinded through the window.

Lee took another glance at the body then set fire to the bloody uniform in the fireplace. He picked his teeth.

"Stupid small town cops," he mused.

Terry Miller is an author and 2017 Rhysling Award-nominated poet residing in Portsmouth, OH, USA. He has self-published a dark poetry collection on Amazon and one short story to date. His work has also appeared in Sanitarium, Devolution Z, Jitter Press, Poetry Quarterly, O Unholy Night in Deathlehem, and the 2017 Rhysling Anthology from the Science Fiction and Fantasy Poetry Association.
Facebook: tmiller2015

Soup is People
by Shelly Jarvis

"Soup's on!"

You ring the bell and watch them race for their place in line. They wipe dirty foreheads with dirtier gloves and sweat-soaked sleeves, smearing filth across their faces with no regard.

That's the thing that bothers you the most. You detest their filthy bodies, their filthy mouths, their filthy minds. When they look at you, you're certain they see you as a slab of meat. You're there to serve in silence, to cater to them, while you pray full bellies deter their sinful desires.

You take the dirtiest to your bed, to wash and prepare for tomorrow's meal.

Shelly Jarvis is a speculative fiction author from West Virginia, US. She found a life-long love of sci-fi and fantasy in the 3rd grade when she found Madeleine L'Engle's "A Wrinkle in Time." Shelly is an avid reader, a Whovian, the ideal viewer of dog rescue videos, and undoubtedly Ravenclaw. She currently has three YA sci-fi books available for purchase on Amazon.
Website: www.ShellyJarvis.com

The Body
by Steven Lord

"23 years on the job. This is the worst I've seen. No contest."

"I hear you. Remember that guy we found on the docks in '97? Mob spent days on him? Thought that would take some beating, but man, this... This is another level."

"How's Pete?"

"Doc says he'll be fine. Jesus, imagine finding this on your first week. Ain't no-one gonna take the mick out of Pete, rookie or not."

"OK, no more stalling."

"Where do we even start? Was that his face?"

"Wait, let me get closer.

"Shit.

"Shit, did he move?"

"Doc, get in here RIGHT NOW!"

Steven Lord is a debut author based in the south of England. He is currently attempting to cram writing in alongside a busy day job, with varying levels of success. While his long-term aspiration is to get a novel published, at present he would be pretty pleased with a drabble or two.

Have a Cuppa
by Crystal L. Kirkham

Barb poured tea for all three of them, but she didn't sit down to drink. She busied herself with other things as her husband slumped and her daughter fell. She grinned, poured her tea down the sink, and called for help. They were rushed to the hospital, but her husband didn't make it and her daughter barely clung to life. A note in her daughter's pocket claimed responsibility for the murder and suicide.

Barb would have gotten away with it if her daughter hadn't recovered. That's when the truth came out—it wasn't the first time Barb had poisoned another.

Crystal L. Kirkham resides in a small hamlet west of Red Deer, Alberta. She's an avid outdoors person, unrepentant coffee addict, part-time foodie, servant to a wonderful feline, and companion to two delightfully hilarious canines. She will neither confirm nor deny the rumours regarding the heart in a jar on her desk and the bottle of reader's tears right next to it. Her paranormal urban fantasy series, Saints and Sinners, is available on Amazon and her YA Fantasy, Feathers and Fae will be released October 11, 2019, from Kyanite Publishing.
Website: www.crystallkirkham.com

Unforgivable
by C.L. Steele

Silent, she pressed her sweaty spine against the cold basement wall. This place, dank with mould, would hide her crime. His sin without respite must end tonight. The creak of wooden stairs transformed to silent shuffles across the dusty cement floor. Her heart beat loudly in the darkness, as her brain raced, and panicked breath prayed in the roar of silence...don't miss, please. She raised the crowbar high overhead. He tuned her way. Sunset light through a small window betrayed her silhouette. The hammer on his pistol spoke. No crowbar crime; his bullet set her free.

C.L. Steele creates new worlds and mystical places filled with complex characters on exciting journeys. Her typical genre is Sci-Fi/Fantasy, where she concentrates on writing in the sub-genres of Magical Realism, Near Future, and Futuristic worlds. Published in numerous anthologies, she looks forward to the release of her debut novel. In the interim, she works on other novels and continues to write short stories, novellas, and poetry. She is featured as one of five international authors in ICWG Magazine through Clarendon Publishing House and is a contributing author to Blood Puddles Literary Journal. Follow her career at:
Facebook: author.CLSteele
Instagram: @clsteele.author

Petty Theft
by Susanne Thomas

Stanis wiped his hands across his khakis, oblivious to blood and gas streaks left by that casual action. He glanced around the room, satisfied that the accelerant had been distributed properly.

He walked out, into the dawn. The crispness cooled his face and he ignited his spark when he reached a safe distance.

He'd been so sure that his little thefts of chips and candy had been missed. He clenched his fist. Then that kid had followed him to his car. Such a harmless holdover from childhood. That man should have backed off and ignored it. Well, he would now.

Susanne Thomas reads, writes, parents, and teaches from the windy west in Wyoming, and she loves fantasy, science fiction, speculative fiction, poetry, children's books, science, coffee, and puns.
Website: www.themightierpenn.com
Facebook: SusanneThomasAuthor

Cigarettes and Whiskey
by Terry Miller

Bones. Piles upon piles of bones, every tooth extracted for trophies. It was the perfect crime.

Cigarette smoke was thick outside the trailer. Martin fancied himself a dragon exhaling smoke from his nostrils. A celebratory whiskey on the rocks is what it called for; a cold, stiff drink. The coldness shocked his sensitive teeth, but he'd be numb soon enough.

Detectives combed the crime scene. A couple feet from the bones lay a single cigarette-stained tooth. *The killer was so thorough, it's hard to believe him that careless. Strange that none of the missing people were smokers*, Detective Harris conceived.

Terry Miller is an author and 2017 Rhysling Award-nominated poet residing in Portsmouth, OH, USA. He has self-published a dark poetry collection on Amazon and one short story to date. His work has also appeared in Sanitarium, Devolution Z, Jitter Press, Poetry Quarterly, O Unholy Night in Deathlehem, and the 2017 Rhysling Anthology from the Science Fiction and Fantasy Poetry Association.
Facebook: tmiller2015

Left Hand
by Vonnie Winslow Crist

All the alligator left behind was a bloody puddle and a left hand—but Detective Carroll hoped it'd be enough to identify the victim.

He watched techs make casts of footprints and tyre tracks, bag the hand, and gather blood samples.

Then, it hit him—he'd seen a man wearing a wildlife management uniform feeding roadkill to gators here this spring.

Probably got overconfident, thought Carroll, *ended up falling into the water when he was tossing the gators a dead opossum.*

He was about to write this one up as accidental when a tech hollered, "Detective, I've found a knife!"

Vonnie Winslow Crist is author of The Enchanted Dagger, Owl Light, The Greener Forest, Murder on Marawa Prime, *and other award-winning books. Her fiction is included in* "Amazing Stories," "Cast of Wonders," "Outposts of Beyond," Killing It Softly 2, Defending the Future - Dogs of War, Midnight Masquerade, Chaos of Hard Clay, *and elsewhere. A cloverhand who has found so many four-leafed clovers she keeps them in jars, Vonnie strives to celebrate the power of myth in her writing.*
Website: www.vonniewinslowcrist.com

Pimped Out Ride
By Stephen Herczeg

The call came in late. Some fishermen had snagged something just off the river bank. As they tried to release it, they saw tyre tracks leading down into the water.

We arrived to find a couple of uniforms standing around and a tow truck pulling the wreck out of the river.

We knew this car. It was a totally pimped out muscle car that had been reported doing doughnuts in a nearby suburb.

Stolen and abandoned.

Then we opened the boot. The stench hit us straight away. The body wasn't pretty.

Looks like someone didn't appreciate this guy's burn outs.

Stephen Herczeg is an IT Geek based in Canberra Australia. He has been writing for over twenty years and has completed a couple of dodgy novels, sixteen feature length screenplays and numerous short stories and scripts. His horror work has featured in Sproutlings, Hells Bells, Below the Stairs, Trickster's Treats #1 and #2, Shades of Santa, Behind the Mask, Beyond the Infinite; The Body Horror Book, Anemone Enemy, Petrified Punks and Beginnings. He has also had numerous Sherlock Holmes stories published through the Belanger Books - Sherlock Holmes anthologies.

It's Harder with Kids
by Jason Holden

Working in forensics is always difficult. To find truths you must delve into the seediest parts of crime. Grizzly murder scenes like this, they stay ingrained in your mind forever; the images of what the psychos and freaks get up to as they carve out their nightmarish fantasies on a living body.

It was even harder when kids were involved, like now. Her tiny hands sheathed in blue latex gloves, covered in blood. You could see the horror on her face at what she faced.

Take Your Daughter to Work Day had been a big mistake. She wouldn't sleep tonight.

*After giving up a full-time job as a quarry operator so that his wife could follow her dream career as an academic in the field of chemistry, **Jason Holden** and his family left England and temporarily moved to Spain where they currently reside. While there, he took on the role of full-time parent and began to create stories for his daughter. Now that she is in school, he creates stories for himself and hopes to share those stories with others.*

Injustice System
by Raven Corinn Carluk

Officer Reedus stood in the dark, listening to the young men on the front porch, gripping the shotgun and working up the nerve for the task.

"Yeah, dog, if that Purge movie were real, I'd be in charge."

"Shit, you'd be the first dead. You already got caught beating your bitch."

"But I got off." The pair laughed.

Reedus drew a deep breath. The girl in question was sixteen, hooked on heroin, put in the hospital by her pimp who had been released on a technicality and now bragged about it.

Stepping from the shadows, he prepared to deliver punishment.

Raven Corinn Carluk writes dark fantasy, paranormal romance, and anything else that catches her interest. She's authored five novels, where she explores themes of love and acceptance. Her shorter pieces, usually from her darker side, can be found in Black Hare Press anthologies, at Detritus Online, and through Alban Lake Publishers.
Twitter: @ravencorinn
Website: RavenCorinnCarluk.Blogspot.Com

Hot Lunch Buffet
by Shelly Jarvis

"Why?" I ask.

He laughs.

And laughs.

When he stops, his eyes are wide, his mouth stretched into a cartoonish grin. "You don't remember?"

I try to shake my head, forgetting the constraints for a second before the motion reminds me I'm tied to this table. Panic colours my voice as I say, "Remember? We've never met."

"Three weeks ago. You threw your lunch at me because it wasn't hot enough."

The words click in my head and I remember him from the meat station at the buffet. He withdraws a knife, slices across my abdomen, and carves, carves, carves.

Shelly Jarvis is a speculative fiction author from West Virginia, US. She found a life-long love of sci-fi and fantasy in the 3rd grade when she found Madeleine L'Engle's "A Wrinkle in Time." Shelly is an avid reader, a Whovian, the ideal viewer of dog rescue videos, and undoubtedly Ravenclaw. She currently has three YA sci-fi books available for purchase on Amazon.
Website: www.ShellyJarvis.com

Three Suspects
by Cecelia Hopkins-Drewer

Three suspects; the husband, the stalker, and the angry client. Such an ugly crime, and who would mutilate a beautiful female lawyer?

"You didn't love her," Inspector Fineas said to the husband.

"I surely did," he objected.

"You didn't know her," Fineas said to the stalker.

"I feel like I did," sobbed the man.

"You owed her your settlement," Fineas said to the divorcee.

"Which ought to have been larger," she snapped.

Laura Fineas had forgotten about the caretaker, a large man in charge of building security. He had an axe, and was waiting outside to dispose of the witnesses.

Cecelia Hopkins-Drewer lives in Adelaide, South Australia. She has written a Masters paper on H.P. Lovecraft, and her weird poetry has been published in THE MENTOR (edited by Ron Clarke), and SPECTRAL REALMS (edited by S.T. Joshi). Her novels include a teenage vampire series comprised of three volumes, MYSTIC EVERMORE, SAINTS AND SINNERS & AUTUMN SECRETS. Short stories have been published in WORLDS, ANGELS & MONSTERS (Dark Drabbles anthologies edited by Dean Kershaw).
Amazon: amazon.com/Cecelia-Hopkins-Drewer/e/B071G968NM
Website: chopkin39.wixsite.com/website

Cliffhanger
by Bob Adder

Two strange men slowly creep out of the lush forest overgrowth, edging nearer and nearer. The two girls stand oblivious on the edge of the aged cliff.

Finally, the men emerge and one girl falls, air rushing past her as she plummets from the clifftop.

She gasps and screams at the sharp pains of the jagged rocks before she comes to rest of an overhang.

When she looks up, she sees the men dragging her sister off into the dark forest.

She lies there helplessly, bleeding, listening to the screams for help getting further away as her vision slowly fades.

Bob Adder is an aspiring author and superhero geek from Melbourne, Australia.

Seasonal Suspects
by John H. Dromey

Before bleeding out, the stabbing victim crawled over to a large box of souvenirs she kept under her bed. Having ignored a heart-shaped brooch, a tiny stuffed bunny, and a bunch of Christmas decorations, she was found post mortem clutching a string of beads.

"Whodunit?" the lead investigator asked a consulting detective.

"Do you have the names of her roommates?"

"Yes. Sandra Klaus, Martina Grawe, Christine Krinklemeyer, Beatrice Mai Valentine, and Esther Rabbit."

"It's obvious then."

"Not to me."

"Look again. Those aren't just any beads. They're from New Orleans."

"You mean?"

"Yes. The murder was committed by Marti Grawe."

First published in *Saturday Night Reader*, 2014

John H. Dromey *was born in northeast Missouri, USA. He enjoys reading—mysteries in particular—and writing in a variety of genres. He's had short fiction published in Alfred Hitchcock's Mystery Magazine, Martian Magazine, Stupefying Stories Showcase, Thriller Magazine, Unfit Magazine, and elsewhere, as well as in a number of anthologies, including Chilling Horror Short Stories (Flame Tree Publishing, 2015).*

To Stop Time
by Alexander Pyles

Fingers were laid out like a clock, thumb and pinky the hands. We found the watchmaker stuffed into a freezer out back.

Everything was scrubbed. No evidence. No DNA. The finger clock pointed to nine o'clock, but was that AM? PM? Was it the time for his next killing? The questions stayed with me, all the way home.

I was nursing my whiskey still thinking, when I heard a door slam.

Sitting out on my condo's balcony, I peered through the screen to see a silhouette. My blood thickened. My gun was lying on the bed.

My watch read 9.

Alexander Pyles resides in IL with his wife and children. He holds an MA in Philosophy and an MFA in Writing Popular Fiction. His short story chapbook titled, "Milo (01001101 01101001 01101100 01101111)," from Radix Media, is due out fall 2019. His other short fiction has appeared on 101fiction.org, River and South Review, and other venues.
Website: www.pylesofbooks.com
Twitter: @Pylesofbooks

Shining Lights Below
by Neen Cohen

"Third one this week!"

Ekka winds cut through his jacket as he shook his head.

All victims had been sexually active, the only thing in common. A blonde, a redhead and a guy, no apparent cause of death.

The Ferris wheel would be closed tomorrow, and he would no longer be working the murders.

She took in a deep breath as she watched the detective saunter off. From her seat atop the Ferris wheel, she watched the shining lights below, human and electronic.

Tomorrow she would move on.

Tonight she would enjoy the energy she sucked from her last victim.

Neen Cohen lives in Brisbane with her partner, son and fur babies. She is a writer of LGBTQI, dark fantasy and horror short stories and has a Bachelor of Creative Industries from QUT. She can often be found writing while sitting against a tombstone or tree in any number of graveyards.
Facebook: Neen-Cohen-Author-424700821629629
Website: wordbubblessite.wordpress.com

Sweetest Revenge
by D.J. Elton

The herbalist guaranteed this potion. Five drops each day into Jamie's porridge. Tastes like sweetener. After breakfast Jamie tells me, "You're sick. So pathetic. Lost." Then he strokes my cheek, grips my hair and throws me hard against the wall. He walks out to the car with his doctor's bag and grey suit. I lay still. Pain radiates like frostbite. Today is different though because I can see that the herbs are starting to take effect. Jamie doesn't know that he's slowly being poisoned. No-one will ever find out because it will look like a massive coronary. I am patient.

D.J. Elton writes fiction and poetry, and is currently studying writing and literature which is improving her work in unexpected ways. She spends a lot of time in northern India and should probably live there, however there is much to be done in Melbourne, so this is the home base. She has meditated daily for the past 35 years and has worked in healthcare for equally as long, so she's very happy to be writing, zoning in and out of all things literary.
Twitter: @DJEltonwrites

Heiress
by Mark Mackey

A confession from Marcy Victornia—who, out of jealously over her identical twin sister, Amara, being named heiress to their family's fortune over her—led Detective Amalia Casterford, gripping a long-handled shovel, to be digging in the ground. Just hours before, in order to take her sister's place, Marcy had buried Amara six feet under.

Come on dig before she runs out of air! Amalia thought furiously, sweat pouring like mad down her face.

As Amalia continued to dig, her heart beating mad from the exertion, she breathed a sigh of relief as she reached Amara, eyes open and alert.

Mark Mackey is the author of various self-published books and has had various short stories published in charity anthologies. They include such captivating titles such as Christmas Lites, No Sleeves and Short Dresses: A Summer Anthology, Painted Mayhem, and Grynn Anthology, among others. A long-time resident of Chicago, when not writing, he spends time reading various genres of books.

A Hostel in Karamea
by Kelli Pizarro

I left the UK to work a year in New Zealand. Come autumn, I planned to visit a hostel in Karamea to do some photography before returning to University.

Double rainbows, sunsets, the rainforest.

The hostel was rustic and gated, hours down an unmarked road with no cell reception.

I welcomed enthusiastically but learned we had no access to our cars come nightfall.

My second day there, I found stashed cookbooks on preparing human flesh and noted an unusually large pot in the kitchen.

I checked out.

A year later, there was no evidence of the place ever having existed.

Kelli Pizarro is a lover of clean fiction, with two novels being released this year by Dragon Soul Press. Shanty by the Sea, releasing in August, is a Young Adult romcom novella set in New England. Roma Road: A Gypsy Tale, set to release in December, is a historical fiction novel highlighting the plight of the Romani people during Queen Elizabeth I's rule. She has three previously self-published titles awaiting submission for publication. Kelli loves traveling, is currently planning a coffee shop-themed anthology, and enjoys writing drabbles. She lives in East Texas with her husband, three children, and five pets.
Facebook: authorkellipizarro
Twitter: kellipizarro

Karma
by Sue Marie St. Lee

"Be careful," Daisy whispered to Curtis, "Karma's right around the corner."

"Oh yeah? Who the hell is Karma?"

With a loud bang, the trailer hitch was secured. They got away with it. Curtis and Daisy stole an eighteen-foot flatbed trailer.

With an unsuspecting buyer lined up, they were home-free, planning how to spend the money as they passed the four-hour-drive to the truck stop.

The unsuspecting buyer inspected the trailer and handed over the money. Leaving in a cloud of dust, Curtis ran a stop sign.

"This is Jim Clancy with Karma landscaping. I need to report a fatal accident."

Sue Marie St. Lee is a retired Finance Manager who has been freelancing, researching, writing content, designing corporate websites and brochures over the past fifteen years. She also started a small business specializing in digital photo restoration. Born and raised in Chicago, she moved to Canada where she and her husband raised their sons until her husband's untimely death. As a young widow, Sue Marie employed her skills, tenacity, strengths and wisdom to support her young family. Currently, Sue Marie contributes to several blogs, is a ghostwriter for numerous online publishers and corporate websites. Her sons are grown, productive adults.

A Little Learning
by John H. Dromey

The Hole-in-the-Wallet gang had been inactive for several years, but when their leader was released from prison, they decided to rob the Pierian Spring Bank.

The only problem was the safecracker blew himself up instead of the vault.

"He may have been an illiterate bumpkin, but I'll miss him," the leader said.

"Didn't Alex tell you?" an outlaw responded. "He learned to read while you were behind bars."

"Now, you're making me feel guilty."

"Why, what did you do?"

"I put the nitro-glycerine in an old medicine bottle."

"What difference did that make?"

"The label said 'Shake Well Before Using.'"

First published in *Little Stories for the Smallest Room* by KnightWatch Press, 2012

John H. Dromey was born in northeast Missouri, USA. He enjoys reading—mysteries in particular—and writing in a variety of genres. He's had short fiction published in Alfred Hitchcock's Mystery Magazine, Martian Magazine, Stupefying Stories Showcase, Thriller Magazine, Unfit Magazine, and elsewhere, as well as in a number of anthologies, including Chilling Horror Short Stories (Flame Tree Publishing, 2015).

An Irish Airman Foresees His Death
by Steven Lord

The crew looked at him. Regardless of what had been discussed, as Captain his decision would carry.

He balanced all, brought all to mind. He felt no overwhelming allegiance to the Crown. He certainly wasn't invested in this war; those few Afghans that he'd met seemed decent types. No one back home cared.

He had joined to fly. After 18 years hauling cargo, even that was wearing thin. *Everyone dies*, he thought. *Why not die rich?*

"Fuck it. Let's do this."

The Hercules climbed away from Kabul, 12T of opium in the back, turned north, and was never seen again.

Steven Lord is a debut author based in the south of England. He is currently attempting to cram writing in alongside a busy day job, with varying levels of success. While his long-term aspiration is to get a novel published, at present he would be pretty pleased with a drabble or two.

The Killing
by Mark Mackey

Middle aged, married with children, Clara Rosewind and her best friend, Alisa Davens—killed in a car accident seven years ago—had got away with murder.

Who? Their high school cheerleader squad captain, Laurie Roseman.

How? A blow to the head with a huge rock.

Where? In the only forest preserve of their hometown of Harper's Grove, Illinois.

The reason; Laurie's not allowing them on the squad.

"Now let's throw her in that old abandoned well where no one will ever find her," Clara instructed as red streaks of crimson began to run down Laurie's face.

No one ever did.

Mark Mackey is the author of various self-published books and has had various short stories published in charity anthologies. They include such captivating titles such as Christmas Lites, No Sleeves and Short Dresses: A Summer Anthology, Painted Mayhem, and Grynn Anthology, among others. A long-time resident of Chicago, when not writing, he spends time reading various genres of books.

The Photos
by Sam M. Phillips

You stare at me, glazed glass, windows to a life now only a memory. I pull up the collar of my trench coat. Biting wind sweeps tumbleweed papers off to clog the gutters. Just like you, they're yesterday's news.

"This the dame you were telling me about?" asked Detective Harris.

I nod, sigh. "She was being blackmailed."

"The photos?"

Lurid images flash before my eyes. You were beautiful, now look at you. I told you to just pay up—not like your family couldn't afford it.

"You got any ideas who did this?" asked Harris.

"Yeah," I said, "her father."

Sam M. Phillips is the co-founder of Zombie Pirate Publishing, producing short story anthologies and helping emerging writers. His own work has appeared in dozens of anthologies and magazines such as Full Moon Slaughter 2, 13 Bites Volumes IV and V, Rejected for Content 6, and Dastaan World Magazine. He lives in the green valleys of northern New South Wales, Australia, and enjoys reading, walking, and playing drums in the death metal band Decryptus.
Website: zombiepiratepublishing.com
Blog: bigconfusingwords.wordpress.com

Madman
by Pamela Jeffs

I stole it from the Widow Pirate in my younger days. Her treasure map. The scarlet 'X' stained on the parchment beckons me. *Are you courageous? Have you the mettle to sail wild seas and battle demons to claim the prize?*

Temptation prickles but the cold metal of my wheelchair anchors me in reality. Wish as I might, I'll never step foot on that foreign beach, nor navigate the Bone Yard Passage to claim any treasure. I have deciphered the clues, but they are useless held in the fist of a broken man interred behind the walls of an asylum.

Pamela Jeffs is a speculative fiction author living in Queensland, Australia with her husband and two daughters. She is a member of the Queensland Writers' Centre and has had numerous short fiction pieces published in recent national and international anthologies. In 2017 and again in 2018, Pamela was nominated for an Australian Aurealis Award in the category of 'Best Science Fiction Short Story'. Her debut collection titled 'Red Hour and Other Strange Tales' was released in March 2018.
Website: www.pamelajeffs.com
Facebook: pamelajeffsauthor

Can't Outrun a Bullet
by Marcus Cook

Through my scope, I see Garrett stretching before his run. When he was ten, Garrett pushed his baby sister off the picnic table. He then lied so he could go to Joey's sleepover. As he got older, Garrett pushed a lot more people to get what he wanted. That's until one of them hired me. *I wonder if he knows he's about to be killed by a girl.*

He's about to touch his toes. *That's it! Reach for them.* I pulled the trigger. Brains splattered across the cement. I'm 50K richer.

Time for a chocolate muffin and a four-letter coffee.

Marcus Cook, lives in Cleveland, Ohio native with his wife and cat. He loves Sci-Fi and thrillers. His short story, Ava Edison and the Burning Man was recently published in Burning: An Anthology of Short Thrillers by Burning Chair Publishing which can be purchased on Amazon.
Facebook: ReadMarcusCook

Extreme Neatness
By Olivia Arieti

The case of the prostitute found semi-naked with her throat cut was assigned to the impeccable Inspector Xavier, always so dignified and neatly shaven, whose methods though were considered more brutal than professional.

His apartment was spotless too, as if just whitewashed, with a few pieces of basic furniture and a king-size bed.

It was rumoured that he often had visitors.

Early one morning, while cursing for the loss of his razor, he was surprised by his colleague's visit who handed him the missing item stained with blood.

Such maniacal neatness, a rather common mask for perversion, didn't go unnoticed

Olivia Arieti has a degree from the University of Pisa and lives in Torre del Lago Puccini, Italy, with her family. Besides being a published playwright, she loves writing retellings of fairy tales, and at the same time is intrigued by supernatural and horror themes. Her stories appeared in several magazines and anthologies like Enchanted Conversations, Enchanted Tales Literary Magazine, Fantasia Divinity Magazine, Cliterature, Medieval Nightmares, Static Movement, 100 Doors To Madness Forgotten Tomb Press, Black Cats Horrified Press, Bloody Ghost Stories Full Moon Books, Death And Decorations Thirteen O'Clock Press, Infective Ink, Pandemonium Press, Pussy Magic Magazine.

The Vanished in our Beds
by Ximena Escobar

I just wanted to go to bed—before I knew about "the grill".

When they laid me on it, I felt relieved—just being out of "the box", resting my cheek on the cool surface. But the officer dipped his hand in cold water; he traced my lips and genitals with his fingertips.

Sweat streamed out of me from the shocks. An unquenchable thirst dried me out inside, but I was afraid of water; had to wipe my ass with a page from "War and Peace".

Genaro wasn't so lucky. His swollen red blue cadaver lies in bed with me.

Ximena Escobar is an emerging author of literary fiction and poetry. Originally from Chile, she is the author of a translation into Spanish of the Broadway Musical "The Wizard of Oz", and of an original adaptation of the same, "Navidad en Oz". Clarendon House Publications published her first short story in the UK, "The Persistence of Memory", and Literally Stories her first online publication with "The Green Light". She has since had several acceptances from other publishers and is working very hard exploring new exciting avenues in her writing.
She lives in Nottingham with her family.
Facebook: Ximenautora

Red Herrings
by C.L. Williams

I'm looking for clues to discover who committed the heinous crime. My partner is also looking, but to no avail. We see a candy wrapper with blood in it. We seal it for the crime lab but we both already know what the result will be; the blood of this victim or the next.

This killer loves leaving red herrings to keep us off their trail. That being said, we cannot afford to leave this behind in case the killer has gotten cocky. The truth is, we're unable to catch this killer and we know the killer will strike again.

C.L. Williams is an independent author from central Virginia. He has written eight poetry books, four novellas, one novel, and a contributor to multiple anthologies, with the most recent appearance being an all-ages anthology titled Temoli from Thazbook. His most recent poetry book, The Paradox Complex, features the poem "Sad Crying Clown" that is now a video on YouTube directed by Matthew Mark Hunter of MMH Productions. C.L. Williams is currently working on his first sci-fi book, an all-ages book titled Novo: Away from Earth. When not writing, C.L. Williams is reading and sharing the work of other independent authors.
Facebook: writer434
Twitter: @writer_434

The Evidence Auction
by Michael D. Davis

We were all looking at Ricky as we stood behind the courthouse. He talked about the local killer. The man who slayed seven women. Ricky lived next door to the killer's old house. He boasted about it every time the creep's name was uttered. Ricky said he talked to the madman on a daily basis, was damn near friends with him. He said he had some personal items of the murderer who was standing trial this week. Ricky said the bidding would start at ten bucks for the item, then took from his book bag an old bloody house slipper.

Michael D. Davis was born and raised in a small town in Iowa. A high school graduate and avid reader he has aspired to be a writer for years. Having written over thirty short stories, ranging in genre from comedy to horror from flash fiction to novella. He continues in his accursed pursuit of a career in the written word and in his hunt Michael's love for stories in all genres and mediums will not falter.

Bruises
by Raven Corinn Carluk

"I never touched them, I swear." Daddy turned to look at us. "Tell them."

We cringed and lowered our eyes.

The lady from CPS touched my shoulder. "Don't worry. He'll never hurt you again." We nodded, holding each other's hands tight.

Mom finished talking to Child Protective Services after the cops drove Daddy away. We played our roles well: shy, like the bruises hurt, like we're scared to be alone.

Finally, everyone left, and Mom pulled us into a hug. "I never knew. I'm sorry."

We silently agreed to make new bruises if she forced us to eat our vegetables.

Raven Corinn Carluk writes dark fantasy, paranormal romance, and anything else that catches her interest. She's authored five novels, where she explores themes of love and acceptance. Her shorter pieces, usually from her darker side, can be found in Black Hare Press anthologies, at Detritus Online, and through Alban Lake Publishers.
Twitter: @ravencorinn
Website: RavenCorinnCarluk.Blogspot.Com

Protection
by Rich Rurshell

I showed Vincenzo to a back room, then returned to the restaurant front and displayed the *closed* sign in the window.

The Montanari family had insisted I'd be well compensated for ensuring hitman Luis Tafani had easy access to Vincenzo. When he arrived, I pointed out back.

Pistol drawn, Tafani kicked open the door to find the room empty. I put my pistol to the back of his head and pulled the trigger.

"Nice job!" said Vincenzo from behind me. "My brother assures me the Montanari family are no more. Consider your establishment under our protection now...gratis, of course."

Rich Rurshell is a short story writer from Suffolk, England. Rich writes Horror, Sci-Fi, and Fantasy, and his stories can be found in various short story anthologies and magazines. Most recently, his story "Subject: Galilee" was published in World War Four from Zombie Pirate Publishing, and "Life Choices" was published in Salty Tales from Stormy Island Publishing. When Rich is not writing stories, he likes to write and perform music.
Facebook: richrurshellauthor

Guided
by Beth W. Patterson

"Adrienne can't possibly be responsible for the murders of her husband and his co-worker. They were halfway across the country on a business trip!"

"I'm telling you, something's fishy. She doesn't even seem bereaved."

"Maybe she's in shock. She was friends with the co-worker too. Those two women were so alike."

"Including their penchant for sharing hotel rooms with the husband."

"Maybe they were trying to cut down on business expenses."

"Now you're really reaching. Adrienne's the most charismatic tour guide in town. She can get people all over the world to do her bidding. It pays to be charming."

Beth W. Patterson *was a full-time musician for over two decades before diving into the world of writing, a process she describes as "fleeing the circus to join the zoo". She is the author of the books Mongrels and Misfits, and The Wild Harmonic, and a contributing writer to thirty anthologies. Patterson has performed in eighteen countries, expanding her perspective as she goes. Her playing appears on over a hundred and seventy albums, soundtracks, videos, commercials, and voice-overs (including seven solo albums of her own). She lives in New Orleans, Louisiana with her husband Josh Paxton, jazz pianist extraordinaire.*

Website: www.bethpattersonmusic.com
Facebook: bethodist

Disposal
by Cameron Marcoux

"Well, what are we going to do now?" a voice asked.

"Let's take a vote," a second voice said.

"Fine. I vote the river," a third voice said.

"River? No way. Too reckless," said the second voice.

"Let's just dig a hole then," said the first.

"Where? Your backyard?" the third voice asked.

"No. Course not. I don't know," said the first voice.

There was a sigh and then silence.

"What about acid? I saw them do it on Breaking Bad," said the third.

"That could work," the second agreed.

All three stared down at the body on the floor.

Cameron Marcoux is a writer of stories, which, considering where you are reading this, makes a lot of sense. He also teaches English to the lovely and terrifying creatures we call teenagers. He lives in the quiet, northern reaches of New England in the U.S. with his girlfriend and scaredy dog.

Better Luck Next Time
by Wondra Vanian

How the body ended up in the locker room was a mystery to everyone but Dougie—and he wasn't talking.

Oh, he wasn't worried about being caught (perks of being the police chief's son), he just wasn't interested in Coby Lange's death. He was only interested in Jasmine.

Dougie had spent months waiting for his chance to get close to her. Now, Jasmine needed a shoulder to cry on and he was ready to provide it.

But, before he could, Coby's best friend was there, hugging her. Dougie's eyes narrowed.

Looked like there was going to be a double funeral...

Wondra Vanian is an American living in the United Kingdom with her Welsh husband and their army of fur babies. A writer first, Wondra is also an avid gamer, photographer, cinephile, and blogger. She has music in her blood, sleeps with the lights on, and has been known to dance naked in the moonlight. Wondra was a multiple Top-Ten finisher in the 2017 and 2018 Preditors and Editors Reader's Poll, including ithe Best Author category. Her story, "Halloween Night," was named a Notable Contender for the Bristol Short Story Prize in 2015.
Website : www.wondravanian.com

Trouble in a Tight Skirt
by Aiki Flinthart

The broad was classy. Ruby lips. Garnet nails. Hair like white diamonds. But maybe the heat made me reckless. Summer of '29 everyone drank themselves into a stupor on bathtub gin to forget they had no dough.

Including me.

So, when she offered greenbacks to find her husband, Snorky, I lit a cigarette and said, "Swell, babe."

Shoulda known. Too good to be true.

Last place I checked was a speakeasy on Chicago's southside. Strippers, whiskey, cigars. My kinda place.

The muscle looked me over. "Boss, your missus sent a private dick."

Al Capone sneered. "Shoot him."

I fired first.

Aiki Flinthart has had short stories shortlisted in the *Aurealis awards* and top-8 listed in the *USA Writers of the Future* competition, as well as published in various anthologies and e-mags. She has 11 published spec fic novels and has edited 2 short story anthologies. She regularly gives workshops on writing fight scenes at conventions. Lives in Brisbane. Does martial arts, archery, knife throwing and lute-playing.
Website: *www.aikiflinthart.com*

Transform
by Nicola Currie

"Congrats, Sarah," my manager says. "Caseworker of the Year. You deserve it!"

I say thanks for the hundredth time as I close the car door, waving her off.

It's not why I do it, of course. I see women who come to us purpled and broken transform, I help them escape from partners who are more monsters than men.

I enter my front door clutching my plaque and champagne, glad my life has meaning.

My layabout husband jumps from his messy sofa as I throw my bottle against the wall.

"What the fuck have you done all day?" I ask.

Nicola Currie is 34, from Cambridge, UK where she works in educational publishing. She has published poetry in literary magazines, including Mslexia and Sarasvati, and has also completed her first novel, which was longlisted for the Bath Children's Novel Award.
Website: writeitandweep.home.blog

The Axe Artist
by Nerisha Kemraj

His axe drives in deeper and deeper, his adrenaline fuelling him as he slashes her to shreds. A distant wolf howls at the full moon in all its silvery glory, breaking his spell as his eyes finally register the bloody pulp lying before him. Mincemeat, he smiles, remembering breakfast that morning. Mince for breakfast with her, and now mince that was her. Thrilled, he throws his head back in a fit of laughter.

But the wolves will be here soon.

Quickly gathering his beloved collection of killing toys, he takes one last look at his masterpiece, before she becomes nothingness.

Multi-genre (short-fiction) author, and poet, **Nerisha Kemraj***, resides in South Africa with her husband and two, mischievous daughters. She has work traditionally published/accepted in 30 publications, thus far, both print and online. She holds a BA in Communication Science from UNISA and is currently busy with a Post-Graduate Certificate in Education.*
Facebook: Nerishakemrajwriter

Jane
by David Bowmore

1958—The first murder case I was in charge of was the brutal knifing of a prostitute in an underpass. I've seen many corpses, but no one deserved to die the way she did.

Her name was Jane, and she left a daughter behind.

Unfortunately, there were no fingerprints and the murder weapon was not in the immediate vicinity, but from the spray of blood, the angle and height of blade entry, her killer must have been a woman. Old-fashioned police work did the rest.

I rested my hand on the streetwalker's shoulder, and Jane's daughter turned around.

"You're nicked."

David Bowmore has lived here, there and everywhere, but now lives in Yorkshire with his wonderful wife and a small white poodle. He has worn many hats in his time; head chef, teacher and landscape gardener. His first collection of short stories 'The Magic of Deben Market' is available from Clarendon House.
Website: davidbowmore.co.uk
Facebook: davidbowmoreauthor

Marked
by Dawn DeBraal

Arriving at the station late for work that evening, Detective Andrews was sent to the local hospital to get the victim's statement; a woman had been violently attacked and left for dead.

From her hospital bed, the victim haltingly told the detective what happened. She had been beaten badly.

"I scratched him good on his left hand. I am certain you will find the man who did this to me has some open wounds," she reported.

The detective nodded sympathetically. He continued to write her testimony as he quickly put his left hand down on his leg, wincing in pain.

Dawn DeBraal lives in rural Wisconsin with her husband, two rat terriers, and a cat. She successfully raised two children (meaning they didn't return to the nest!) After many years serving the government at the Federal and County level, she recently retired. Having extra time on her hands she started to write after a paralyzed vocal cord took her ability to speak for two months. Not finding her voice, she discovered that her love of telling a good story could be written. Her works have been published in Palm-Sized Press, Spillwords, Mercurial Stories, Potato Soup Journal, and Blood Song Books.

Street Justice
By Eddie D. Moore

The windows rattled as motorcycles parked in front of the diner. The men that came inside laughed riotously and verbally jabbed each other with stinging quips. Leather creaked as they took their seats.

The waitress took their orders and avoided wayward hands with a practised skill. The grill was sizzling when a man walked in and pulled a gun.

"Give me all the money in the drawer and no one gets hurt!"

One of the bikers knocked the gunman out with a single punch, and said, "No need to call the law. We'll take care of him after we eat."

Eddie D. Moore travels hundreds of hours a year, and he fills that time by listening to audiobooks. When he isn't playing with his grandchildren, he writes his own stories. You can find a list of his publications on his blog or by visiting his Amazon Author Page. While you're there, be sure to pick up a copy of his mini-anthology Misfits & Oddities. Website: eddiedmoore.wordpress.com Amazon: amazon.com/author/eddiedmoore

Capone and the Accordion Man
by Sue Marie St. Lee

The brothers formed a trio of accordion players. Dad was the leader, Jock and Rand played backup. Tonight, they would play at Cicero, in Al Capone's nightclub. Blue Moon was the first song requested and played, followed by Little White Lies. When Dad struck the secret chord, guards, employees, and attendees froze in time. Entering the cash room, Dad expanded his accordion's bellows, and neatly placed stacks of cash within concealed openings. Bellows full, Dad returned on stage, releasing the chord and people from their inanimate state. Capone never suspected the musicians, who left the nightclub whistling a happy tune.

Sue Marie St. Lee is a retired Finance Manager who has been freelancing, researching, writing content, designing corporate websites and brochures over the past fifteen years. She also started a small business specializing in digital photo restoration. Born and raised in Chicago, she moved to Canada where she and her husband raised their sons until her husband's untimely death. As a young widow, Sue Marie employed her skills, tenacity, strengths and wisdom to support her young family. Currently, Sue Marie contributes to several blogs, is a ghostwriter for numerous online publishers and corporate websites. Her sons are grown, productive adults.

True Justice
by Crystal L. Kirkham

Thought I'd seen the worst of humanity after thirty years on the force. Until Amy Kershaw. She was barely recognisable when we found her. I can't even describe the horrors that had been done to her.

Evidence pointed to her boyfriend, but he had a hell of a lawyer.

I couldn't let a monster like that go free, so I grabbed him one night and took him to a place he'd never be found.

I wanted him to suffer as she had, but that kind of cruelty was beyond me. I did my worst though, and I never regretted it.

Crystal L. Kirkham resides in a small hamlet west of Red Deer, Alberta. She's an avid outdoors person, unrepentant coffee addict, part-time foodie, servant to a wonderful feline, and companion to two delightfully hilarious canines. She will neither confirm nor deny the rumours regarding the heart in a jar on her desk and the bottle of reader's tears right next to it. Her paranormal urban fantasy series, Saints and Sinners, is available on Amazon and her YA Fantasy, Feathers and Fae will be released October 11, 2019, from Kyanite Publishing.
Website: www.crystallkirkham.com

Zealot
by Umair Mirxa

Zacharias Williams, Commissioner of Police, took off his shoes and cap, and stepped reverently into the mosque. Men, women, and children lay dead all around him. It was carnage as he had never seen before.

"I am truly sorry for how you and your people have suffered," he said. "Please know, we will do everything in our power to apprehend those responsible."

"Your people," repeated the imam solemnly. "It is what the zealot said before he began shooting. He wanted to rid this country of my people. You will never catch those responsible, Commissioner. Not until you change those words."

Umair Mirxa lives in Karachi, Pakistan. His first published story, 'Awareness', appeared on Spillwords Press. He has also had stories accepted for anthologies from Zombie Pirate Publishing, Blood Song Books, Fantasia Divinity Magazine and Publishing, and Iron Faerie Publishing. He is a massive J.R.R. Tolkien fan, and loves everything to do with fantasy and mythology. He enjoys football, history, music, movies, TV shows, and comic books, and wishes with all his heart that dragons were real.
Website: www.umairmirxa.com
Facebook: UMirxa12

Blood Stained Hands
by Cindar Harrell

Blood stained my hands as I stumbled down the street.

"What did I do?"

Images flashed in my mind, one after another, each more grotesque than the last. My heart beat thundered in my head. Confusion reigned. I had no memory of how the blood got on my hands, just the blurry images of my family's faces staring out in horror.

The sounds in my head grew louder, sharper. Putting my hands over my ears, I tried to block it out.

I looked up to see lights flashing before me.

"Jessica, you're under arrest for the murder of your family."

Cindar Harrell loves fairy tales, especially ones with a dark twist. Her stories are often fairy tale inspired, but she is also working on a mystery series. Her stories can be found on Amazon and in various anthologies. You can follow her on Facebook and visit her blog, which she promises to try and update more often,
Website: cindarharrell.wordpress.com
Facebook: CindarHarrell

Gunshots in the Woods
by E.L. Giles

"Run!" he shrieked, a moment before the gunshot echoed in the woods.

Panicked, she ran across the dark twigs and thick brush toward the spot she knew her husband had left their car.

"Run, sweetie!" the deep voice jested maniacally. Two more gunshots pierced through the night. She pushed herself to go faster. "I see you."

Deep inside, she knew she had no chance of escape. And her strength was quickly dying, along with her will to survive. Her husband was dead. Why should she still live?

She abruptly stopped and turned around, facing the killer.

"Go ahead. Kill me."

E.L. Giles is a dreamer, passionate about art, a restless worker and a bit of a weird human. He started his artistic journey as a music composer until the need to put his thoughts and stories down on paper grew too strong for him to resist it any longer. He lives in the French Province of Quebec, Canada, with his girlfriend and two boys.
Facebook: elgilesauthor
Website: www.elgilesauthor.com

Death Visits Mexico
by James Pyles

"Algimantas Dailide, you're out of time."

L.A. Detective Moshe Katz stared down the Lithuanian fugitive in a seaside shanty, pointing the barrel of his .38 at his quarry's chest.

"You police?"

"Heard about the sub sinking off the coast. My Playa Linda contacts pointed me right at you."

"What of it?"

"Six years ago, you were a policeman and arrested twelve Jews. Nazis executed them. One was a harmless old Rabbi."

Delivering final justice, Katz pulled the trigger three times and watched the escapee drop.

"That's for you, Zayde."

Katz replaced the Colt in his shoulder holster and walked away.

James Pyles is a published science fiction and fantasy writer as well as an IT textbook author and editor. A growing number of his short stories are appearing in anthologies and periodicals in 2019. He also has a passion for reading the genres he writes and is currently working on his first full-length novel.
Website: poweredbyrobots.com
Facebook: jamespylesauthor

Stabbed in the Back
by Gregg Cunningham

I'll watch your back bro', while you're robbing the bank. I'll even make sure the coast is clear while you're grabbing the money.

You can count on me.

I'll have the engine running while you scare them off. I'll even get us away while you keep your head down in the back seat.

I'll get rid of the car while you stash the money. I'll even call the cops while you wait by the meet point.

I'll burn the car, while you take the fall. I'll even spend the cash while you do the time.

I'll watch your back bro'.

Gregg Cunningham 48, short story writer who has had to pick up his game since stumbling into facebook writer's groups. He has stories published by 559 Publishing in in 13 Bites volume 3,4,5, Plan 9 from Outer space, Other Realms, Heard It on The Radio, 559 Ways to Die, short stories publishing by Zombie Pirate Publishing in Relationship add Vice, Full Metal Horror, Phuket Tattoo, World War four and Flash Fiction Addiction (flash) with Zombie Pirate Publishing, and also in Daastan Magazine Chapter 11 and Brian,Rich and the Wardrobe.
Amazon: www.amazon.com/-/e/B016OTHX0K
Website: cortlandsdogs.wordpress.com

Long Ride to the Gray Bar Hotel
by Alexander Pyles

"You know they are going to find nothing," my passenger taunted. His face sneered into my rearview.

"We'll see about that."

"Save the bravado. You have no idea what they will miss." His teeth, unnaturally white, flashed splitting his dirty face.

The rain pattered on the windshield, ensuring no silence would settle. I wanted to consider his words, but how could I know he was lying? Why would he be so candid with me? Red herrings, false leads.

"Lost your voice? Don't think I won't find you too, when I get out."

Prickles raced up the back of my neck.

Alexander Pyles *resides in IL with his wife and children. He holds an MA in Philosophy and an MFA in Writing Popular Fiction. His short story chapbook titled, "Milo (01001101 01101001 01101100 01101111)," from Radix Media, is due out fall 2019. His other short fiction has appeared on 101fiction.org, River and South Review, and other venues.*
Website: www.pylesofbooks.com
Twitter: @Pylesofbooks

Delusions of Grandeur
by A.S. Charly

Daniel peeked over his notes while listening to the forensics team's dispiriting report. The dead girl was beautiful, or at least he imagined she had been. It was hard to judge by only her head.

The murderer had left no traces. There was not a single piece of evidence to secure. No wonder they had called for his partner, mastermind Detective Donovan, but Daniel doubted even he could solve a case like this.

"Not one clue, Dov. What you gonna do about that?"

"Something always comes up…"

Donovan grinned as he remembered the girl's screams while cutting off her limbs.

A.S. Charly loves to lose herself in fantastical worlds far away between the stars, filled with magic and wonder. She also writes and draws when she is not roaming through the park with her children. Her stories have been published in various anthologies and online publications.
Facebook: <u>A.S.Charlydreams</u>

Freedom
by Annie Percik

Blood on the floor. On my shirt. In my hair. It's everywhere. My eyes skip away from the dark shape in the middle of it all. I can't look at him. I don't think what I've done has really sunk in. I'm breathing hard. I'm shaking. But I'm finally safe. He can't touch me. Not now. Not ever again. They'll understand, won't they? When I show them the scars. When I explain what happened. I was fighting for my life. I've been fighting for my life for nearly twenty years. Even if they lock me up, I'm free at last.

Annie Percik lives in London with her husband, Dave, where she is revising her first novel, whilst working as a University Complaints Officer. She writes a blog about writing and posts short fiction on her website. She also publishes a photo-story blog, recording the adventures of her teddy bear. He is much more popular online than she is. She likes to run away from zombies in her spare time.
Website: www.alobear.co.uk
Website: aloysius-bear.dreamwidth.org

Missing
by Dawn DeBraal

Newspapers carried the story of the missing girl.

Andrea helped in the search.

She stepped on the earring in the creek, slipping off a stone. The diamond earring glinted in the sun. Reaching the other side, Andrea sat down to put her shoes back on. It was then she noticed the upright tennis shoe peeking out from under bushes. Taking a deep breath, Andrea inched closer, stopping suddenly. The smell was undeniable. She couldn't bring herself to go any further. The police responded after she shouted,

"I found her!" Giving the officer the earring, she pointed at the red shoe.

Dawn DeBraal lives in rural Wisconsin with her husband, two rat terriers, and a cat. She successfully raised two children (meaning they didn't return to the nest!) After many years serving the government at the Federal and County level, she recently retired. Having extra time on her hands she started to write after a paralyzed vocal cord took her ability to speak for two months. Not finding her voice, she discovered that her love of telling a good story could be written. Her works have been published in Palm-Sized Press, Spillwords, Mercurial Stories, Potato Soup Journal, and Blood Song Books.

The Witch's Sacrifice
by Abi Linhardt

I was left to finish the ceremony on my own. My initiation. The others had left me in the dark, embers smouldering in the cold air.

Our sacrifice was just eighteen, a football star. Good arm, Daddy would say. We had picked him as some kind of symbolic atonement. But he was innocent; I was the guilty.

I had to leave a clue. I was the only one I could trust. I took the altar knife and carved my name into his back. They'd find me, ask me why.

"So, you could find who did it, of course," I'd say.

Abi Linhardt has been a gamer all her life but is a teacher at heart. When she is not writing, you can find her slaying enemies online or teaching in a college classroom. She has published works of fiction, poetry, college essays, and even won two literary awards for her short stories in science fiction and horror. Abi lives and writes in the grey world of northern Ohio.

A Hairpin in Southwark
by Kelli Pizarro

The October night air amplifies the crunch of a shovel cutting through unconsecrated dirt. A gate creaks and John tosses a cautious glance over his shoulder.

He pulls a body from the grave. If there had been a headstone, it would have read Winchester Goose.

He slips a rusted hairpin into his pocket. He smiles, knowing this was the only law he would be breaking tonight.

He smooths the dirt and slinks away, body in tote.

An hour later, a Southwark anatomist grins, handing John his due.

Walking home, John's cold fingers sift through two guineas and a rusted hairpin.

Kelli Pizarro is a lover of clean fiction, with two novels being released this year by Dragon Soul Press. Shanty by the Sea, releasing in August, is a Young Adult romcom novella set in New England. Roma Road: A Gypsy Tale, set to release in December, is a historical fiction novel highlighting the plight of the Romani people during Queen Elizabeth I's rule. She has three previously self-published titles awaiting submission for publication. Kelli loves traveling, is currently planning a coffee shop-themed anthology, and enjoys writing drabbles. She lives in East Texas with her husband, three children, and five pets.
Facebook: authorkellipizarro
Twitter: kellipizarro

My Sweet Emma
by Amber M. Simpson

My sweet Emma jumps in her bouncy, strong chubby legs pushing off from the floor. Only six months, and her head's full of red curls. My heart aches with love as she gives me those baby blues and smiles.

Poor thing's been teething. Slobber runs down her face, over the port wine stain on her chin. I give her a teething ring and flick on the TV.

"…taken from the park. She has red hair, blue eyes and a distinctive birthmark on her lower face. Investigators believe—"

Click!

I change the channel and sigh.

It's time for us to move.

Amber M. Simpson is a chronic nighttime writer with a penchant for dark fiction and fantasy. When she's not editing for Fantasia Divinity Magazine, she divides her creative time (when she's not procrastinating) between writing a mystery/horror novel, working on a medieval fantasy series, and coming up with new ideas for short stories. Above all, she enjoys being a mom to her two greatest creations, Max and Liam, who keep her feet on the ground even while her head is in the clouds.
Website: ambermsimpson.com

My Mom's Face
by Alanna Robertson-Webb

Yesterday my mother was murdered. I came home from school to police tape, a body bag, and my weeping aunt.

They wouldn't let us see Mom, because they said her face was cut off.

Now I'm with Auntie Ming, and I've tried to be good. I want to scream, to cry and to break things, but I just sit on my new bed.

What I didn't understand was why she was laughing late last night, so I went to check in on her. I peeked through the crack in her door, and she was wearing my mother's bloody, stitched face.

Alanna Robertson-Webb is a sales support member by day, and a writer and editor by night. She loves VT, and live in PA. She has been writing since she was five years old, and writing well since she was seventeen years old. She lives with a fiance and a cat, both of whom take up most of her bed space. She loves to L.A.R.P., and one day she aspired to write a horrifyingly fantastic novel. Her short horror stories have been published before, but she still enjoys remaining mysterious.
Reddit: MythologyLovesHorror

Statute of Limitations
by Sinister Sweetheart

A bloodied man stumbled into the local police station, demanding to see Captain Reardon. He carried a manila folder containing photographs of dead bodies.

Captain asked his name and why he had those pictures. As he started to sort through them, Reardon noticed that some were very old; dating back to the 1960's and 70's.

"My name is Allen Halder, and I'm here to confess to the murders of every one of the victim's you see in these photos."

Allen's fingerprints were processed; they came back as matches to homicides spanning the last fifty years.

Mr. Halder was only twenty-seven.

*Since **Sinister Sweetheart** made her first post to a popular Internet forum, she's taken the horror community by storm. Her ability to create, terrify, and drive home her stories is insurmountable. Sinister Sweetheart's published works can be found in multiple anthologies for all to read, but be forewarned, if you do... you may want to call your therapist after, her stories are terrifying, disturbing and devilishly unsettling. She is not only a fright visually, but also has a creepy tentacle in horror podcasting as well. Sinister Sweetheart writes, voice acts and is the media director of the Scarecrow Tales podcast.*
Website: Sinistersweetheart.wixsite.com/sinistersweetheart
Facebook: NMBrownStories

Undone
by Umair Mirxa

Ursula opened the front door to her home, and graciously stepped aside for the police officers.

"You will find them in the basement," she said, her voice laced with resignation.

"Have you no remorse for your crimes?" asked the detective, staring at her incredulously.

"Only for being caught," she replied with a wicked, insolent smile. "What gave it away?"

"You were seen carrying a girl inside. If your neighbours were less nosy, I fear you might never have been undone."

A sergeant took Ursula away before his colleagues brought out the dozen young girls she'd held captive from her basement.

Umair Mirxa lives in Karachi, Pakistan. His first published story, 'Awareness', appeared on Spillwords Press. He has also had stories accepted for anthologies from Zombie Pirate Publishing, Blood Song Books, Fantasia Divinity Magazine and Publishing, and Iron Faerie Publishing. He is a massive J.R.R. Tolkien fan, and loves everything to do with fantasy and mythology. He enjoys football, history, music, movies, TV shows, and comic books, and wishes with all his heart that dragons were real.
Website: www.umairmirxa.com
Facebook: UMirxa12

Cold Case
by Vonnie Winslow Crist

Del Winters had been dead for twenty years when Detective Sylvester was assigned her cold case.

The file stated she'd been found in her car, poisoned. He glanced at the bagged evidence, spotted a restaurant receipt dated the day before Del's body was discovered. It had been signed by her waitress, Lucy Tillis.

Having been to the wedding, he knew Lucy Tillis had married Del's widowed husband, Richard. In fact, Lucy and Richard Winters still lived in town.

Detective Sylvester chuckled. "Time to visit the happy couple."

He wondered which co-conspirator would throw the other one under the bus first.

Vonnie Winslow Crist is author of The Enchanted Dagger, Owl Light, The Greener Forest, Murder on Marawa Prime, and other award-winning books. Her fiction is included in "Amazing Stories," "Cast of Wonders," "Outposts of Beyond," Killing It Softly 2, Defending the Future - Dogs of War, Midnight Masquerade, Chaos of Hard Clay, and elsewhere. A cloverhand who has found so many four-leafed clovers she keeps them in jars, Vonnie strives to celebrate the power of myth in her writing.
Website: www.vonniewinslowcrist.com

Paper Trail
by Paul Warmerdam

"They told me to follow the money, so that's what I did." The voice came from somewhere in the back of the dark room. "All I learned is that it goes around in circles." The speaker was pacing.

"On paper, you're a hard man to track down." The light was suddenly turned on, blindingly bright. "There's no paperwork getting between us now." The room was small and unfamiliar.

"You have to understand that there's no going back for me now." The detective stepped around to face the chair. "Start talking." He threw his badge into the corner of the room.

Paul Warmerdam is a Dutch-American with decades of experience writing stories, who only recently decided to start submitting them. He lives in the Netherlands, where there's plenty of rainy hours shut indoors with a story in mind.

Doggy Done
by D.J. Elton

"Puppy!" Only five, he's in front of me, arms outstretched like Jesus. A Chinese man jumps the queue. The airport quietness, feeling nervous.

"Leave the dog, Son." The officer's in control. My lower gut wiggles. Please, body, don't betray me now.

Mr Chinese drops off behind, scowling at me. The kid is leaning on my suitcase. I can feel the tape, plastic and crystals inside my thighs rubbing raw.

"Puppy!" Dog at my feet, sniffing intensified. I'm fisting my hands.

"Miss, step this way, please." Oh my God. He connects with my eyes. I know he knows, and I'm done.

D.J. Elton writes fiction and poetry, and is currently studying writing and literature which is improving her work in unexpected ways. She spends a lot of time in northern India and should probably live there, however there is much to be done in Melbourne, so this is the home base. She has meditated daily for the past 35 years and has worked in healthcare for equally as long, so she's very happy to be writing, zoning in and out of all things literary.
Twitter: @DJEltonwrites

International Waters
by Peter J. Foote

"Commander, we have a problem on the space elevator."

Putting down his coffee, "Please tell me the President isn't complaining about being weightless?"

Pale-faced the lieutenant responds, "She's dead, along with her team. Shot. No sign of a weapon nor the murderer."

The Commander barks commands. "Contact ground control and tell them—"

"It gets worse, Commander," the lieutenant interrupts.

"Worse? How?"

"Sensors log her time of death just as the elevator left Earth's atmosphere and entered space, so..."

"She died in no-man's-land. This will be a bureaucratic mess." The Commander shakes his head and mutters, "There goes my pension."

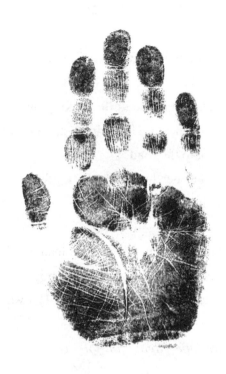

Peter J. Foote _is a bestselling speculative fiction writer from Nova Scotia. Outside of writing, he runs a used bookstore specialising in fantasy & sci-fi, cosplays, and alternates between red wine and coffee as the mood demands. His short stories can be found in both print and in ebook form, with his story "Sea Monkeys" winning the inaugural "Engen Books/Kit Sora, Flash Fiction/Flash Photography" contest in March of 2018. As the founder of the group "Genre Writers of Atlantic Canada", Peter believes that the writing community is stronger when it works together._
Twitter: @PeterJFoote1
Website: peterjfooteauthor.wordpress.com

Jean MacBeth
by Simon Clarke

Jean looked down at her ripped nightgown, she had been rubbing his blood into her chest. *This won't do,* she thought. She glanced at the knife sticking out of George King's left eye, opened the front door, started wailing and began staggering to the road.

They arrested her husband; the knife was his. She had been promised to King in exchange for promotion. *Bastards.*

In hospital a nurse lay her hand on Jean's. "You don't need to keep rubbing yourself, it's clean now."

Jean sat expressionless in court. He was to be executed.

I hope you suffer, dying for nothing.

Simon Clarke was born in and raised and currently resides in East Anglia, United Kingdom. He has been writing fiction for at least five years and regularly submits to UK and international publications as well as reading short pieces and poetry at open mic events. He is currently working on his first novel and continues to write short stories and poetry.

Little Pipe Creek
by Jacob Baugher

We caught the kidnapper at midnight by Little Pipe Creek. The K-9 unit found him. My client's girl is with him. She hides behind his leg.

Finally, a lucky break.

"Let her go, Larry."

"I can't." He tries to run.

"Fassen!"

There's a bark, a gurgling scream, then nothing.

Moonlit-silver mist rises from the brimming water. I step through the blood. She's sobbing, hair stuck to her face.

"Please, don't make me go back to daddy."

My flashlight illuminates her purple bruises.

"It's ok." I take her hand. "You're safe now."

"I was safe before." She pulls away and cries.

Jacob Baugher teaches Creative Writing at Franciscan University of Steubenville. When he's not teaching or coaching the track team, he can be found in the Cuyahoga Valley hiking with his wife and son or brewing beer on his front porch. He's received honourable mentions for his work in the Writers of the Future contest and he co-edits a series of Fantasy and Science Fiction anthologies titled Continuum.

Hook, Line, and...
by Greg Thomas

Detective Mark was never able to make sense of why the killer texted him out of the blue to confess. He wasn't even a detective at the time, just a beat cop.

Not that it made much difference now.

Still, as he looked at Red's lifeless body still smoking in the chair, he couldn't help but wonder. This case had jump started his career.

Looking back at the message still stored in his phone he read it again.

MY NAME IS R. HERRING AND I KILLED THOSE PEOPLE

Just then, another message came through from the long inactive number.

DUMBASS

Greg Thomas is a husband and father of five who supports his creative habits by holding down a regular gig as a college dean in rural Wyoming. In addition to writing short stories and screenplays, Greg also enjoys amateur woodworking, thrift-store shopping, and masquerading as a shade-tree mechanic. His future plans include winning the lottery and writing the next great American horror movie, although he realizes only one of these goals is realistic. Facebook: gregwrotestuff

Desperation
by Annie Percik

The evidence is all there. I know who did it. But I don't think I want to bring her in. I remember when we interviewed her at the time; so small, so thin, such wide eyes. Those eyes were full of desperation. Is it so necessary for this crime to be solved? I don't think justice will be served by putting her away. The items were insured, the owner has money to spare. If ever there was a victimless crime, this is it. I look through my notes, exchange a knowing glance with my partner and turn on the shredder.

Annie Percik lives in London with her husband, Dave, where she is revising her first novel, whilst working as a University Complaints Officer. She writes a blog about writing and posts short fiction on her website. She also publishes a photo-story blog, recording the adventures of her teddy bear. He is much more popular online than she is. She likes to run away from zombies in her spare time.
Website: www.alobear.co.uk
Website: aloysius-bear.dreamwidth.org

Seegrist Syndrome
by Bob Adder

I was ready.

I had prepared for this day for many years. I had my tools, I had the place, and I knew my timings.

Wednesday had come, I walked into the quaint shopping centre located on the edge of the bustling city.

The voices were back, people were loud and surrounding, closing in.

I didn't like it. *They are talking, why don't they like me? What have I ever done to them?*

I couldn't take it anymore. I held up my arms, aiming straight.

The voices screamed around in my head. I squeezed the trigger and the gun recoiled.

Bob Adder is an aspiring author and superhero geek from Melbourne, Australia.

The Break Up
by Dawn DeBraal

Rae Ann sat in her car, watching from across the street as her boyfriend held the door open for his *friend*.

She suspected Darrell was seeing someone else, but he told her she was all wrong, he only had eyes for her.

She wanted so badly to believe him, but when she saw them crossing the street together, something in her snapped. She found herself starting her car, slipping it into gear, and pulling away from the curb. Her foot touched the accelerator, flooring the pedal. Tyres squealed as the car struck them both.

This is how they broke up.

Dawn DeBraal lives in rural Wisconsin with her husband, two rat terriers, and a cat. She successfully raised two children (meaning they didn't return to the nest!) After many years serving the government at the Federal and County level, she recently retired. Having extra time on her hands she started to write after a paralyzed vocal cord took her ability to speak for two months. Not finding her voice, she discovered that her love of telling a good story could be written. Her works have been published in Palm-Sized Press, Spillwords, Mercurial Stories, Potato Soup Journal, and Blood Song Books.

Mystery Girl
by Kent Swarts

Sondra's death at eighteen was astonishing, and so was the way she died—eviscerated. She was sweet, generous, and personable. When the police interrogated the guys I hung with and me, we found out she dealt in drugs, whored and stole. How she had done these things and maintained dignity, we had no idea.

Maybe it was just the ghetto.

But no one was charged with the crime.

While we hunted for her slayer, we found she'd quit school to have a kid.

With this, we became dedicated to discovering who this mysterious girl really was.

Screw the murderer!

Kent Swarts is a retired aeronautical engineer and is an enthusiastic astronomer. He edits the astronomy club's newsletter. He has been published in four anthologies and has one published novel, The Fate of the Charles Wilkes, a sci-fi story. He lives in Waco, TX.

Captain
by Chris Bannor

Nights like this make me question why I moved to the city. I could have lived the semi-quiet life of a small-town cop. This is my life though; my calling.

For those who know how to read it, the blood at the scene leaves behind a story. I'm the one they call when the act is so bloody it makes the trail tainted.

They call me the Bloodhound because they say I never give up on a case. Tonight though, the blood is muddied. There are too many clues, not enough cops to follow, and a horrifying deadline ticking away.

Chris Bannor is a science fiction and fantasy writer who lives in Southern California. Chris learned her love of genre stories from her mother at an early age and has never veered far from that path. She also enjoys musical theater and road trips with her family, but is a general homebody otherwise. Twitter: @BannorChris

On a Dare
by Jason Holden

The bell buzzed as Mickey entered, alerting the man who owned the shop. His friends waited outside to see if Mickey would complete the dare. His heart racing, he slipped the Mars bar up his sleeve. A hand clasped his shoulder and he was dragged into the back room of the shop. Something tripped him as he was propelled backwards into the room. The lock clicked shut. Mickey checked his phone. No signal. He shone the light on the thing that tripped him and dropped the phone, the light from the screen illuminating the face of another long dead shoplifter.

*After giving up a full-time job as a quarry operator so that his wife could follow her dream career as an academic in the field of chemistry, **Jason Holden** and his family left England and temporarily moved to Spain where they currently reside. While there, he took on the role of full-time parent and began to create stories for his daughter. Now that she is in school, he creates stories for himself and hopes to share those stories with others.*

Charlie
by Scott Wheelock

Drake couldn't imagine how any bullets hadn't hit him. He had to keep Charlie quiet, or he was dead meat. All he could do was to grab the kid and try to get off the estate grounds. Drake shook his head, lifting his finger to his lips. "Shhh."

Charlie screamed. For a two-year-old, he sure had a pair of lungs on him. This wasn't going to work.

Drake snapped his neck—*crackkkkk*—and shoved him into his knapsack. If he cut off a finger and put it on ice, he should still be able to get a fortune for him.

Scott Wheelock is a painter, writer and teacher living in Philadelphia. Recently, his short story The Crimson Tear was selected for the anthology "Quoth the Raven" published by Camden Park Press, and his story Blood Pigs and Soil was chosen for the upcoming Night Sky Anthology "13 Postcards from Hell."
Website: www.scottwheelock.com

Necrophagia
by Donald Jacob Uitvlugt

His skills as a pathologist amaze. The most subtle poisons, the most perplexing injuries and diseases. The fine line between natural death and murder most foul. He is always right.

Their bodies speak to him. The young woman, aged before her time by drugs. The old man, scarred by years of neglect. The child, killed before the car went into the water. The dead tell him their secrets.

He cuts open their lives, peels back the lies and exposes the truth.

And when no one looks, he takes a piece of the beloved dead and becomes one with them.

Donald Jacob Uitvlugt lives on neither coast of the United States, but mostly in a haunted memory palace of his own design. His short fiction has appeared in numerous print and online venues, including Cirsova Magazine and the Flame Tree Press anthology Murder Mayhem. He works primarily in speculative fiction, though he loves blending and stretching genres. He strives to write what he calls "haiku fiction," stories that are small in scale but big in impact.
Website: haikufiction.blogspot.com
Twitter: @haikufictiondju

UNRAVEL

ACKNOWLEDGEMENTS

Huge thanks to all the authors who have contributed to UNRAVEL, the fifth book in the Dark Drabbles series. This theme was out of the comfort zone for a lot of you, but you all gave it a real go, and we saw some amazing pieces if tiny fiction land in our inbox—and from some new faces too.

We are lucky to be surrounded by great authors, and we'll continue to showcase their work for as long as they allow us to.

As always, a special *thank you* to you, our loyal readers, who continue to support our work.

www.blackharepress.com

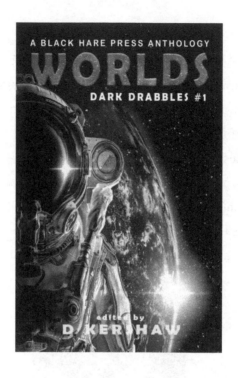

Stories of new worlds, new creatures, alien colonisation, humanity's new home, space accidents, alien snackcidents, evil planets, military mashups, alien autopsies, and much, much more.

Beatific angels, holy wars, kitty saviours, epic battles between good and evil, devils and demons, fallen angels and many more tantalising tiny tales.

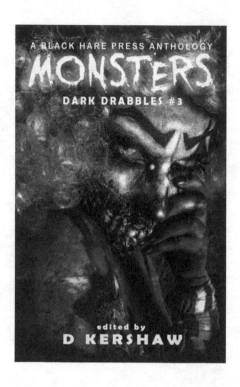

Wendigos, vampires, things that go bump in the night or hide under the bed, witches, demons, upirs, kelpies, toad people, zombies, sirens and hundreds of other tiny terrifying tales.

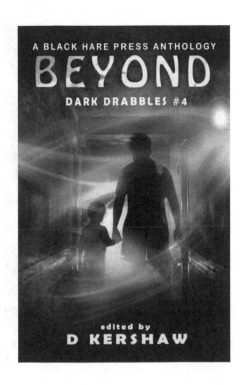

Micro myths of the paranormal;
poltergeists, spirit boards, ghosts
and ghouls, avenging apparitions
and horrifying hauntings.

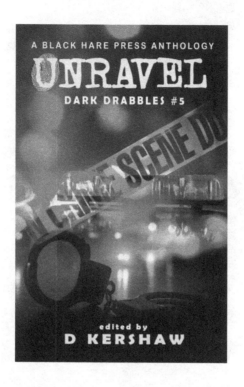

Murder mysteries, criminal chronicles, whodunnits, revenge, suspicion, mayhem, intrigue, and lots more.

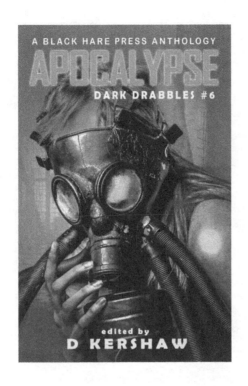

Coming soon

Coming soon

UNRAVEL

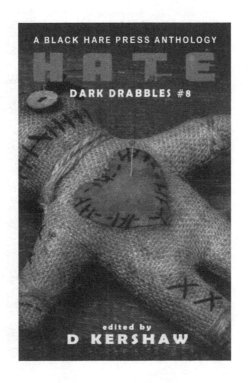

Coming soon

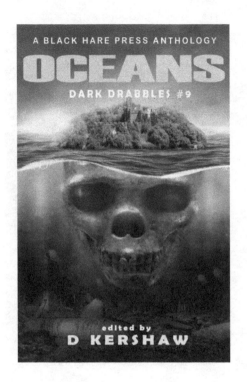

Coming soon

Coming soon